# The writing is evocative!

*"This book is sssoooo good."*— Doris Maxwell

*"This story is so good, I am sending it to everyone I know."* -- Racquel Lyle

## SPIRAL

*"Evil comes to him who searches for it....*
*He who brings trouble on his family will inherit only*
*wind, and the fool will be servant to the wise."* —
Proverbs 11:27 & 29

by Denise Turney

# Spiral

Published by:  Chistell Publishing
7235 Aventine Way
Chattanooga, TN 37421

Cover:  Morris Publishing
Cover Photography Copyright © 1997 by Morris Press
ISBN: 9798834560982
Library of Congress Catalog Card Number: 2002108146

Printed in the USA by
Morris Publishing

3212 East Highway 30 * Keamey, NE 68847 * 1-800—650-7888

# Dedication

For my son.
I love you, Gregory.

# Acknowledgements

Thank you to the Creator! Thank you to my family here on earth and to those I love so dearly who have transitioned. Thank you to everyone who has supported me and my books, my newsletter, The Book Lover's Haven, and my website at www.chistell.com. I appreciate each of you very much. I think it's impossible for you to ever know how much your support means to me. I am deeply grateful for you because I know that there are a zillion choices you could have made and you chose to support me. Thank you! Enjoy <u>Spiral</u>!

## PART I

<u>Chapter One</u>

The summer of 1934 was an unusual summer in Louisville, Kentucky. It was the summer that children became scared to go outside and play. Although they never said a word, not even amongst each other, the children knew, through the many warnings that their parents gave them, that something more fierce, dreadful and evil than ghosts and imaginary monsters was outside ... maybe at the park, just around the corner from their family home, perhaps at the edge of the school yard.

"Come here, Sweetheart," a wiry, middle-aged man said while he curled his finger. "I ain't going to hurt you. I know you're going home from school. It's a long way. Come with me. I'll give you a ride home, so you don't have to walk all that long way. Your mom and dad asked me to pick you up today. They're busy with work and didn't want you to walk all the way home by yourself."

The freckle-faced girl grinned shyly at the man who was leaning out of the side of a rusty, old pick-up truck smiling at her.

"Come on," the man smiled. "I'm a friend of your mom's and dad's. I've seen you playing at your house when I was talking with your dad. You probably don't remember me, but I know your parents really well."

A moment later, the little girl sat on the passenger seat with the man. She giggled each time he reached over and tickled her.

In between a burst of laughter, the girl looked up at the man and asked, "What's your name?"

## PART II

Chapter Two

Ten years later, like a bad dream that would not end, evil snaked its way to Memphis, Tennessee and Tammy Tilson, a fiercely strong-willed woman, moaned, "God, help me," as she made her way from her bedroom to the bathroom. Everything in front of her was blurry. She closed her eyes and breathed deeply. "Oh, God," she whispered while she neared the bathroom, "Who killed that little girl?"

It started yesterday evening when the news aired. Tammy had been in the kitchen cooking cube steak and mashed potatoes when she heard, "News flash." She turned away from the stove and turned the radio up. "All of Memphis, a little girl is missing. The child was outside playing in front of her parents' home on Monroe Avenue when neighbors say they saw a man pick her up in a truck. Before the little girl's neighbors could race to her rescue, the man grabbed her and sped down the street. The little girl hasn't been seen since..."

That was last night. Now it was morning, and men were still being ordered from their homes or right off the street to report to the police precinct. There, angry police officers lobbed a series of questions at them in loud, threatening voices. "Where were you last night, boy? I didn't ask you where you were in the morning, you stupid moron. Don't want to hear another word about morning. Damn it! I'm asking you where you were between the hours of ten and eleven last night! You work? You got a job? Got your own car? Did you drive that car last night? Where'd you go? For how long? Were you gambling last night, boy? Do you like little girls? Ever killed before, boy?"

The possible answers to the questions only brought more questions to Tammy. After all, her husband, Philip, was one of the men rounded up early this morning. He told her that he had been working at their grocery store when cops came down to the store, their car sirens blaring, grabbed him by the back of his neck and snapped a pair of tight handcuffs around his wrists. They drove him to the police precinct and questioned him for five long hours.

Tammy glanced at a clock on the wall. It was six o'clock in the morning and her husband had only been home for two hours. She went into the bathroom, closed the door and sat on the toilet with her head between her knees. Life had never been easy for her. She'd grown up the daughter of a woman who took ill with "bad pressure" when she was only seven years old. Tammy couldn't remember a time when her mother played with her or spent longer than two hours out of bed.

Oldest of her eleven siblings, from the age of seven, Tammy grew up taking charge and working as hard around the house and on her family's farm as a grown man. Even now, she couldn't remember a time when she wasn't working. Not until she was grown and married did the hard work bring a reward.

She and her husband were the first Coloureds in Memphis to open their own business at the center of town, a place usually reserved for companies owned by wealthy entrepreneurs and adult children of former politicians who hadn't outgrown riding their father's coattails. They were the first people in town to go door to door asking for signatures to sign a petition to have "mysterious" house fires on the poor side of town fully investigated. They stood up to the mayor when he told them "y'all ought to be grateful folks support y'all and allow y'all to thrive in these parts. Truth be told, in a lesser town, y'all would've long been dead ... shot or something another."

After she sat on the toilet with her head between her knees for several seconds, Tammy looked up. She watched a caterpillar inch down the window and thought about her husband. He was good to her and their four children. She knew that she was the only person he trusted. All his life he'd "made-do" and kept his deepest thoughts to himself. He was like a locked door that would only open for her. If not for her, he wouldn't have told a soul, outside his father, that he was the one who came upon his mother hanging from the barn loft.

He was only six years old. All he knew to do was to scream and run. Mothers didn't kill themselves, he told himself while he ran to tell his father to hurry and get his mother down from the top of the barn. His mother wasn't dead. She was just swinging in the air. It was all so easy to believe until his father raced back to the barn with him. The tortured look on his father's face and the hard groans moving up out of his mouth made him step back and hide behind his father's thick legs. After he told Tammy the story when they were first married, he never said the words "my mother" again. To Tammy it was as if her husband had no mother. It was as if he had been born straight out of his father's rib.

Seconds later, when Tammy heard her daughters talking in their bedroom, she stopped recalling the past, stood from the toilet and washed her face. She'd keep moving. She'd stand with her shoulders tall and walk like she didn't fear anything. For her children, she would.

"It's gonna be all right," she repeated to herself until she entered her bedroom and saw her husband, Philip, wrestling in his sleep. Her husband had never been in trouble with the law. The cops had no right to embarrass him in front of their customers, handcuff him and force him to go with them to the precinct, a place where justice was never allowed for the poor or the Coloured. While Tammy watched Philip try to sleep, she thought back to their first grocery store.

If not for the store, her husband and she would just be farmers who'd never break even despite how many hours a day they worked. She almost smiled. She was the one who had talked Philip into purchasing the large grocery store that they bought seventeen years ago. She didn't even argue when he demanded that the store be named after his kin. Two weeks later, the store was torched and burned to the ground. Tammy ran after the hooded men in the trucks and two police cars as the nightriders laughed and cursed their way back down the street, away from the burning store. "You bastards! God'll get you for this! God'll get you for this!" she shouted while she threw heavy rocks at the trucks and cars. She didn't stop throwing rocks until she heard one of the car windows shatter.

"We'll get another store," Philip told her that night while he sat next to her on the front porch cradling a shotgun in his lap.

"Do you know how much money we're out? Insurance company ain't gonna give us no money for the store. They'll say it was our fault the store burned to the ground."

"I know. I know." He reached out and tapped

her hand. "We'll build a new store. And if those ignorant asses burn this one down, they're gonna get a load of what's in this here shotgun."

With the help of men in the community, they did build another store, nearly twice the size of the first one. The grand opening of Tilson's Grocery Store in Greasy Plank, a small town in Memphis, Tennessee's Shelby County, was the first story on the cover of *Memphis Prize,* the city's only Coloured newspaper at the turn of the century.

Most houses in Greasy Plank were small, wood structures. Most women in the town still pushed their laundry up and down splintered, wood boards before they dipped the laundry in tin pails of soap and water and hung the clothes on the line in the back yard. Roads were narrow and seemed to stretch for miles with there not being many businesses or shops nearby. Greasy Plank was country, a place where grass, dirt and weeds ruled over brick, mortar and concrete. The closest highway to Greasy Plank was twenty miles from the town. Strangers didn't stay in the town long. Old timers ran them out with hard stares and bitter gossip.

It was a town that consisted of the memberships of four churches, New Mount Holly, the church the Tilsons attended, being largest of the four. Everyone in Greasy Plank went to church. Children from the town grew up and married former classmates. Adults stayed in the town until they died. The biggest business in town was Tilson's Grocery Store. More Greasy Plank residents shopped at Tilson's each week than made deposits and withdrawals at the bank, visited the theatre or went shoe shopping on Beale Street.

Every night, with a loaded shotgun nearby, Philip and Tammy cleaned out the grocery store cash registers and counted money customers exchanged for clothing, household goods, meat and produce. Tammy placed the money inside a tin box beneath their bed. Monday, she climbed inside the family truck and drove through the business districts paying invoices. Other revenue remained locked in the tin box until she had time to get uptown to Beale Street to Shant's Savings & Trust Company and deposit the money in Philip and her account.

Winter Tammy didn't go to the bank. Instead, Philip and she gave money to the poor. Within the last month, twice, after the police chief refused to investigate a series of house fires, they lent two neighborhood families money to rebuild homes nightriders had burned to ash. They also donated a large sum of money to a home for retarded children. Every donation they made was in the memory of a little girl named Bobbie Long. "Keep this quiet," Tammy ordered when she dropped the checks off.


Tammy turned and watched Philip run his hand across his face. She reached out and stroked his back until she felt his muscles relax. "Mama warned me," she whispered while she rubbed her husband's back. "Mama warned me a day like this would come." She sighed. The first seer in the family — that's what her mama was. She saw things happen long before they ever did. She went around trying to warn people. "That's what's so hard about bein' a seer," she told Tammy when Tammy was a little girl. "When don't nobody else see what you be seein', folk go 'round callin' you crazy. Seers get their root off family trees, Tammy. Trace the root, Chil'! Trace the root!"

All those years ago as a small girl, Tammy shook

while she watched her mother's eyes roll in her head. Then, she watched her mother press her head into her bed pillow, cough and wipe spots of blood away from the edges of her mouth. "Be careful who you let be on our family tree, Tammy. I done told ya. I done told ya. If you don't, gurl, you gonna help to birth a thing called crazy. Yes. Yes." Then, her mother closed her eyes and died.

Shaking thoughts of her mother further into her memory, Tammy sat erect and reminded herself how much work had to be done. A man was coming by the store at one o'clock. He telephoned from Louisville, Kentucky yesterday morning. He told Philip that he peddled written works for a living, particularly essays authored by Carter G. Woodson and Frederick Douglass, and thought Tammy and Philip could sell the books and pamphlets. Tammy argued and shouted with Philip for a whole ten minutes when he told her about the man.

"You don't even know who that man is," she said. "We can't afford to go around trusting people, especially people we don't know, Philip. How many business people were calling us before we made a success of the store? Wasn't nobody coming around here before. Since we opened the store, all kinds of people knocking on our door. People want to take a free ride on our name. That ain't happening. Nobody wants to see us win, Philip. Nobody.Every single prominent man right here in town wants to see us fall. No," she added, shaking her head. "We don't need no outsiders coming around to stir the pot."

When Philip responded to her with silence, she lowered her voice. "I just want us to have what we builttogether stay between the two of us. We did this together, Honey. It's ours, our children's and our grandchildren's, right on down the line." When he smiled at her, she reached out and took his hand inside hers.


"Mama?"

Tammy rubbed her husband's back one last time, then she pushed off the bed and walked into the hallway and looked inside her sons' bedroom. "What, Son?" She looked at the closed curtains and sniffed the strong odor of musk coming out of the bedroom. "Please open those curtains and windows."

David pushed the curtains apart.

Tammy stood akimbo. "I'm waiting."

In one jerk, he finished parting the curtains and pushed the windows up. The lines in his forehead had deepened since his mother had entered the room. "Mama, I'm doing the best I can."

"I'm not talking about the curtains. What do you want?"

"Nothing. Never mind."

"Child, what all has been going on with you lately? Don't you know I've got enough on my mind as it is? I don't need you adding to my troubles." She went out of the room, then she turned back and entered it again. "And if you think you're grown enough to come creeping in here any ol' time you feel like it, you best do some more thinking. I know you were out late last night. Don't think I don't know." She looked at him with a pointed brow. "Ain't nothing out late at night but trouble. Make sure you're in early from now on. Things are happening around here. Only fools stay out late at night." She mumbled. "Sixteen years old." Then, she shook her head, turned, walked to the end of the hall and went downstairs.

David scowled.

At his side, his younger brother, Jonathan, sat up. His hair was disheveled; the corners of his eyes had a hard white crust on them, evidence of a long night of sleep.

Peering over his shoulder and looking at his brother, David mumbled, "Lay on back down, Jon."

"Who were you talking to?"

"Mama, and so what?"

"I just asked."

Silence.

Jonathan gazed at his brother. "In a funk?"

David was silent. If he had to describe his feelings for his mother, he would say, "I love her. I hate her." His mother had always been hardest on him. These last few months, he'd heaped his greatest disappointment upon her. He fell in love with a girl by the name of Margaret Armstrong, the daughter of a man his mother hated.

Jonathan looked over his shoulder at David. "Mama?"

David lowered his head into his hands. He was angry with himself for not having gentler, warmer feelings toward his mother, but he couldn't bring himself to deepen his love for her. Each time he tried, it seemed that she hurled an insult or a comment that relayed how deeply disappointed she was in his behavior at him.

He peered up at his younger brother. "She's my mother. I'm supposed to love her." His jaw trembled. "I'm trying so hard to do that."

"You still leaving?"

"I don't know." He sighed. "I want to. That's the only way I'm ever going to learn to love Mama. I

14

have to leave."

"Life ain't no fun when you live it full of regret, Man."

David was silent.

"Everybody up!" Tammy shouted from the kitchen. "I'm cooking breakfast! If you're not down here soon, you won't eat!"

Philip jammed the pillow over his ears. He felt nauseous and thought about running into the bathroom to vomit.

Glancing at the small, rotary clock on the nightstand, he saw that it was six-fifteen. His eyelids felt like they weighed two pounds each. If he had left the store when he normally did, the cops would never have cuffed him. He'd have been home, and he knew that no one wanted to confront him and his wife when they were together. His wife knew the law and would sue, but him — alone, all he could do was argue and plead for more time to set things straight.

He'd been at the store late because one of the regular customers was shaking so badly when he came by the store last night that Philip felt that he had no choice except to stay with the customer. He'd listened while the customer talked about seeing a group of men climb out of a truck up on the railroad tracks. While his eyes ballooned, the customer swore to Philip that he saw the men dump a body into the river that ran just over the cliff at the back of the tracks.

"Keep it to yourself," Philip coached the customer. "So long as you're living, don't you ever tell one soul what you saw. If you tell it, these backwards cops'll only think you did it, and you'll be the one to end up in jail or swinging from some tree with your neck broke out in the middle of nowhere."

Pushing off the bed, Philip swallowed rising vomit until it burned in his throat.

Down the hall, his daughter, Melinda, hurried out of the bathroom. "Janice, you ready to go downstairs?"

Her twin sister, Janice, stood behind the bedroom door so that her brothers wouldn't see her snapping her bra closed. "Yes. Mama said we have a lot of work to do today."

"We always have a lot of work to do."

Her bra fastened, she tossed Melinda a pair of wool gloves. "Here. Catch."

A vase of yellow tulips decorated the center of the large newly hewn kitchen table. The flowers seemed like a decoy, a sign of how much effort Tammy was putting into convincing her family that everything was all right.

Above the flowers, sunrays came through the windows with a strong glare, and yet an ominous foreboding pointed at the family. The kitchen was numb with silence. A little girl was missing. She lived on Monroe Avenue. Her father was a lawyer. Investigators were already out knocking on doors.

Buster, the family's black and white spotted mutt, was in the back yard eating from an old dinner bowl that Tammy had decided she no longer needed. Tammy glanced out the back, screen door at Buster and wished that someone at the table would speak.

David stared at the wall clock so hard that he saw the minute hand move.

Beneath the table, Janice nudged Melinda with her foot.

Tammy turned from facing the screen door and

sipped tea. "Nice day, isn't it?"

"Sure is," Philip answered.

David chewed on the hot cakes. "So, Dad, you going to the fights tonight?"

"They're only on Saturdays," Philip answered.

Tammy pursed her lips. "Ain't nobody going nowhere at night no time soon in this here family."

Philip chuckled dryly.

"We cannot afford to get caught up in anything bad."

Philip raised his hand to signal his wife to be silent. Then, he resumed eating his syrupy hot cakes.

She stared at him blankly.

"I ain't seen or heard nothing. You know what kind of night I had." He shook his head and grimaced. "I was only at the store late on account of working so hard. I don't know nothing about no missing girl."

"The kids might believe—"

He banged the table with his fist. "I work hard. I ain't never broke no law, and you know it. I'm not gonna sit here and let you try to sayI was wrong for what happened last night. I ain't gonna stand for it."

Tammy was silent.

Philip sat against the spine of his chair.

Tammy jerked her head away from her husband and looked out the screen door.

After he cleared his throat, Philip said, "Doctor told you about worrying so much. Why you think your pressure's up? You keep on. You're gonna work yourself into a real bad heart attack. Doctor done told you."

Tammy looked hard at her husband, as if she could stare the truth into him. "I know you haven't done anything, Philip. That's not what I'm trying to say. But I don't want this going on and on." She ran her hand across her face. "When them people come knocking, Philip, you gotta get to the bottom of this. You know they're coming back. You gotta tell them things just so they'll go away and stay away. If you don't, we could be going on with this forever."

"Let's not talk about this madness in front of the kids."

Tammy sat still for a moment. Images of a little girl running through weeds and tall grass, hurrying away from death, flashed across her mind's eye and she cringed. She looked at her own children before she said, "You're right." She pursed her lips and nodded. "We'll talk about it later." She stood. "I hope you all liked breakfast. I made hot cakes because I know how much you all like them. If you're all finished eating, we gotta get moving. We have a lot of work ahead of us. Melinda, you and Janice, get these dishes cleaned up. Jon and David, go with your father. There ain't time for any of us to be fooling around." Her shirtsleeves were rolled to the elbows. "Girls, I'll be upstairs. We're going to strip these floors and clean the bed linen." She talked while she walked out of the kitchen. "Janice, you wash. Melinda, you dry. You two do it better that way."

After her father and brothers left the kitchen, Janice listened to the sound of her mother's footsteps until she could no longer hear them. Then, she rested her chin in the palm of her hand. "I thought I heard Mama up last night. I don't think she slept at all. Somebody kept coming by here knocking on the door. Mama must have talked to I don't know how many people last night."

Tammy was standing outside the bathroom door when she shouted, "Stop the yakking and get to business!"

The sisters lowered their heads while they waited for the sink to fill with sudsy water. "I thought I heard Mama crying last night. I've never heard Mama cry before," Melinda's said.

"You didn't hardly hear Mama crying. Mama never cries. Never. Nothing can make Mama cry. Mama's tough. Mama's strong."

"Yes," Melinda added with a tight brow, "But she's also human. When are you gonna see that? She's only human, Janice."

Tammy raised her voice. "All right! I told you once!"

Janice whispered, "What do you think she meant about Dad telling things in a way so the cops won't come back? Dad doesn't know anything about that girl from Monroe Avenue."

Melinda pressed her finger against her lips. "Ssshh, Mama's coming downstairs."

Tammy stepped inside the living room. "You two almost done?" She ran her hand across the coffee table. She frowned when she turned her hand over and saw dusts on her fingers. She exited the living room and then the kitchen as quickly as she had entered them. "Hurry and finish." With her back turned, she didn't see Melinda roll her eyes. She went outside into the shed next to the rear of the house. She tossed rags and moved old pieces of furniture and boxes. "Where's that bucket?"

Janice hunched her shoulders and covered her mouth with her palm. "So, what do you think Mama meant?"

"I don't know. Dad must know something. Somebody must have told him something." She raised then lowered her shoulders. "Maybe he saw a stranger around town or something. I don't know. I heard there's been some strangers coming around here." She stared into the sink. "Maybe Mama's trying to scare Dad into not staying down at the store so late anymore." She sighed. "I don't know."

The back door swung open. The porch area surrounding the back door, the area the family dog huddled and slept in, was dirty with paw marks and loose dog hair. Tammy wiped her brow while she walked through the back door carrying a bucket. It was eight o'clock in the morning.


At four-thirty that afternoon, Melinda, Janice and Tammy were finishing the last load of laundry—the bed covers. The brown and white house on Jeanette Place in Shelby County was clean.

House chores completed, Melinda and Janice stood on the front porch staring into the sweating face of an angry police officer.

"Told you to let me in, Girls. I need to talk to your folks about some important business."

"My dad is away and my mama isn't down here right now."

Tammy ran down the living room stairs. "Melinda! Janice! Didn't you two hear me calling--"

The officer smirked when Tammy met his glare. "How, you doing, Tammy — Mrs. Tammy Tilson? How you doing?"

"Go upstairs, Melinda and Janice. Please. You two go now. Leave me alone to talk with the officer."

The police officer laughed. "Oh, now, Tammy, don't be like that. We're all family around here. Small town folk. We all know each other. You know better. Call me Henry right out. Just say Henry."

Melinda and Janice were upstairs leaning around

the top corner listening hard to what their mother and the police officer had to say to each other.

"You ain't got no right coming around here bothering my children, and you know that. I ain't gonna stand for it. You and your other officer friends ain't about to harass me and my people. You ain't seen a fight yet, you come snooping around here again. It's bad enough y'all kept my husband down at that hell of a place last night." She squinted. "You better not ever cuff none of my people again. Do and you'll regret it like nothing you can ever think of."

The officer rolled his cover around in his hand. "You just make sure your husband's got a good explanation for why he kept your store open longer last night than the city permit allows."

"Permit—"

"And you make sure your husband comes down to the police station to tell us what that good friend of yours, one of your faithful customers, told him last night." When he turned to leave, he pointed at her. "You make sure all that happens, Mrs. Tammy Tilson."

Tammy stood on the porch like a deep-rooted oak tree. She didn't move until the cop drove down the street. Then, she started wiping her brow and wondering why the last few summers in Greasy Plank were so hot, so full of the devil's bite.

She closed the front door and lowered her head. She choked back emotion until she heard her daughters calling her, at which time she stood tall and walked toward the stairs.

"Is everything okay, Mama?"

"Yes, Melinda. Now please stop asking so many questions and you both come down here and help me pull something together for supper."

While they watched their mother move away from them and closer to the kitchen, Melinda and Janice looked at one another. So often when they communicated with each other, they didn't utter a sound. It was as if they were joined at the soul the day they were conceived. When challenged, they defended each other with loud arguments or with an eerie silence.

As soon as Tammy entered the kitchen, the back door swung open.

"Did the three of you finish cleaning up?" Philip asked. His sons followed him. Mud and dirt splattered their pants. "We sure busted our rumps out on the farm and at the store today. I even tuned that raggedy truck. Cut my hand good on one of them wires doing it too."

Tammy didn't speak. Despite her worries, she promised herself that she wouldn't burden her children with the recent, unexplainable events in town. Since the day that her children were born, they'd known safety. She was angry with herself for mentioning the missing girl in front of them at the breakfast table. She vowed to do so no more. Despite their advancing ages, she wanted her children to know and to especially feel that they were safe.

"We got everything done. We're just getting—" She peered over her shoulder at her daughters. "Supper ready. And," she added, "How did it go with that man who was visiting from Louisville?"

Philip laughed. "He didn't even have any books. He just kept asking me a whole lot of questions about your father and especially your mother."

Chapter Three

On the top row of the splintered bleachers at Booker T. Washington High School, David Tilson, one of the city's brightest students and, thanks to his parents' role in business, politics and social life, one of Shelby County's most well-known sons, clenched his fists. David was only sixteen and already in the twelfth grade. "The boy with the dreams," that's what his classmates called him. Late last night, David's life took him beyond books, ambition and ideals. Last night, David became a witness to a murder.

Leaning forward on the bleachers, David frowned. He felt numb while he watched the basketball game unfold in front of him. His sisters were more than ardent basketball fans; they were two of the best girl basketball players in the state of Tennessee.

David watched his sisters sprint up and down the court stealing balls, blocking shots and scoring. Despite the fact that the game was close, he knew that his sisters would find a way to earn their team a win. While he stared at the court, making sure to nod and smile every now and then in effort to mask his mounting fear, he asked himself why he came to the game.

He could have easily walked to his girlfriend Margaret's house and spent the afternoon with her. "No," he whispered shaking his head. He didn't want to trouble her with a heavy heart.

Family, friends and classmates surrounded him. The bleachers were crowded, and yet David felt alone. He knew no one else around him had ever seen a murder. What his eyes had seen and what his ears had heard set him apart forever. When it came to what he was forced to experience simply because he had chosen to be out late last night drinking, he knew that he would always feel alone. He couldn't tell what he'd witnessed last night, ever — not to a soul. If he did, he knew that people would always want to know more, would always think that he was concealing something. The more he told, the more they would want to know. It would become a story that had no end.

He'd been up on the railroad tracks drinking with a new teenager in town. The boy's family consisted of no more than the boy and his father. They hadn't been in town for two days when David and the boy struck up a friendship. The boy told David that he'd gotten into trouble with the law for petty thefts and other non-violent misdemeanors while his father and he had lived in Chicago. Then, one day three weeks ago, his father walked inside the house, told him to start packing and said, "Come on. I've had enough of all this trouble and carrying on up North. We're getting out of here. We're goingback South."

Cheering fans distracted David, pulling his attention back to the basketball game. David's sister, Melinda, scored and David raised his hands and cheered when everyone else did.

A second later, David started recalling last night's events and his thoughts about why he'd found himself at the wrong place. For starters, he'd been raised to believe that drinking was a sin and that sin brought punishment, hard, unrelenting punishment straight from God. It would have been enough had he been made to bear this burden alone, but he'd brought the new boy in town into it by encouraging him to go up on the tracks with him so that they could drink freely without being discovered. They'd laughed, talked about the gossipy women in town, told each other what they disliked most about their parents and drank pure Tennessee whiskey straight out of the bottle.

In the bleachers, David cursed beneath his breath.

24

He was exhausted. The night had proved long, and it was taking a lot out of him to convince himself that he'd imagined everything that he knew he saw last night. He'd been drunk he kept trying to tell himself. He only thought that he saw a truck pull up against the edge of the tracks about one hundred yards away from where he and the boy had drank whiskey. He kept trying to convince himself that it was all in his mind. Nothing really happened last night. He was just dreaming again.

A second later, a chill raced up his spine and he told himself that he'd seen the ghost older folk talked so much about. "Yea," he whispered with a nod while he watched his sisters jog to the side of the court after their coach called a time-out.

He'd seen Bobbie's ghost. He'd seen the ghost. He smiled. He had seen nothing more than a ghost, and he was right for coming here. Being at the game would distance him from the cops.

He wouldn't be home if investigators came pounding on his parents' front door again. He'd only made one mistake last night. His wallet had fallen out of his pant pocket.

He was running so hard after he saw what looked like a body being dumped into the river that stretched along the back of the railroad tracks. He didn't realize his wallet was missing until he woke this morning and stuck his hand inside his pockets, hunting loose coins.

"Damn," he cursed beneath his breath. "How could I have been so dumb? I should have gone back first thing this morning to hunt for my wallet."

A second later, he swallowed hard and told himself that seeing something wrong was not the same as doing something wrong, and besides, he wasn't even sure that he saw what he thought he saw. He'd been drinking.

Hearing his friends and classmates talk kept his

mind from racing with detail over crazy events that he knew he'd never fully make out. He clenched his jaw and stared at his hands. Even now sitting in the bleachers, he knew that if he lived to celebrate the age of forever he would never forget the shrilling screams that came out of the girl's body while a group of men hoisted her into the air. He would never forget seeing the men clasp their hands around the girl's flailing arms and her swinging legs.

He closed his eyes and squeezed back tears. He didn't look up until his girlfriend sat next to him.

She crossed her arms. "Are we still going to the dance, David?"

Before he could answer, another student called out, "David?"

David turned sharply and faced the top of the bleachers. It was the new boy. "I gotta go," David told his girlfriend, Margaret. "I'll be right back."

"But—" Margaret started to say as David stood.

"I didn't even know you were here," David tried. "I thought you said you weren't coming to the game. I'll be right back." When her gaze didn't soften, he leaned over and kissed her softly on her forehead. She smiled and he nodded at her. "I'll be right back."

Then, he hurried to the top of the bleachers. "Why are you all the way up here by yourself?" he asked the boy.

The boy stared at his feet. "My dad said we're going back to Chicago."

"What?"

"Yea," the boy nodded.

"But you just got here."

The boy shook his head. "Too much is going on," he told David. "I told my dad what we saw last night."

26

David's eyes ballooned.

"Don't worry. I'm not going to tell nobody else. I won't tell another soul as long as I live. I'm gonna work hard to forget what we saw last night. I'm never talking about it again. I'm going to pretend it didn't happen. But my dad said we've got to go. He doesn't want to be a part of this. When the hammer comes down, somebody's gonna pay real good. I ain't staying around to let it be me."

"But we didn't do anything—"

"--Doesn't matter, David. Don't you get it?"

When a few of the students sitting at the back of the bleachers looked in his direction, the boy lowered his head and his voice. "It doesn't matter what we did. We saw something bad happen. If they never catch who really did it, you might as well say that we did."

"What?"

"We were there."

"But we didn't—"

The boy shook his head. "You've been living in a small town too long. You don't know how it works."

David stared at the boy.

"We can be placed at the scene. We were there. If the cops don't find out who really did it, and they find out we were there."

"Yes. Yes," David nodded. "Now I understand."

"So, my dad said we're out of here. Going back to Chicago."

"Three weeks, Man."

"I know," the boy said. "My dad and I were only here for three weeks, but after this, we can't stay to live out a fourth week here."

"Well," David said, looking down the bleachers at Margaret. She continued to watch the game. "If you have to go, you have to go. B u t keep in touch. When you get to Chicago, mail your number or something. No reason we can't stay friends just because you're leaving. As a matter of fact," David added while he reached inside his back pant pocket. "Here. I'll write my number and house address down for you. I can write it on the back of this envelope."

The boy chuckled when he saw the heart shaped drawings on the envelope. He looked down the bleachers at Margaret. "She really likes you."

David smiled. "Yea."

"You two live in the same small town and you write each other letters?"

"She was just writing me something. You know how girls are. It's no big deal." Shrugging, he handed the boy the envelope. "That's my address on the top part, and my phone number is on the bottom."

"All right," the boy said with a nod and a smile. Seconds later, he waved to David one last time, then he walked down the bleachers and hurried away from the basketball court leaving the sting, the cut, of a hard memory as far behind him as he possibly could. At the edge of the school grounds, the boy crumbled up the envelope and threw it onto the ground, then he started running. He didn't stop running until he reached home. Before the basketball game ended, he and his father were in their car on their way out of Tennessee.

"Who was that?" Margaret asked when David returned to her side on the bleachers.

"Just a friend. It's no big deal."

"Well, why didn't he come down here with everybody else?"

"Margaret, you see how crowded it is at this game, in these bleachers. Besides, like I told you, it's no big deal. He was telling me something. Plus," he told her, "I don't ask you everything you and your friends say to each other."

"Okay. I was just asking. I wasn't trying to be nosy. Sometimes you can be so to yourself, like you don't want anyone to bother you or talk to you or be around you or anything. You remind me of my father when you get like that." Tears pooled in her eyes. Silence moved between them like a ghost. They couldn't see what was separating them, but they both knew that something was there and they were too afraid to face it. They sighed when they heard one of their classmates talking behind them. It wasn't until the girl mentioned the old Lenox barn that David stopped thinking about the railroad tracks and listened intently to what the girl sitting behind them was saying to a group of friends.

The girl was always creating stories, saying things that everyone knew couldn't be true. David tried not to listen, but the girl had clearly mentioned the old Lenox barn. Despite his efforts to ignore the girl, he couldn't distance himself from the sound of her voice. It worked like a magnet and drew him further into the story that she was telling.

Even while he listened to her, he thought about how the last story that the girl told had cast such a shadow over her family, her mother thought about sending her up North to spend the summer with her aunt. Yet the girl stuck to her story. For two straight weeks, she'd told classmates that she'd had a run-in with a ghost.

She'd said that while she'd been outside playing alone one hazy afternoon, she rode her bicycle over a little girl's grave up by Lenox's, an abandoned barn that hadn't been used in more than fifteen years.

"I didn't know it was a grave until my tires got stuck going over the hump of the tombstone. Soon as I looked down and saw — Bobbie Long — March 21, 1922-August 28, 1930, I took off. I mean, I got in the wind. I pedaled out of there like I was crazy. It wasn't even three nights later before I was in bed at night trying to fall asleep when I heard my door creak open. I looked up and this little Coloured girl was standing in my room. I sat up and asked her what she was doing there and how did she get in. She just walked right toward my closet kind of like she was floating and took a sweater. Then, she left. Next night it was a shoe. Next night it was a dress. One night I followed her and you know she went right back to Lenox's and put those clothes and that one shoe under a tree close to that tombstone. It wasn't until I promised her I would never, never, never step on that tombstone again that she stopped coming to steal my clothes late at night."

Margaret shook her head and tsked while she listened to the girl talk. "Always looking for an audience," she whispered.

David peered at Margaret. "Soon as the game's over, I'm outta here. You hanging around or are you coming with me?"

"Where are you going after the game's over?"

He shrugged. "I don't know. I thought 1 might go for a walk. You know," he shrugged again. "Maybe I can walk you home."

"Okay. That'll be nice," she smiled.

When they were silent again, they heard the girl talking behind them.

"I don't care what you all say, I am never changing my story," the girl said. "I know what I saw up by that old Lenox barn. My mother couldn't even make me change my story. You see something like that and you wouldn't change your story either.

I saw that little girl. I saw her ghost. She walked right in my room. I know what I saw."

David heard another girl say, "Donna, you're always making stuff up. This is probably just as made up as those poems you're always writing. You've just got a big imagination."

"That's true. I have a big imagination," Donna said. "But I didn't make the story up."

"You're always fishing for attention. You're always trying to get somebody to brag on something you've done. That's the only reason you put so much time into those poems you're always writing."

"I like to write. What else am I going to do? I'm the only child in this whole town who doesn't have a brother or a sister. My mom's always sending me off to my room. If I didn't write, I'd probably lose my mind."

"One thing I know is you better stop using that word inyanga' in all your poems," another girl told Donna. "English teacher already told you. I heard her tell you to never use that word again. She wasn't playing either. I heard her when she told you, and you know better than to use that word anyway."

Donna folded her arms and rolled her eyes. "I'll write what I want to write."

"And you'll believe what you want to believe too," Margaret mumbled.

"Hi, David and Margaret," a trio chorused.

David looked up at Melinda, Janice and Jonathan. "I see you all won again, Melinda and Janice. Congratulations. And where have you been, Jon?"

"I was down by the court. You and Margaret always sit so far back."

Melinda reached out and hugged her oldest brother. When she stepped back, Janice embraced him next.

31

"This was a hard win."

"It didn't look that way to me," David laughed.

Melinda chuckled. While she wiped sweat off her forehead with a towel, she looked up into the bleachers and asked, "So, is everyone going to the dance tonight?'

Donna answered first. "I am, Melinda."

"Why don't you and Evelyn come by our house? You two live so far from here. I get scared sometimes knowing you both walk so far to get home."

Donna chuckled. "Besides a ghost or two, there's nothing to be scared of. Ain't nothing in Greasy Plank except a whole lot of nothing fun to do. But yes. I'll come over. It'll be nice to see your mom and dad again."

Jonathan looked at Donna. "So, you're going to the dance?"

Despite her smile and high-pitched laughter, Jonathan saw how much pain Donna had known. It showed all over her face. He'd heard students at school making fun of her. They said that she was spoiled, jealous, selfish and always looking for attention. The youngest son of powerful parents who'd given their last bit of extra time to their children a few years after the twins were born, Jonathan was acquainted with hurt. He learned of the times his parents played outdoors with their children through his siblings. Tammy nor Philip ever played with him or took him for long nature walks the way they had with David, Melinda and Janice. He'd been born after the store became a success, after his mother's and his father's days filled up with one too many chores. He'd been born too late. Donna's pain intrigued him. He wanted to be able to do or say something to make her pain go away. But he didn't try. Instead, he asked her, "So, are you going to the dance

32

or not?" again.

"I just told your sister Melinda I was going. I'm coming over to your house to get ready for the dance. I just have to go home first and let my parents know."

David laughed when he looked up at his brother. Soon other students in the bleachers started laughing too.

Janice teased, "Jonathan must be sweet on Donna, wanting to know if she's going to the dance and all."

"Doesn't matter. Everyone's going to the dance," Donna snapped.

"Donna, you still pass Lenox's when you go home?" Janice snickered.

Other students laughed.

"    Yes, Janice."

"That place is old."

"I know, Janice," Donna said. "Let's don't get started on that again, please."

"All the old folk claim they've seen a little girl's ghost up there," Janice said. "I think they're just superstitious. That ghost story is older than we all are."

Donna looked at Janice for a long time. When she spoke, her words came out slowly, almost as if they were being dragged up onto a long, muddy riverbank. "You all better not go up there by that barn. You all better not."

Her friends turned, looked at her and burst out laughing.

Two hours later, David was home, stretched across his bed. He wished that he hadn't walked Margaret to her parents' house. If he had waited, let a few days pass, he was certain that when he walked to school on Monday the envelope would have been gone. The wind would have picked it up and pushed it across the road into the woods.

At first, Jonathan had offered to walk with them being that Donna lived out by Margaret, then suddenly he changed his mind and turned around. It wasn't long before Margaret and David were alone. David took Margaret's hand inside his. He told her that he would return to get her and take her to the dance at seven o'clock that evening. "Be ready," he told her. "Be on time." They exchanged light conversation and enjoyed the frequent cool breezes that brushed their skin and blew through their hair until they reached the end of the school grounds. It was there that the wind blew the envelope over the top of David's shoe. He picked up the envelope that he'd given his Chicago bound friend and flattened it in the palm of his hand. He stared at his own name, address and telephone number until a hard lump formed in his throat.

He'd made the discovery over an hour ago. Now at home and shaking away thoughts about his walk to Margaret's following the basketball game, David sat up on his bed when he heard his mother call out, "Dave."

"Yes, Ma'am?"

"Will you please go see who's at the door? Somebody's knocking. I don't have time to do no yakking. I have work to do on the farm. Check the door. See who it is." As soon as she heard David's bedroom door squeak open, she said, "And watch the banister. Your dad painted the banister while you all were at the game, then he went right back to the store."

"I know, Mama. I smelled the paint as soon as I came home from the game."

After he heard his mother go out the back door,

David descended the stairs. "Who is it?" he asked through the closed door.

"Was that your mother who just left? I just saw a woman in a truck drive away from your house."

"Who are you and what do you want?"

"You don't remember me?"

"I remember you," David said, glancing through a crack in the living room curtains. " You're the man who came by the store yesterday. My dad said that you said you wanted us to sell books and pamphlets at our grocery store, but you didn't have any books or pamphlets. Who are you?"

"I want to talk to your mother. She'll know who I am."

"You can't talk to my mother." David leaned against the door and locked it slowly, quietly. He let out a deep breath when he heard the lock catch. "Get off of our porch. Get away from our house." He raised his voice to a shout. "Leave now or I'll call the police."

The man laughed. "I don't think you want the police coming around here, especially you."

"Who are you? What's your name? How do you know my family? We don't have family or friends in Louisville, Kentucky where you said you're from."

"Where did your mother go?"

"Who are you?"

"What time is your mother coming home?"

"I think you better leave before you regret it." He listened while the man walked off the porch. Then, he went to the living room window, parted the curtains and peered out onto the street. His gaze followed the man down the street. Up-down, up-down the man moved as he walked away from the house and further down the street leaning heavily upon his shiny cane that was decorated with a color that matched the tint of his dyed hair — silvery gray. Club foot -- that's all that David could think while he watched the man walk. As soon as the man neared the end of the street, David saw the resemblance. He made quick mental notes: short, broad shoulders; long, narrow head; short arms. The man's arms were so short that David told himself that they belonged on a child. "I don't know why I didn't realize it yesterday,"he mused to himself. "I saw you before yesterday," he thought while he watched the man climb inside a long, black car. "It was you."

The front door opened and closed. "David, who are you talking to?"

Closing the curtains, he said, "Nobody, Melinda. Where's Janice?"

"I heard you talking to somebody, and why were you looking out the window? You didn't even answer us when we came up on the porch and asked you to open the door. The way you were staring out the window like you were in a trance, it's a good thing Janice had her key."

"Who was that man walking away from our house?" Janice asked as soon as she entered the house.

David hurried toward the living room steps and his bedroom, the place from where he shut out the realities of the world and dreamed until he felt like he was someplace else. He hated questions, because he hated people getting to know him. Since last night, he wished that he could live in his room, recline on his bed and dream himself through heroic accomplishments, imagine that he was free of fear, pretend that he was someone he was not.

Janice didn't have time to trail her oldest brother with a string of questions. Someone was at the door. "Who is it?" she called out while she hurried across the floor.

"It's Donna and Evelyn."

"Hurry up and let us in." Donna banged on the front door. "Hurry up. Let us in."

Janice pulled the door open with such haste that Donna nearly fell into the living room. "Sorry, but you sounded like you couldn't wait to get in and you were banging on the door."

"I was. We ran all the way over here. Where are your parents?"

"They're probably at the store," Melinda answered. "They weren't home when we came—"

"Who's here?" Donna asked.

"David. He's upstairs in his room. Jonathan went over a friend's house after the game. He'll be home soon though. If he wants to get ready for the dance in time, he better get home soon. David's driving us and you know he's not waiting."

Now that Donna and she were no longer running, Evelyn started to feel how fast she was breathing. "Donna was so mad when she left her parents, she just started running." Evelyn leaned over and worked to catch her breath. "I didn't have any choice but to run with her. If I didn't run, I would probably only be halfway here by now."

"Even running I don't see how you made it here as fast as youdid. Are you sure you both went home after the game?"

"Yes, Janice," Donna answered while she rolled her eyes. "My mom and dad were fighting because my dad stayed out late again last night, so we hurried up and got out of there. I don't want my friends to have to listen to my parents screaming, hollering and fighting. It's bad enough I have to do it. After we left my house, we went to Evelyn's, got her stuff and came over here.

We ran all the way over here."

Evelyn crossed the floor and sat in the rocking chair next to the window. "A lot of men were out late last night," she said. "That's all my dad talked about when he came home from work. My dad didn't get any sleep last night either."

Sure that her friends didn't respect her father's decision to remain on the police force, Evelyn started rocking back and forth in the chair until the chair began to squeak. She talked about how hard her father worked to ensure that men arrested from Greasy Plank really did commit a crime. She talked about the long hours that her father put in late nights at home working for free while he poured over every detail of a case before he went out and cuffed a man. She repeated bits and pieces of conversation she overheard her father having with the head of the department, conversations that passionately defended poor men, it didn't matter what side of the tracks the men lived on.

She talked about the latest case with the missing girl and how she knew some cops were prejudiced but wanted justice more than they wanted to hurt a Coloured man. Rocking back and forth, back and forth in the squeaking chair, she told them over and over again that she knew, she just knew that the case was going to turn out right. What she didn't tell them was that she wanted them to think that her father was a good man. She wanted them to think that her father was just like them, one of them. She wanted the color of her father's skin to mean something to them. "My dad didn't like asking his friends so many questions last night. It's hard asking your friends so many questions when you know they didn't do anything wrong."

"Your dad's a police officer, Evelyn. It's not his

fault he works for a bunch of idiots."

"Melinda."

Stung by her sister Janice's rebuke, Melinda sat back on the sofa and held her tongue.

"Imagine what it feels like to be the only Coloured police officer in all of Shelby County."

"My dad likes being a cop, Donna. He just," Evelyn sighed. "He just doesn't like questioning so many of his own friends like he's having to do with this case."

"Tell me your father doesn't think this case or any case in this town has been handled the right way."

"Melinda, will you stop?" Janice tried.

"My dad wasn't out late because of a case. Everybody knows he cheats on my mama," Donna blurted.

A long silence filled the room. To counter the awkwardness, Donna added, "Do you know he had the nerve to tell Mama that he was at the store talking to your father about the Joe Louis fight, Melinda and Janice? He kept saying it over and over."

Turning, she said, "Didn't he, Evelyn?" She didn't wait for Evelyn's answer. "My mama got so mad after he kept lying, she picked up the bedroom lamp and threw it at him. I heard that lamp smash against the wall. That's when I decided it was time to get out of there. We went straight to Evelyn's after that. Her dad was at work, and her mama was cooking. And I don't care how we tried, Evelyn's mama would not call her brother to come get us and drive us to your house. Your mama is something when she's cooking, Evelyn."

Evelyn peered at Donna. While she looked at her

friend, she wondered if she was aware of her own quiet, strength, if she admired herself for the way that she bounced back after each of her parents' marathon fights. It pained her to think of Donna as an only child living in a large house with parents who fought more than they lived in peace with one another. As the daughter of a police officer, it was at times like these, with the missing girl case being investigated, when she herself felt alone. She almost said, "I'm sorry," to Donna while she worked to distance herself from the hard names that she'd overheard Donna's parents shout at each other less than an hour ago.

Now that they had revealed why they were out of breath, Melinda wanted to know why Evelyn had fear in her eyes. She leaned forward on the sofa and asked, "You all right, E? You didn't look right when Donna and you first got here. You okay?"

"I'm fine. I'm just tired from running over here. That's all. I'm not scared of nothing. I'm all right. Do you know when David's going to drive us to the dance?"

"We'll get to the dance," Melinda assured Evelyn while she tapped her knee. "You know we won't be late as many places as we've gone together."

"I was just wondering what time we were leaving, that's all."

"We'll leave in about an hour." She looked into Evelyn's lap. "Is that your dress?"

Evelyn lifted the dress off her lap and shook it once. "Yea. My mama made it. I actually like it. I can't believe my mama made a nice dress. She always makes such old timey looking clothes. She sends me to school looking like a librarian or an old school teacher."

Janice laughed. "Donna, where's your dress?"

"In this bag I brought with me right here on the

floor."

"You both can change over here."

"That's the only way to do it," Donna said. "We're not about to run back home just to get dressed. It's getting dark."

"Yes," Janice said. "And you shouldn't go near the railroad tracks, neither one of you. I've been hearing things, and you know it's never been safe up there. Whoever was up on those tracks the night that girl turned up missing probably took the girl. If you ask me, they ought to look around those tracks and stop only asking men from around here all kinds of stupid questions. Anybody in town can go up to those tracks. All kinds of people go up there. The cops know that."

"If we had gone away from the tracks, it would have taken us more than an hour to get here and we didn't want it getting dark on us," Donna said. "We would have really been scared then."

Janice listened to the chair squeak louder and in shorter intervals while Evelyn rocked faster, harder.

"I'm not going by the tracks no more."

"What makes you say that, E?" Melinda asked.

Evelyn stopped rocking the chair. "No reason."

Donna looked at Melinda and Janice with a blank stare.

"It's a funny smell up by the tracks," Evelyn said.

"I didn't smell anything—" Donna began.

"Something foul is over by the river," Evelyn repeated. "The smell. I could hardly breathe. Soon as I get home tonight, I'm going to tell my dad."

Janice leaned across the sofa until the distance between Evelyn and her narrowed considerably, until she felt the heat fromEvelyn's opened mouth rush up her nose.

"I didn't go looking around." Evelyn said. "I

41

haven't walked over here in a long time. Today I remembered how far it was. When I smelled that awful odor, I started running faster. It's so quiet out there by those tracks. You never know who's up there. I know some of our brothers go up there drinking, but don't tell it." She shook her head. "I never will. All of our brothers would get a beating if our mamas and dads found out."

Janice looked at Evelyn and thought, "You're hiding something," but so as not to bring her friend discomfort, she spoke not a word. Instead, she sat across from Evelyn smiling and nodding politely. She hated that Evelyn wouldn't tell them everything she knew, everything about this case she'd overheard her father talking about with colleagues on the telephone and with her mother late last night at home.

"I ran so hard trying to keep up with Donna. My legs were hurting. I kept reaching down to rub my thighs, and one time when I was reaching down, I heard a noise coming from the woods."

Janice sat across from Evelyn partly daydreaming, partly listening to what Evelyn was saying. While Evelyn talked, Janice thought back to when she was younger and played with her siblings down by the riverbank until their father found out. "Don't go down there anymore," he told them. "You could slip into the river and drown." Ten years had passed since Janice last went up on the railroad tracks or descended the incline at the back of the tracks and walked along the edge of the river. She remembered the smell coming off the river. The air was always fresh then. The water was the color of blue that she read about and saw in pictures in children's books. That was years ago. Now sitting across from Evelyn and Donna, Janice wanted to know more. "You and Donna, you didn't walk on the tracks.

You were on the ridge below the tracks?"

"We were careful."

"It's been raining a lot. Was the river at flood level?"

Donna shook her head. "No, Janice. The water was high, but you could see the river wasn't anywhere close to flooding even if it rained some more."

"I'm never going to forget that noise," Evelyn said while she stared into her lap.

"What do you think it was?" Janice asked.

Evelyn looked up and met Janice's gaze. "What if she's still alive?"

"Who?" Janice asked.

"That little girl who turned up missing last night? What if she ran real hard and got away from whoever snatched her? What if she was moving in them woods and I heard her?"

All the girls silenced when they heard a door upstairs squeak open. Then, they listened while David said, "Will you all please keep it down? I'm trying to get some rest before the dance."

"Sorry," Evelyn called up the stairs. "I didn't know I was talking so loud. I didn't mean to wake you."

"It's nothing," David said with a wave of his hand. "Just change the subject, please." He turned away from the stairs, glad that the girls couldn't see him. They couldn't see his hands shaking or take notice of the red in his eyes. He had a hard lump of emotion in his throat.

He returned to his room and closed the door. He hoped that Jonathan wouldn't come home soon. He needed time to think. He hadn't been in the woods; he'd been on the railroad tracks last night when he saw the men dump what looked to him like a small girl's body into the river. If he hadn't seen the men run over the tracks and down toward the river, he would have believed that the girl might be alive.

"They made sure," he told himself. Seconds later, sitting on the edge of his bed, he asked himself a hard question, "Why didn't you try to stop them?"

The question jabbed at him, especially considering that it was too late to go back and look for whomever it was that the men hoisted into the air and dumped in the river. He sat on his bed until he convinced himself that the wind and the current had pushed the body downstream, until he convinced himself that there really was nothing that he could have done.

Last night his balance was wobbly from drinking. If he had tried to run after the men to struggle with them to leave the girl alone, he would only have lost his balance and fallen. By the time that he'd gained his footing again, it would have been too late.

Even if he had made a different choice where the men and the running girl were concerned, the outcome would have been the same. He hadn't done anything wrong, and what good would it have done if he had died too? If he had shouted at the men to stop, they would have seen his friend who was with him on the tracks. He'd have put another innocent person's life in danger.

He reclined on his bed and wondered what it was about this death that refused to leave him alone. He'd been to funerals. He'd heard his parents talk about elders in the community and their own parents, his grandparents, when they died, but that pain eventually released him. This, he feared, would not. Knowing you were near someone seconds before they died was a hard thing to live with.

"I don't know what's wrong with him," Melinda said downstairs in the living room. She waved her hand. "Don't pay him any mind. David gets like that when he's sleepy. He can be moody sometimes." A second later, she asked, "Donna, did you hear anything in the woods while you and Evelyn were walking over here?"

Donna sat still for a moment. "No. I might have heard some leaves moving around, but I didn't hear anybody walking or running in the woods. I don't know what Evelyn heard."

"I heard something," Evelyn repeated. "And I'm going to tell my dad as soon as I get home tonight after the dance. I'm going to tell him what I smelled too."

"Your daddy can't solve everything," Melinda said.

"And neither can yours," Evelyn quipped back.

"Come on, you two. Stop." Janice stood. "And we better take a bath and get dressed if we want to make it to the dance in time." She started walking toward the stairs. "I don't want to rush at the last minute."

Donna, Evelyn and Melinda followed her.

"So, Donna," Janice asked when they reached Melinda and her bedroom, "Are your aunt and uncle still coming to visit your mama, dad and you this Christmas?" She smiled while she asked the question. She already knew what Donna thought of her aunt and uncle.

Donna turned up her nose. "As much as I wish they wouldn't, yes, they're still coming. They just want to be there in case Mama and Dad have one of their knock down drag out fights. They're like an audience, two bug-eyed spectators. After they get enough of seeing what Mama's done new to the house, eating up

45

all our food, telling us how good they've got it living in Detroit and listening to Dad's corny jokes, they'll be ready to head back North. I wish they'd just stay up there. Mama always gets sad when they come. They always manage to embarrass her and hurt her feelings, showoffs that they are."

"Your mama does know how to keep a home. My mama and all the other women in town talk about how nice your house looks," Evelyn said while she hung her dress on a hanger. "Your mama is blessed that your grandfather left her that big house. That is one big house you all live in."

"It's too big if you ask me," Donna said. A second later, she closed the door and pulled off her shirt.

"I know you're going to get washed up before you get dressed," Melinda said. "You both said you were running."

Donna laughed. "Yea. I'm gonna wash up, Girl. I can wash off after I put my dress on."

Melinda twisted her mouth. "Girl, you better do things right and wash off before you get dressed."

All the girls laughed.

After Donna pulled her slip down over her head, she said, "I wish Granddaddy didn't give Mama the house. There's only three of us and Mama almost didn't have me. The house is too big. It's not like it was when Granddaddy and Grandma lived there when Mama and all my aunts and uncles were still kids. There were so many of them. Maybe Granddaddy thought Mama would grow up and have alot of kids, but she didn't. She couldn't."

Evelyn pulled her hair into a ponytail. "I don't care what you say, you have a gorgeous house. It's like a mansion. I wish I lived there. You can live where I live." She laughed. Then, she shook her head. "Your grandfather was rich, a doctor. You must really look up to him. And he was so nice to everybody around here when he was living." She bumped Melinda's shoulder. "Remember those free dental visits he gave us on Christmas?"

The girls laughed again.

"The dental visits didn't hurt," Donna said. "My granddaddy never hurt anybody when they stepped inside his doctor's office."

The girls continued to laugh. "I'm going to wash up first,"Evelyn said while she grabbed her dress and headed toward the bathroom. "We're going to have a good time tonight, Melinda, Donna and Janice."

Melinda stopped digging through the bedroom closet for her dress, so that she could turn and smile at Donna. "And it's about time."

"I know," Janice said while she ran her hands over the front of her dress in effort to flatten a few wrinkles bunched at the center of the dress. "There's hardly anything to do around here. I'm shocked the school helped put this dance together. All we do is work, go to school, come home, play basketball and go to church."

"After last night and especially after my mama and dad fighting today, I'm due a break," Donna said. "It started off with you two playing a good game of basketball, but what's new about that?"

"I can't remember a time when we didn't play basketball," Janice said while she watched Evelyn exit the bathroom. "Look at you," she said when Evelyn entered the bedroom. "That is a pretty light blue dress, E. You look nice."

Evelyn smiled so hard, she started blushing.

"You do look nice, Evelyn," Donna said while she picked up her dress and carried it toward the bathroom.

"I'm next. Janice, you and Melinda are taking baths after that basketball game,so you two are going to take the longest in the bathroom. Me and Evelyn should go first."

"My mother would never let me play basketball," Evelyn said.

Melinda watched Evelyn sit on the edge of her bed. "My mama said she wants us to be strong," Melinda said. "She wants us to be able to do a woman's work and a man's work. Ever since we were little girls, my mama said that she wanted us to be strong."

"But basketball?" Donna asked with an upturned nose."What's lady like about basketball?"

"Go in the bathroom and wash up, Donna," Melinda laughed."Miss Dainty."

Forty minutes later, all the girls were dressed. They sat on Janice's and Melinda's bed talking about their dates and envisioning the romantic conversations, slow dances and soft gazes that they hoped to exchange with their dates before the night was over. While they talked, their worries over what would happen to their fathers after last night's investigation lengthened, began to work into a quiet interlude.

Only thoughts about the dance moved their thoughts away from the investigation, causing the soon approaching dance to work like a magic potion, helping the girls to forget that trouble was around them.

They told jokes and asked each other questions just to keep talking and to keep each other laughing, just so that they could keep their minds on the dance. It worked until they began to run out of questions and found themselves with no more jokes to tell. A moment of awkward silence went between them, then Donna sang a song softly, "A little girl went into the woods down by the railroad tracks. Railroad tracks. Railroad tracks. A little girl went into the woods down by the railroad tracks. Railroad tracks. Railroad tracks. Railroad tracks."

Evelyn looked at Melinda and Janice, then she arched her brow and peered at Donna. The soft way that Donna sang the lyric almost made the words to the song seem innocent, as if they could do no harm.

None of the girls spoke. They spent the next few seconds examining each other's reaction to the song and to the fact that one of them had created it.

Evelyn struggled to calm her emotions while she looked hard at Donna. She'd seen the drained look in her father's face when he came home and told her mother that he had to tell a parent that their child was dead. Just having to tell someone death had stepped outside the shadow of tomorrow, pushed through the distant future of another day, and found a loved one was exhausting. Evelyn could only imagine what it would feel like to be the recipient of such tragic news.

Donna started singing again. "A little girl went into the woods down by the railroad tracks. Railroad tracks. Railroad tracks. Railroad—"

"--Will you please stop singing that stupid song," Evelyn snapped. You're not going to finish it anyway. Always going overboard. Always trying to get under a spotlight. Always trying to feel important."

Donna walked close to Evelyn and laughed. "I'll finish it. A little girl went into the woods down by the railroad tracks. Railroad tracks. Railroad tracks. And she was never heard from again."

The girls jumped when they heard the bedroom

door swing suddenly open. David stood in the doorway. "I told you all once," he shouted. "Stop talking about it." The veins at the sides of his head swelled. "Stop talking about it." He turned away from his sisters' bedroom as abruptly as he'd entered it. He crossed the hallway and stormed inside the bathroom. The door banged to a close behind him.

Tuning her back toward the doorway, Donna called out,"Inyanga."

Moments later, the girls left the bedroom and went downstairs. Jonathan was coming through the front door when they entered the living room. He laughed at his sisters and their friends and the dresses that they wore. "Don't we look nice?" he teased in falsetto. "Dave!" He hollered up the steps. "Come down here and see these girls trying to be women." He laughed again. "Look at you four, trying to look halfway decent." The second that they started hurling insults at him, he ran up the steps. "The dresses are pretty," he said when he reached the top stair, "But you all still have work to do. Take a tip. Start with your faces."

"You ready to go?" David asked when he opened the bathroom door.

Jonathan hurried into David's and his bedroom. "I just got home."

"You knew we had to be leaving soon."

Jonathan watched his older brother go into the closet and pull out a neatly pressed white shirt and a pair of navy blue pants. "We'll get there on time, Man." He chuckled. "You can't stand to be two seconds late to a place, can you?"

"It's gonna be crowded, Jon."

Pulling his shirt over his head, Jonathan reiterated, "Two seconds late, Dave."

David sat on the edge of his bed. He laid the pants and shirt across his lap. "I'm tired, Man. I almost don't feel like going to the dance. I'd kinda rather just stay home."

Jonathan finished pulling a fresh yellow knit shirt over his bare chest. "Aw, Man, you've got all kinds of time just to sit at home. Go to the dance. You know Margaret wants to go. If you don't take her, Man," he shook his head. "She's not going to forgive you. You know how women are when they get their mind set on something."

"Alright," David said when he looked up at his brother. "But we've got to let Mama and Dad know when we're leaving and when we'll be back.

"We can run by the store on our way to the dance. You know that's where they're at."

It was six-thirty in the evening when David, Jonathan, Melinda, Janice, Evelyn and Donna pulled up to the front of Tilson's Grocery Store. Dirt billowed at the back of the car that David drove. The store parking lot was so full that some trucks and cars were double-parked directly in front of the store, others were parked on the grass and dirt at the sides of the store. Heat in the day scorched the flowers and plants that Tammy pushed into the ground at the start of spring in effort to beautify the property the grocery store was placed on. It was sticky hot outside.

David was glad when he peered up into the sky and saw dark clouds grouping, threatening the area with rain. Inside the store, customers milled about and made it difficult for David to see his father standing midway down a center aisle restocking shelves with fresh rice and cereal.

"Dad."

Philip turned. "Come to help your old man fill

these here shelves?"

David chuckled. "Not this time, Dad. Just wanted to let you and Mama know that we're all heading to the dance."

"Got the car?"

"Yes, Sir. We'll be back around eleven o'clock tonight."

Philip bent and picked up another five-pound bag of rice. "Your mama see you come in the store?"

David shook his head. "No, Sir."

"Good." After he placed the rice on the shelf, he turned and faced his son. "You know your mama doesn't want you riding that girl around in our car."

"Dad."

"Now, Son, you know your mama don't like that girl. She don't like that girl's people. If your mama sees that girl in our car, she's gonna have a fit, and I don't feel like dealing with it. She's just gonna go on and on." He let out a deep breath, then said, "Tell me that girl's not sitting outside the store right now in our car."

"She's not. I'm going to pick her up on my way to the dance."

"Can't that closed mouth father of hers take her?"

"Dad."

"Okay. Alright." He nodded. "Just don't let your mother find out that girl was in our car."

"I won't." After a pause, he told his father, "That man came by the house too, after Melinda's and Janice's game."

"What?"

"I was home by myself. He kept trying to get me to open the door."

"What man?"

"The man who came by the store saying he had

books and pamphlets he wanted Mama and you to sell."

Philip stared blankly at his son.

"I told him to get going or I'd call the cops. He finally left. He left right before Melinda and Janice came home."

Philip placed his hand on his son's shoulder. "Good and don't worry about it, Son. I'll handle it."

He smiled at his father. "I know you will. And Dad, Margaret's father's name is Ramsey, and he talks sometimes. Mama and you ought to give yourselves a chance to get to know him. He's not odd the way people keep making out. He's alright, Dad."

His father released another deep breath and lowered his shoulders. "Alright. Alright," he added with a pat to his son's back, "Go have some fun at that dance, and don't stay out too late. Be back home by eleven o'clock like you said you would."

No sooner did he tell his father, "I will," than his mother rounded the corner and walked next to him. She held a stack of clothes in her arms. "Heading for the dance?"

"Yes, Mama. I gotta get going," he said while he stepped around her. "If we're going to make it there on time, we better leave now."

"You taking that girl?" She looked at him hard, not a smile, a frown, a sigh — just a hard look.

"Mama, I have to go." He picked up his pace and hurried out the store's main door. His mother stood behind him watching him go out the door.

After David picked up Margaret, he drove all the way to Booker T. Washington High School with the accelerator pressed to the floor. Margaret, Donna,

Evelyn, Janice and Melinda begged him to slow down, but he ignored their requests and sped passed the entrance to the woods that lead to the railroad tracks. While his girlfriend and sisters shouted at him to press the brake and slow down, David swallowed hard and stared at the trees. They were coming up on the spot where he saw the men pushing a little girl into a truck. He only recognized one of the men by sight, the man with the cane and the pronounced limp. The man who had been on his parents' front porch earlier in the day, the man who'd come to the grocery store yesterday asking questions about his mother and her family.

Voices ... it was the other men's voices that sounded familiar to David. He'd heard their voices when he went to the foundry to pick up two specially ordered metal pieces for the grocery store.

David closed his eyes. Tight. When he opened his eyes again, he grabbed the steering wheel and turned a hard right to keep from veering off the road.

"You alright?" Jonathan asked him.

"Yea," David answered with a nod. Then, he pressed the accelerator and continued driving down the road. He clutched the steering wheel and tried to make the voices stop. "Get her in there!" the voices kept saying. About a quarter mile up the road was the entrance to the river.

While his siblings and their friends talked about the dance, David stared blankly at the road. "Get her in there!" He'd heard one of the men shout to the others after they caught the kicking, screaming girl. She had been running. Running hard. Away from the river.

Last night, David had knelt behind a tree and watched the girl try to free herself from the men with the strength of her small legs and arms. She had clawed one of the men's eyes and kicked two of the men in the face, arms and groin. David almost cried while he watched the ribbons in the girl's hair blow in the wind. He'd figured that she'd leaped from the truck somehow and thought to make her way over the tracks and further into the woods to a place where she could get quiet and hide, but the men caught her. Seconds later, firmly in the men's grasp and still kicking fiercely, the little girl's leg scraped a tree. Hard. Even now as he neared the spot in the woods where he'd seen the men struggling with the girl, David held his breath. He remembered the smell of blood. His friend and he had waited until the men were gone, then they ran to the side of the road where the men and the little girl had struggled. It was so dark outside when David stretched forth his hand that he couldn't make out the mark on the tree. But blood — he smelled the blood. Moments later and further down the road, he'd heard something heavy splash in the river.

Duke Ellington and his orchestra were playing one of their hits on the radio when Donna's arm sprung forward. "David, don't forget to take that turn!"

David pumped the brake and sent everyone's head crashing against the back of the seat. A second later, he leaned forward and ran his palm across the window, "Sorry."

"It's so foggy out," Jonathan said.

"I can hardly see." David swallowed hard and looked at his watch. It was five minutes before seven o'clock. "Sorry. We're almost there." Fearing his thoughts were translucent, he created small talk. He didn't want anyone to sense his fear. He smiled while he listened to the song on the radio.

When they reached the school, David sat inside the car while everyone else climbed out.

"Aren't you coming?" Margaret asked.

"I'll be back." Then, he put the car in reverse and sped back to the river.

Margaret stood outside the school waiting for David to return until Janice grabbed her forearm and said, "Come on, Margaret. He'll be back. I think he has a lot on his mind right now. He probably just needs to think. David gets like that sometimes. He's my brother. I know it's hard, but it's just the way he is. Come on. Come inside with us. He'll be back."

Twenty minutes later, David sat in the cafeteria next to Margaret. His shoes were wet where he'd washed them in the river to clean off mud that had caked his shoes when he climbed down the incline behind the railroad tracks.

"Where did you go?"

"Margaret, please."

"No," she whispered. "Where did you go?"

"I thought I lost something when I was out last night, so I went to see if I could find it."

"Lost something where?"

"Just lost something, Margaret, he raised his voice. "Now stop talking about it, so we can have fun."

Several of the students turned and looked in their direction. When they did, Margaret lowered her head and covered the side of her face with her hand. On the other side of the cafeteria, four of the six teachers who had volunteered to chaperon the dance stood with their backs against the wall. Next to them was the refreshment table. It was loaded with food that the students' mothers had prepared. Colored paper strings hung from the ceiling. Long, skinny balloons bobbed back and forth on the tabletops. Shiny musical instruments lined the front wall.

The other two teachers who'd volunteered to chaperon the dance stood close to the two open cafeteria doors. They watched students pull chairs away from tables and sit. Because it was eighty-two degrees outside the school and even hotter inside the cafeteria, every operable window was pushed open.

It was seven twenty-five. Noise filled the cafeteria as friends told jokes, gossiped and talked about the basketball game.

Evelyn lifted her elbows to the table, folded her arms and asked Melinda, "Are we going to eat here or go to Mama Blue's Restaurant after the dance?"

Outside, clouds threatened to group and storm. The temperature had dropped ten degrees since late afternoon. One of the students looked at Evelyn, pressed a finger to her mouth and filled the cafeteria with one long, "Ssshhh."

The entire cafeteria became silent when the band's lead singer walked behind one of the five microphones and tapped its crown.

A chaperon closed the windows and shut the cafeteria doors, thunder pealed so loudly.

The trumpet player blew two notes through his trumpet. Beside him, the band's lead singer stepped to the microphone and called, "One-two. One-two." He pushed his mouth close to the microphone and shouted, "Hello!"

The students shouted back, "Hello!"

"How're you doing?" He adjusted the microphone while he worked the crowd.

"All right!"

"Feeling all right?"

"Yea!"

"Said, you feeling all right?"

Some of the students stood. "Yea!"

Leaning behind her boyfriend, Keith, toward her sister, Janice, Melinda whispered, "He's cute."

"Which one?"

"The drummer."

Janice stood and titled her head until she spotted the drummer. "He is a looker, but I think the lead singer's easy on the eyes myself."

The lead singer shouted, "I'm Kevin, and I'm glad to be here! We're gonna set this place on fire!" A second later, he stepped back and waited for the audience to roar. His greatest response came from Janice and Melinda. The sisters leaned against the backs of their chairs and screamed.

Once Melinda's laughter silenced and her breath evened, she looked down the table. "Margaret, why are you sitting all by yourself? Where did David go?"

Margaret sighed. "He went to the bathroom. He'll be right back."

Janice leaned closer to Margaret and said, "Don't look so sad. We're at a dance. He only went to the bathroom." She sat against the back of her chair and laughed.

"David seems different." Margaret lowered her gaze before she asked, "Janice, did anybody come by your house today?" She peered into her lap. "Asking questions?"

Janice leaned into the spine of her chair. "What kind of questions?"

Margaret pulled on the ends of her hair. "Police questions."

Janice asked, "About what?"

Margaret stared into her lap. "You know. About the little girl that's missing?"

Janice twisted her mouth. While she watched

Margaret stare into her lap, she thought back to her own childhood and the time when she felt lost and alone. She was playing hide-and-seek with her siblings and got stuck in the closet. She figured that she was five years old at the time. She cried until her mother heard her calls for help and came and opened the closet door. Her brothers teased her, but even now, she wouldn't close a closet door all the way. The dark inside a closed closet and the feeling of being away from her mother scared her that much. She couldn't bear to think of another little girl being afraid, alone and crying out for her mother. She looked at Margaret and waved her hand. "Let's just have fun. The questions will stop. It'll go away, Margaret. It always does." She clinched her teeth and prayed for the little girl to be okay. "We didn't have crime here until a few years ago."

The band's lead singer called out, "We've put together some tunes we know you'll enjoy. A little something from Duke Ellington, one of Tennessee's own, W. C. Handy, Memphis' own, Jazbo Brown and Jelly Roll Morton." Because he wanted the students on their feet, he gripped the neck of the microphone and shouted, "Joseph Oliver! Cab Calloway! We also wrote two of the songs we'll perform tonight. But before we begin, let me introduce the guys."

In the audience, Margaret leaned close to Janice. "Something's different about this time."

Janice waved her hand. "No it's not. It's the same as before. In two to three weeks, it'll be a gone issue. Watch and see." She lowered her head. "I just hope that little girl's okay." She looked up. "I hope she's okay."

Margaret arched her brow. She stared at Janice. "How does something like a murder just go away?"

Janice shook her head. "You ain't figured it out yet? The police are so convinced that the person who snatched that girl is from around here, they won't look any place else for clues. When they don't get enough evidence on anyone from Greasy Plank, they'll say the case is still open but won't have any detectives assigned to it anymore. It'll just drop. It'll just go away. Watch and see. It'll happen again. It always does." When Janice peered at Margaret and saw her folding and unfolding her napkin, she changed the subject. "Do you think they're going to play songs we can jitterbug and lindy-hop to?"

Margaret smiled. Her voice was soft and sounded faraway. "Cab Calloway. Yes. They'll play some good dancing music."

Janice sat forward on her chair. "Yea, and listen. They've started. I'm getting on that dance floor." Before she stood, she turned and grabbed her date's hand and said, "Come on."

The music blared. It sent the students' bodies into a dancing frenzy. Knees raised, hips jerked and swayed, heads bobbed and feet slid across the buffed floor. "Go, Donna! Go, Donna! Go! Go!" Janice cupped her hands around the corners of her mouth and joined Melinda to cheerlead Donna's sharp dance steps. Across the cafeteria, Jonathan and his date did the cakewalk. David stood next to Jonathan and his date clapping his hands to the beat of the music and the rat-tat-tat of Jonathan's and his date's feet. At the front of the cafeteria, the Dixie's pianist stroked the piano keys.

Two hours passed. The lights grew a heat all their own. Not even the rain falling to the ground outside could weaken the heat in the lights. At the band's request, an hour ago, one of the chaperons opened the cafeteria doors and, to keep them open, placed a large rock at the bottom of each door.

The band's lead singer scanned the cafeteria. "We're going to slow it down a bit." He crossed the platform and shook his head at no one in particular. "You young folks can dance." His voice was milky soft. "Thank you for your support. Thank you. You've been one of our best audiences, and we've played a lot of gigs. Now, like I said before, we want to slow it down a bit." He tightened his grip on the microphone. "Next, we're going to do a Nat King Cole tune." He backed away from the microphone and bowed his head. When he stepped toward the microphone again and raised his head, the pianist started strumming the piano keys.

S e c o n d s later, the large rocks that held the cafeteria doors ajar were hurled through the cafeteria windows. One of the chaperons placed her hand against her pounding heart as she watched the glass shatter. She listened to feet scamper across the ground outside and heard a man's voice scream, "You darkies better tell yo' fav'rite meddling mammy, that manish looking, Tammy Tilson, not to go sticking her nose in on this one!"

Chapter Four

Evelyn's father, Detective Robert Cramer, knocked on the front door at 77 Monroe Avenue, then he turned and eyeballed the neighborhood. All of the houses were four stories with large, wide front porches. All the front yards were well manicured. When Detective Cramer looked into the backyard of the house next to 77 Monroe, he wondered if the yard had an end. "All of these houses are sitting on no less than three acres," he said aloud to himself while he waited for someone to answer the front door.

While he stood on the porch, he wondered if the little girl who used to live in this house was the only child on the street. It was the middle of a summer's day and he didn't hear one child laughing, talking or playing. The street seemed too still to even have people living on it.

As he looked around the neighborhood, he wondered what it was about people with financial wealth that made them think the places where they lived ought to appear sanitized and quiet. This time of day where he lived in GreasyPlank, adults would be outdoors working on their farm and children would either be working alongside their parents or running, singing and playing near the edge of the road. Noise would fill the neighborhood; it definitely wouldn't be quiet.

"May I help you?"

He smiled cordially at the ebony skinned woman. "Is the man or the woman of the house available?"

"The woman of the home is here. May I ask who is calling for her?"

"Oh, yes. Please do excuse me." He extended his business card. "I'm Detective Robert Cramer from the Memphis Police Department." He took notice of the woman's features and her accent. "You're not from around here, are you?"

The woman blushed behind the attention that Detective Cramer gave her. "No. I wasn't born here. I'm from Jamaica. I live here with the Baxters."

"No wonder I haven't seen you around town. You didn't look familiar." He smiled cordially at her. "Do you mind going to get Mrs. Baxter?" Reaching inside his shirt pocket, he showed her his police badge. "I have a few questions I would like to ask her?"

The woman shook her head. "This has been a terribly hard time for the family."

"I can imagine." He paused, glancing around the woman and peering at the foyer. "Mrs. Baxter, please," he said as he craned his neck and peered further inside the house.

The woman turned. She left the front door open while she went to look for Mrs. Baxter.

While she was away, Detective Cramer stood on the porch inspecting the foyer and the living room. He admired the original European art decorating the living room. "French design," he said while he looked at the furniture in the main room of the house.

A tall, slender woman with a long pointy nose and brunette hair that scarcely reached to her shoulders approached the front door. "Who are you?"

Detective Cramer extended another of his business cards. He also made a point to show the woman his badge. "I'm Detective Cramer from the—"

"--Where are your colleagues?"

"I'm working this case—"

"--I didn't know Memphis had Coloured police officers."

Detective Cramer smiled. "I understand, Mrs. Baxter. It's a surprise to a lot of people—"

"--How long have you been working for the police department?"

"Ten years—"

"--Is this what my husband and I get for all the taxes that we pay in this city, for all the money that we give to community events and charity in this city?"

"Excuse me, Ma'am. 1 don't think I understand what you're saying--."

"--My daughter is missing, and the police department sends over a Coloured to investigate?"

"Ma'am, I'm one of the highest ranking detectives—"

"--I want to speak with the head of the department right now. I want to speak to your boss. Now."

He tilted the crown of his head toward the business card the woman held in her hand. "The number to the main office is on that card I gave you, Mrs. Baxter. If you'd like to call, feel free to do so. I'll wait until you're finished if you'd like. I have a few questions that I'd like to ask you."

She turned the card over in her hand. Then, she looked up at Detective Cramer. "Come in. My husband's a prominent attorney, you know," she said while she waved her hand toward a chair opposite the long living room sofa. "Have a seat."

"I'm aware of that. Yes," Detective Cramer said with a nod. He gave the room and the tall, winding stairs several yards to the right of the chair a long sweep. As he sat, he said, "I understand that your husband is a well respected man in Memphis and in Mississippi, if I may add."

She smiled. "He is. He's very good at what he does."

"I'm glad to hear that."

"Have they found my daughter?" Her words came

out flat, like heavy bricks falling to the ground.

"Ma'am, that's what I came here to speak with you about."

"Have they found my daughter?" she asked again, this time with a hard scowl.

"No, Ma'am. We have not found your daughter yet, but we are working around the clock to do just that. We want to get her back to you safely and as soon as possible."

Mrs. Baxter sat forward on the sofa and squinted at him. "Why am I hearing that this has become a murder case?"

"I don't know, Ma'am. People talk. Your daughter has not been found."

"She needs me."

"I understand. All children need their mother." He opened a small notepad and took a pen out of his shirt's right breast pocket. "If you don't mind, I'd like to ask you a few questions. It'll help with the investigation. It'll help us to locate your daughter and return her safely to you and your husband."

She bit down on her words. "She's my daughter."

Detective Cramer nodded. "I understand."

"No, you don't understand. You sound like a damn parrot. You keep saying you understand when you do not understand. Joycelyn is my daughter. Her father only thinks that she is his."

Detective Cramer sat forward on the chair. His brow went up only to lower a second later. He made a mental note that she was telling him something that she may not have told her husband. "Excuse me?"

"Do you like to hear everything get repeated?"

"I'm just trying to make absolutely certain that I get the facts straight, Ma'am. I don't want to misinterpret anything. That's all."

"What I just told you is not for note taking."

"When did you last see your daughter Joycelyn?"

Mrs. Baxter looked into her lap. A second later, she straightened her spine, sat erect and looked Detective Cramer in the eyes. "Two days ago."

Detective Cramer swallowed his frustration and asked her another question. "Do you know what time of day it was two days ago when you last saw your daughter?"

"Lenora," Mrs. Baxter called over her shoulder in a raised voice while she leaned back on the sofa and gazed into the dining room.

The maid, Lenora, hurried to the edge of the living room. "Yes, Ma'am?"

"What time was it when you last saw Joycelyn before she disappeared?"

Detective Cramer looked from Mrs. Baxter to Lenora.

"I don't remember. I had been outside watching her while she was playing when I came inside for a moment to check on the afternoon meal. It seemed like it was about one or two o'clock to me. It must have been around one o'clock, because we hadn't eaten the afternoon meal yet."

"What time do you normally eat lunch?"

"Twelve or one o'clock, but lately it's been more close to one o'clock," Lenora told Detective Cramer.

"Any particular reason?"

"I just haven't had the afternoon meal prepared in time to eat earlier," Lenora shrugged. "That's all."

"We've been remodeling," Mrs. Baxter said while she ran her hand across the sofa.

"Do you know anybody who might know your daughter who I should talk to, Mrs. Baxter?"

Mrs. Baxter sat back and crossed her legs. "No."

"Do you know anyone who your daughter may have gone to visit or play with?"

"No."

"Has she ever walked off before or gone inside a neighbor's house without telling you--"

"--No."

"Can you think of any place where she might possibly be—"

"--Are you trying to get me to do your job, Detective?"

"No, Ma'am."

"And are you telling me that you have found absolutely nothing regarding my daughter's disappearance? After two days you know nothing more than you knew before she turned up missing? Is that what I'm hearing? Is that what you're telling me?"

"Ma'am, we are combing the woods and every inch of this city in search of your daughter. It will help if you can give me as much information as possible about your daughter, especially all you know just before you last saw her."

"I wasn't with her when she disappeared." She pointed the crown of her head toward the maid. "Lenora was. Like she told you, they were outside together when Lenora came in to check on the afternoon meal."

"Lunch?"

Mrs. Baxter closed her eyes tightly. "Yes. Lunch."

"Well, Mrs. Baxter, the last time that you, specifically you," he added, glancing at Lenora, "did see your daughter, what time of day do you think that was?"

"About nine o'clock in the morning," Mrs.

Baxter answered.

"And you didn't see her again the entire day?"

"Lenora is our live-in maid and nanny. We pay her very well."

"Excuse me, Mrs. Baxter. Do you work?"

She sat against the spine of the sofa hard, obviously offended. "No."

"I apologize," Detective Cramer said while he wrote notes on his pad. "I didn't mean to offend you."

Mrs. Baxter was silent.

"Just a few more questions, if you will. What was your daughter wearing when you last saw her?"

"I don't remember." Glancing across the room, she asked, "Lenora?"

Lenora leaned around the kitchen corner and looked into the livingroom at Detective Cramer. "She was wearing a yellow blouse and a pair of dark blue pants. She had yellow and blue ribbons in her hair. She was also wearing white socks with ruffles on them and a pair of blue and white sneakers. Her hair was pulled back in a ponytail."

"Thank you," Detective Cramer nodded at Lenora. Turning on the chair, he faced Mrs. Baxter. "Do you mind if I have a look at your daughter's room? Seeing the layout of her room and some of her favorite belongings will help me to understand her better, what motivates her, what she likes which may, in turn, play a role in helping us to find her."

"Lenora," Mrs. Baxter said, sitting tall on the sofa but not standing. "Escort Detective Cramer to Jocelyn's bedroom."

Detective Cramer spent half an hour in the little girl's bedroom. Stuffed animals filled the top of the bed. Board games that a child could play alone were stacked on the dresser. D o l l s filled a toy box at the foot of the bed. A bedspread with a cartoon design covered the bed. Curtains in the room were custom designed with cartoon characters. The clothes in the closet were neatly pressed. Plastic dry cleaner bags covered all the clothes.

"Thank you for letting me see the room," Detective Cramer told Lenora as he turned to leave the bedroom. On his way out the door, he looked back at the dresser. Photos were paper clipped and scotch taped to the sides of the mirror above the dresser.

Detective Cramer walked back inside the room and studied the photos. There was a silver-haired man in two of the photos leaning on a cane. He stood next to the girl.

Chapter Five

Tree limbs stabbed the girl's arms. Tall blades of wet grass cut her legs. Wind moving with the speed and noise of a freight train pushed at her face, but she didn't stop running. She could hear the men coming, running hard behind her. She pumped her arms faster. Her mouth opened into a chilling scream. Just as the first man grabbed her and wrapped his arm about her waist, a lighter in his back pocket flipped open and fell to the ground. The little girl tossed dirt into the man's eyes. Her face was burning; her legs were hot from the fire. "Mommy! Mommy, Janice!" the little girl screamed while she ran with her arms raised.

Janice sprung up in bed. Her face was drenched with sweat. "Melinda!" she hollered into the night. She breathed deeply until her heart stopped racing. Then she leaned on her side and cried.

Hauntings ... nightmares that came to her with an unrelenting regularity. "Dear, God," she sobbed. "Why does that little girl always turn into Melinda? Why?"

A recent high school graduate, Janice spent most of her time cleaning the house and working at the store or visiting her boyfriend. Wherever she was, she often felt deep pain and loss. In the mornings, she didn't want to get out of bed. At night, she cried herself to sleep. She couldn't stop the images and the voice of her sister, a week-old newlywed, from entering her mind. She was always lonely for her sister. Besides the loss of her twin, Janice felt nothing changed in her life since she'd graduated from high school. Twice since graduation, she left Greasy Plank and went uptown to large, local businesses and filled out job applications, but the women peering at her from behind their thick horn-rimmed glasses didn't seem to care that she had a diploma at home.

The night before her sister and her high school graduation, her mother tried to comfort her. She'd come into the room that she had shared with her sister, Melinda, since the day that she was born. Her mother had just taken a bath. She was wearing a light blue robe; a story filled her head. Melinda was at the Daisy Theatre with her fiancé, Keith, watching a Bill "Bojangles" Robinson hit.

Although Janice bowed her head in effort to duck her mother's shadow, Tammy made her way inside the dark bedroom. "Hi, Baby," she said while she sat beside her daughter on the bed, and, pulling her hairbrush from her robe pocket, began to brush Janice's long, thick hair. "You know, I'm proud of you and Melinda. Your father and I both are. All of you kids have done so well. You've made us happy." She continued to brush Janice's hair, oblivious to the fact that Janice had moved closer to her side. "You know, I didn't graduate from high school."

Janice peered up at her mother in disbelief.

"Your father didn't either. I dropped out of school in the sixth grade to help my folks. We had a twenty-acre farm and taking care of it took more than four hands. Your father dropped out of school in the fourth grade to help his father. His mother died when he was just a child. Your grandfather, your pop's father, raised ten children by himself. He was a tall, proud, powerful man, someone I admired." She stopped brushing Janice's hair and placed her hands on top of Janice's. A heat like that found in fire came away from their bodies when they joined hands. "We're proud of you, Baby, and you'll be fine even though Melinda's getting married. Now I may not agree with her choice for a husband." She shook her head. "Really thought I taught you kids better." She sighed. "But you'll be just

71

fine." Lowering the brush to the bed, she turned and wrapped her arms around her daughter's shoulders. She concluded the talk by saying, "You'll get along, and you'll have fun again. You'll do just fine, and you'll stop spending most of your time at the store."

"But Mama, I miss her and so much is changing. It's not the way it used to be." She didn't mention her nightmares about the little girl who'd turned up missing over a year ago. She pretended that she'd forgotten as had everyone else in town -- as if time could make a little girl's life no longer matter.

After six months of investigating the case with fervor, one domestic violence related murder, a theft related murder, rapes, burglaries and rumors of political indiscretions pushed the missing girl case off newspaper front pages and closer to the back of open police files.

Unaware of her daughter's nightmares, Tammy lowered her gaze. "Everything is changing, Sugar." She looked up. "It's the way life is."

"I can't even get a job."

"You can always work at the store."

"I want to get out on my own, Mama."

"You ain't got to live here to work at the store."

"But I don't want to live all by myself. It's not safe. People are always trying to hurt us because we stand up for what's right. We're not cowards who just go along with the tide. So many people hate that about us. And I don't want to be lonely either." She looked up. "Mama, I don't want to be lonely."

Tammy massaged the top of Janice's hand "Oh, Child."

"I'm losing my best friend, Mama." She stared at her mother's hand resting gently atop her own. "I'm never going to get her back the way I used to have her."

While rubbing her daughter's hand, Tammy spoke softly. "You remind me of my own mama in ways, Janice. You have a strength for connecting into the spirit of the universe. You can feel things before they happen, before they actually come true. Mama would call you a seer." She smiled. "She was the first one in our family, you know. Mama was." She shook her head. "She saw things long before they happened. Mama always said no coward could ever be a seer. Said cowards was afraid of the truth. Run straight from it. Mama said a coward'll do anything to fit in, to make like they belong. They just so scared. Cowards are scared of who they even are. They scared of themselves and everybody else too." She laughed. "Seers can see right through a coward, a whole family or group of them, Mama said, right through them. See right through them even when the coward's busy trying to hide from the truth."

Silence passed between mother and daughter, then Tammy asked, "You see things, Janice? Things that are to come?"

Without looking at her mother, Janice lowered her shoulders and whispered, "She's gone."

Chapter Six

Detective Robert Cramer leaned over a back counter in a small room at the rear of Tilson's Grocery Store. "The Brown Bomber's not what he used to be." He sipped on a can of soda. "I say he needs to retire."

Philip laughed. "He just knocked out Johnny Paycheck. What more you want from the man? And besides, what's a boxer going to do after he stops fighting? Those guys should start building on a career outside the ring while they're still young."

Another of the six men that filled the small, back room belched and said, "Joe Louis still has a lot of fight left him in. Just because a man loses a few fights doesn't mean he's done and that there's no more winnings left in him. Don't give up on Joe so fast. He's already champ again."

"I lost a lot of money on that fight," another man said. Then he gave Robert a quick glance and added, "I wasn't doing nothing illegal, Cramer."

Robert chuckled. "I didn't say anything." He smiled and lowered his head, then he shook it. "I don't know why you all keep doing that to me. Just because I'm a cop. Man. I'm just like you all. I'm one of y'all. I'm not watching every single thing you all do."

"Betta not be watching nothing I do," another man in the room laughed and said.

"We know you're one of us, Cramer. Everybody from Greasy is family except for that Ramsey Armstrong. He don't never come around." Another man in the room looked over his shoulder at Philip. "Sorry, Man. I know David's seeing Ramsey's daughter, Margaret, but you know Ramsey's one tight-lipped brother."

Philip nodded slowly. "Yea." Then he nibbled on a mouthful of ice. "You all are shot out, Man. Just shot out. Now hush, so I can hear this fight on the radio."

The men spent the next two hours listening to sports broadcasts on the radio. They didn't think about their jobs, disagreements they were having with their wives or how they were going to pay for a new outfit their children wanted. Philip didn't even think about his oldest son David's upcoming wedding to his girlfriend, Margaret Armstrong, an event that his wife had tried to stop for months. The men laughed and shared in the special brotherhood t h a t  they had created when they all were just little boys growing up in Greasy Plank, the same way that they did when they bumped into each other at the barbershop.

These Friday night gatherings were therapeutic for Robert most of all. They allowed him to believe that the men of Greasy Plank still considered him a friend even after he and his colleagues questioned them for weeks after the little girl from Monroe Avenue turned up missing. He comforted himself with the thought that each time he called one of his friends into the interrogation room, he always referred to him as "Mister." Not once did he belittle or ridicule them. But the questions, he'd asked them so many questions that toward the end of the interrogations, he himself had started to cringe.

"Alright," one of the men said as he stood to leave after Philip reached across the counter and turned off the radio. "I'm gonna be getting along. If I don't get home soon, my wife'll throw a fit."

Another man racked in the loose deck of cards on the table that they'd been playing spades on, then he folded the table and placed it behind a filing cabinet. "I know what you mean. I have to be going myself. I don't know what it is about eight o'clock. I can come home any time before eight o'clock and

75

my wife won't say a word beyond, 'did you have a good day?' But let me come home after eight o'clock." The man pursed his lips and shook his head. "And I'll never hear the end of it."

Robert stopped and looked up at the 'Picture and Notice Board' on his way out the door into the main area of the grocery store. "Philip," he called after the rest of the men had exited the small room.

Philip started to turn the light off.

"No. Wait," Robert said. He pointed to a picture on the board. "Do you know this man?"

Philip squinted and looked at the picture of an elderly white man. "He comes in here sometimes." He pulled the picture off the board and crumpled it in his hand. "I don't know how that picture got up there."

"But do you know him?" Robert asked while Philip and he walked out the door, exiting the small room.

"He came down to the store once. He called and said he had some books and pamphlets he thought Tammy and I might be able to sell. I came all the way down here one day to meet him. He said he was from Louisville."

"Kentucky?"

"Yea. Thing was he didn't have any books, pamphlets or anything with him. He spent the entire time he was down here asking questions about Tammy and her family, especially Tammy's mother."

"That's odd."

"You're telling me."

"Ever hear from him again?"

"David said he came by the house once. I wasn't there. He's been in the store maybe twice since. Can't stop a man from shopping at a store."

"Did he have a cane when he came into the store?"

"Cramer, you're always a detective. I don't know, Man. I don't remember. He might have had a cane. He might not have had a cane. Why?"

"Just asking, Man." Robert paused then asked, "What did he want to know about Tammy?"

"I don't know. I forget. That was more than a year ago, Cramer. I've got too much to think about day to day. I don't have time to be keeping up with what happened a year ago."

"Was he alone when he came into the store or was he with a tall, slender brunette?"

Philip gawked at Robert.

"Alright, Man. Alright," Robert said as they walked out of the grocery store together.

## Chapter Seven

Although her parents and her brothers continued to live at home with her, Janice felt empty each night when she walked through the front door. Being separated from her sister was an injury that time did not heal. She wasn't three years old like she had been the day that her parents first brought her to the grocery store. All those years ago, Melinda was always right at her side. When they were little girls, they'd sit on the stool that Tammy placed beside the cash register with their hands open. Customers stuck pieces of hard candy inside their palms after they paid for their goods and grabbed their grocery bags before they walked out the door. The girls would stick the candy inside their pockets and giggle.

Today, because she woke up with a migraine, Janice stayed home. Heat filled the kitchen from the floor to the ceiling. Seeking relief, she turned from where she stood in front of the stove grilling a cheese sandwich and faced the radio. While she fanned her face with her hand, she listened to the broadcaster's voice. As did most Southerners, the broadcaster chopped his words, cutting out syllables here and there. Words the broadcaster didn't chop, he drug, "More men'll be coming home from the war, home for good. And now for local news. Last night a yellow blouse and a blue and white sneaker that is thought to belong to the missing Baxter girl was found . . ."

Janice lunged across the kitchen table and turned the radio off. Images of her future sister-in-law, Margaret Armstrong, moved to the front of her mind. She almost burned the grilled cheese sandwich -- her mind went off into unfamiliar territory and remained there so long. Turning off the stove, she walked toward the table.

When she sat, she thought about her future sister-in-law's father, Ramsey. Quiet and somewhat forlorn, he appeared to be a devoutly religious man to her. He seldom spoke or smiled, and he walked with his head down. He came off as a serious man. He wasn't one for socializing or telling jokes; that much she knew. He kept company with misfits and other men ostracized by larger society. She thought about the little girl who turned up missing last year.

Tears pooled in her eyes. She'd started thinking about looking for the girl on her own. Leave the store and instead of going home, go up by the railroad tracks and down by the river. In her dreams, she'd heard the missing girl crying. She kept her awake at night. She haunted her. When Janice crawled into bed at night, she reached beneath her mattress and pulled out a flashlight. She pushed the flashlight beneath her bed covers and kept it on all night. She was terrified to be in the dark. She feared that the thickness of night would bring dead things around her. Sometimes when she was home alone, she swore that she heard a child whimper, "Help me. Help me." She recalled one of the pictures of the Baxter girl that was copied onto flyers taped to storefronts across town. A second later, she grimaced and told herself, "Margaret's father's not evil."

Before David's and Margaret's wedding, Janice met Margaret's mother, Rebecca, once. *Porgy and Bess* was showing at the Orpheum Theater. Everyone in Shelby County talked about the musical. The line of people waiting to see the show went around the side of the theater.

Though Rebecca smiled, Janice could tell that the older woman spent more than a few late nights crying.

Bags were beginning to form under her eyes. When Janice lowered her head to keep from having to look at Rebecca, she saw knots atop the older woman's knees. "Long hours of prayer for her soldier son," Janice mused to herself.

She looked at the ground. A flyer promoting United States Savings Bonds blew across the sidewalk over the tops of her feet. "She doesn't want to be a soldier's mama," Janice told herself when she stopped glancing at the flyer and peered up at Rebecca. "She's scared some Army General's gonna come banging on the front door early in the morning to let her know her son's dead."

Janice turned the radio on again. The broadcaster's Southern drawl boomed, "Today, September 2, 1945, is a great day in history. General MacArthur, General Umezu, the Japanese foreign minister, and government officials from France, Australia, New Zealand, Canada, the Netherlands, Russia and China gathered to sign the documents that ended the war."

Across town, Margaret, David's soon to be wife, peered inside her family's dining room. Her mother continued to talk to the town gossip on the telephone. "Don't you know it? That figures just right for her. She's always been that kind."

Margaret rolled her eyes and walked inside the kitchen. A box was on the floor next to the cupboard. She smiled when she glanced at the box. She was glad that her favorite aunt had sent her parents and her home with a plate of food. Now that she didn't have to cook supper, she could unpack the contents of the box.

"Oh, Girl, stop kidding yourself. You know that woman's always been mean and nasty. She ain't changed one bit. Stop and think about it. Remember what she said about that out-of-town preacher?" Pulling the receiver closer to her mouth, she whispered, "And as if that's not enough, I heard she's been running around with one of the married men in town." She sat back in the chair. "The things I have heard that conniving woman has been doing late at night." She clucked her tongue. "You know word around town is that some of these married folk don't hardly sleep in the same bed no more and haven't in years. The things I have heard. Girl, the folks in this town sure know how to carry on."

Listening to her mother gossip, Margaret hung her head and wished, "Let Mama be off the phone by the time I finish eating a piece of chocolate cake." After she cut the cake, she sat at the kitchen table and listened to the sound of her mother's voice. She overheard her say, "Child, you know I don't like talking on the phone, but you know his wife's been running around on him, don't you?" There was a pause. "Yes, Child. For at least five years now. She's been having extra long meetings with one of them traveling preachers. Sure has. You can look right at that youngest son of hers and see it ain't her husband's. You can look straight at that child and see that." She laughed. "And she's always going around telling folk she got the perfect marriage. Always standing up testifying long and sanctimoniously every Sunday morning."

Margaret looked into the dining room. While she watched her mother laugh, it seemed strange to her that her parents laughed all too infrequently and vacationed only twice since as far back as she could remember. Both times they had visited her favorite aunt in Atlanta, Georgia. As a child when she asked her father why they didn't vacation more, he'd stared at her and, speaking in monotone, told her, "Because something might happen. That's why."

Margaret looked into the dining room long enough to see her mother lean forward and smile a crooked smile. A chill went up her spine. She worried that her mother was teaching her that, in order to be a "good wife" it was necessary to ignore her husband's most destructive habits. Despite the sharp and lasting pain that her father's emotional distance brought to his children, her mother not once asked him to open up, play with the kids more, take them to a movie-- nothing. When she was around her father in the house alone, she felt cold and empty, almost like a paper doll. Her father never hugged her. He never told her or her siblings that he loved them. To Margaret, her father was just a man who worked hard and came home before the sun went down every night. She had no other frame of reference with which to describe him. "The man who was just there." That's what he was to her.

Her mother's laughter echoing in her ears, Margaret turned her back to the dining room and unfolded a note that she had taken off the front door when her parents and she had returned home from driving her younger brother and sister to their aunt's and uncle's.

*Dear Margaret, David Tilson came by your house. Says it's very important, and for you to telephone him soon. He scared me the way he was breathing so hard. Looked like he ran all the way to your house. Better call that boy soon as you and your folks get back in. Seen some cops peeking through your back window too. They was looking down by y'all drainage pipe. Even went down to the creek at the back of y'all yard and looked around real good. Maybe y'all best not go away nowhere far for awhile.*

*Good day. Your neighbor, HW*

Margaret faced the kitchen window. It was pitch black outside, certainly too late to run to the Tilson's and ask David about the note. She refused to think about the cops. Doing so only made her ill and beyond throwing up and losing sleep, she knew that there was nothing that she could do to right whatever wrongs there were that existed around her, wrongs rooted right in her own family. She stared at the note again and wondered what David knew that she didn't. "It's gotta be about Alex," she mused. Last week her father told her mother and her that her oldest brother, Alex, called him at the foundry. He said that Alex kept apologizing for missing the birth of his youngest son. "Don't forget to visit Sharrie and the boys," he had reminded their father.

Margaret's brother, Alex, worried about his wife, Sharieffa. They had been separated for two years. Margaret speculated that her brother's heart ached when he felt his wife's loneliness; especially when he read his wife's letters.

Sharieffa wrote Alex weekly. In her writings, she described their young sons in detail. She wrote and told Alex that their sons, Karl and Michael, were "growing like collard greens". Then, she asked Alex if he remembered how big her eyes were and told him that Michael's eyes were bigger and that both boys were "as cute as they wanted to be." She would continue and say, "Michael's potty trained and has eight teeth. Karl learned to ride the tricycle the neighbors gave him as a present on his second birthday. He likes pulling Michael in the wagon you sent from Europe last summer. I won't let him take Michael outside in the wagon, but I allow the boys to play plenty in the basement when I'm down there scrubbing laundry."

In her last letters, she wrote Alex less about their sons and more about her longing to see him. "Can't you come home, even for a few days?" she asked midway through her letters. Nearer the end of her letters, she began to plead. "I pray for you to come home. The boys and I need you. Please come home soon."

The despair and rage that had fashioned itself from the shreds of plea that she'd unthreaded several long paragraphs earlier would become a scrawl of, "The President and the nation will likely do little to reward you Coloured servicemen and servicewomen for your heroic efforts in this bloody war. We still won't be able to sit down and eat at the counter of Georgie's or McNutt's or get a table at Lydia's on a Friday night. None of the businesses on Riverside Drive'll want to serve us. You'll still be a 'nigger' to them."

Her anger would break and she would write, "I'm still working at Johnson's Cleaners. It's hard, real hard around here right now. They never did find that little girl that turned up missing last year. If somebody ask, cops say they're still looking for her, but I don't believe it. Men in Greasy even went looking for that girl. It's almost like that girl never existed. Like she was no more than a ghost. I watch the boys real close, because you just don't know. Nobody wants to believe a killer is living right around us, but somebody took that little girl."


"Mama? Dad?" Margaret called out from the

kitchen twenty minutes after she heard her father come home.

Rebecca released Ramsey's hand. When she did, her own hand become suddenly cold. She pulled down on her dress' hem.

Leaving the kitchen and entering the living room where her parents sat on the sofa, Margaret peered at the note before she handed it to her mother.

While Rebecca read the note, Ramsey looked at Margaret. He twisted his mouth. "Who is the note from?" His hands shook while he stared at his daughter.

Margaret shook her head. "No. The note's not from Mr. Robinson." She turned away from her father.

Rebecca re-read the note, then she asked, "Margaret, what is this?"

Margaret shrugged, "I don't know."

Pulling the note close to her chest and away from her husband's prying eyes, Rebecca asked, "Well? Did you call Dave?'

Margaret struggled not to judge. Yet, her finger seemed to straighten and point at her mother on its own. "You were on the phone."

"I've been off the phone for over half an hour."

"Not that long," Ramsey injected.

"Ramsey, I know when I got off the phone, and Margaret, you could have called Dave."

Margaret mumbled, "I know."

Rebecca peered into her daughter's eyes. "Tammy?"

"Right." Margaret crossed her arms.

Rebecca folded the note and stuffed it inside her dress pocket. A second later, she looked over her shoulder at Ramsey and nodded, "Tammy." Then

85

she added, "I shouldn't say this, but Tammy's a little too much for me. Nothing our family does is good enough for her." She scowled. "If you don't call Dave, I will."

Margaret shook her head. "No. I'll call him."

While she watched her daughter walk to the telephone, Rebecca called out over her shoulder, "If Tammy starts in with the million questions, give the phone to me. Hear?"

"Yes, Ma'am."

Margaret sat in the dining room staring at the telephone.

A few moments passed before Ramsey whispered over his shoulder, "Margaret?'

Margaret waved and gripped the receiver. "Not now." Again facing the telephone, she raised her voice. "Dave, when did you leave the note?"

"About one o'clock. I knew you all were out of town visiting your aunt and uncle, so when I saw your neighbor out back, I figured I'd tell her. Can you believe Alex actually called me at our house?"

"And you told me to call you soon. I figured it must be important."

"It is," David shouted. "Call Sharieffa and tell her the good news."

"What good news?"

"Alex is coming home."

Margaret let out a scream. Fumbling with the receiver, she turned and faced her mother. "Al is coming home!"

## Chapter Eight

Stephanie Baxter hurried across the parking lot to a burgundy Jaguar. After she unlocked the car door, she slid across the creme colored leather seats. Despite her husband's repeated vows to stand by her and support her through this, their greatest crisis, she felt her marriage was coming undone. She'd lied enough to know when a person believed her. She'd lied to her mother when she was five years old and the family dog darted away from the back yard and took off for the house yelping loudly. She'd stuck the dog with the two large safety pins that decorated the plaid skirt that she wore. Yet, when her mother asked her if she knew why the dog was crying, she looked her mother straight in the eye and told her the dog had gotten stuck in one of the bushes and that she'd tried with all her might to free him.

From petty thefts that she'd wrestled her way out of by crying loudly and begging forgiveness and reminding law enforcement that she was the daughter of a prominent physician to threatening suicide to teasing men with her sexual advances only to later claim that the men were too aggressive with her, Stephanie lied. Her life was a circle of lies. One untruth after another. It was the reason that she didn't flinch when her husband visited her at the hospital the day that Jocelyn was born and, holding her daughter in her arms, she had raised her in the air and told her husband, "See how precious your little girl is? Thank you for giving me such a beautiful gift."

Now in the parking lot, Stephanie felt that her lies were catching up to her. Age was taking a toll on her figure; she couldn't hide behind her good looks the way that she used to. She was beginning to feel like just another woman and she hated that.

She gazed into the rearview mirror and combed her

polished fingernails through her hair until her hair lay flat against her head. Then, she leaned forward and applied another layer of lipstick to her mouth. After she dropped the lipstick inside her pocketbook, she turned the key in the ignition. A second later, she turned the car off and sat against the seat.

Her husband had just come in from visiting a client when she'd stepped off the elevator half an hour ago. He had looked surprised to see her.

"Hard at work?" she had asked him just before she leaned and kissed his face.

"I went to see a client," he had said without a smile or any response to the kiss that she'd given him.

She'd tugged on his forearm. "I know she's gone, Honey, but we have to go on with our lives. Jocelyn wouldn't want to see us like this. For her, she'd want us to go on with our lives."

"She was a little girl. How do you know what she wanted?"

"I was her mother."

He'd pulled his arm out of her grasp and hurried toward his office. "Don't you do this."

She'd followed him. "You're right," she'd said. "I can't continue to live like this." Her voice had started to break. "I shouldn't continue to live like this and neither should you. She's gone, and it will certainly do us no good to continue to put our lives on hold as if doing so will bring her back. I'm her mother. How terribly awful do you think I feel? You don't feel half as badly as I feel. You can't. And I can't keep going like this." She'd started to cry. "I can't keep suffering like this, hoping like this, waiting like this.

"Every time I hear the front door open, I look to see if she's coming home. It's almost like she went outside to play for a long time. I swear every time our front door opens, I hold my breath and my heart starts racing. I can't breathe sometimes, especially at night." She'd raised her voice. "You think I don't hurt?" She had pounded his chest with her fist and said. "I hurt. She was my daughter. She was my little girl."

He'd swallowed the anger that had risen after he discovered that it was his wife who had demanded that the police department not publish information about the investigation, information that detectives felt would generate renewed interest in the case which could help lead them to Jocelyn's kidnapper.

"Come here," he'd said while he opened his arms and embraced his wife. He'd stroked her back and told her, "I know this has been hard on you. I don't blame you for what's happened. I know you loved Jocelyn as much as I did. We'll get through this. Somehow we will. We just have to do all that we can to get the investigation started again, so we can find Jocelyn. We cannot afford to let this go." He'd shook his head. "We can't stop fighting to find our little girl until she's back at home with us again."

She'd stepped away from him and shook her head. "No. No. No. I'm not going to do this. I do not want the investigation re-opened."

"It's never been closed."

She'd blinked several times. "I-I-I didn't mean re- opened. I meant exploded in the media again. It'll be in the papers. It'll be on the radio. I can't live through that all over again." She'd started to cry. "I can't. I just can't. How many times can a parent re-live their child's disappearance? How many times should any parent have to live through that hell?"

"I understand, Sweetheart. I'm just saying let the detectives, particularly that Detective Cramer — he has a lot of interest in this case and has never fully stopped looking for Jocelyn anyway — Sweetheart, let him give the case all he has. Let him find our little girl and bring her back safely to us."

"You don't love me," she'd stammered as she'd turned to leave. "I can't believe you'd put me through this hell again."

"Just give it a few more months, please. Six months. At least six more months, Sweetheart. That's all I'm asking."

She'd hurried out of the office without answering him, and now she sat in her Jaguar wanting to say, "I'm sorry." He'd loved her daughter like she was his own since the day that she was born. But why wouldn't he, she told herself, "He thinks that she is his daughter."

She sat in the car awhile longer, then she started the engine and put the car in reverse. She was halfway out of the parking lot when she slammed on the brakes and nearly sent the car careening into the side of her husband's office building. She stared at the silvery-gray haired man in disbelief. When he leaned against his cane with one hand and waved at her with the other, she turned the steering wheel and pressed the accelerator until it touched the floor and sped, the Jaguar's tires squealing, out of the parking lot.

Chapter Nine

Margaret laughed hard into the telephone receiver after Evelyn Cramer told her a joke. Of all the people who Margaret knew, Evelyn was the one she trusted most. She liked Melinda and Janice, but they were Tammy's daughters.

She loved David, but he reminded her so much of her father. David was good to her though. He didn't have a temper and he was a hard worker. He'd make an excellent father to the children she hoped to have. Like her father, when things troubled David, he didn't talk; he went into his room and closed out the world. It was tough, but during their courtship, she had managed to get him to at least begin to open up. It scared her to think that she'd have to spend the rest of her life assuring David of her love for him and encouraging him not to shut her out when he was worried or troubled. On the other hand, she believed that, with lots of prayer and affection, she could get him to change, change until he no longer reminded her of her father.

She also knew that Tammy called her names and said cruel and untruthful things about her when she wasn't around. It was bad enough that Tammy rolled her eyes at her when she visited David. The Tilson house seemed cold to her; she knew it was a place where she wasn't welcomed. Tammy *tolerated* her. Margaret didn't need anyone to tell her that. If not for Evelyn, Margaret doubted that she would stay in this town. People talked about her father. They said that he was too quiet, kept to himself too much. What they didn't seem to think was that if her father was the type of man that they said he was, Evelyn's father would be watching him, and he wasn't.

Margaret crossed her legs and laughed. "Evelyn, you are always cutting up. Is there anything you won't say?"

"Just remember what I told you. Make sure you keep David on your side, because with a mother-in-law like Mrs. Tilson, you're gonna need every ally that you can get."

Margaret chuckled. "If I ever find myself in a situation where I haven't got one soul in the whole world who believes in me and who will support me, I know I can always count on you to be my forever friend."

"That's the truth. I don't care what happens, we're friends forever."

"Forever friends," Margaret added with a smile. Then she said, "Talk to you later, Evelyn."

Seconds after she returned the receiver to its cradle, the telephone rang again. Before Margaret could ask who the caller was, Tammy blurted, "Make sure you're at the house by noon today so I can start on your wedding gown. You know that pretty yellow dress at the store? Well, I made that. Evelyn's mom bought it two days ago. And those blue and white skirt sets the Henrik girls wear that everyone loves, I sewed those one evening when Janice was minding the store. Ask anybody. They'll tell you how good I am. I'm the best seamstress in all of Greasy Plank. I made near all of my children's clothes when they were younger. Sure, I did. I made the cutest outfits for David when he was a little boy."

She laughed. "You should have seen him. I kept my children looking like they were somebody because they are. Even after Philip and I built the grocery store, I sewed my children's clothes so they'd feel like they were somebody. Sure did." She cleared her throat. "And now, Margaret, I know you didn't have nothing to do with where David and your

92

wedding is going to be. I know you'd of had your wedding at the church that David grew up attending, especially since you and your people ain't from around here, being as you all are from Kentucky and all. I know you're not a dumb girl. I know you've got enough sense to know that little church your people go to ain't hardly no place to have a decent, respectable wedding."

"I know that, Margaret, but I gotta do something. I was just telling Philip the other day how much I feel like our hands have been tied and that we're getting to do next to nothing to help prepare for our oldest son's wedding. I know you don't have nothing to do with it. I would just hope that your mother and father would let go of some of the control they're forcing with my oldest son's wedding. I know, Margaret. I know. I know your father's friend, if that's what you can call him — that Mr. Robinson — gives your people money. Sweetheart, I know."

"I mean, I know he's helping to pay for the wedding and all, but your mother and father can be more friendly and not throw the fact that they can afford a decent wedding with a lot of Mr. Robinson's help up in me and my people's faces." She chuckled. "I mean, it's not like you're marrying yourself, you know. And it's surely not like people get married every day. This is a lifetime thing, Margaret." She didn't so much as pause or give Margaret the chance to speak. "Ain't no turning back. And being as your mom and dad didn't give Philip and me no say in where our oldest child'll be married, I just gotta sew your grown. It would tear me up something awful if I couldn't. Even though your mother and father might not like it, I gotta do something. I'm sewing David's tuxedo. I have to sew your gown. It wouldn't be right if I didn't. After all. Think about it. If it wasn't for my son asking you for your hand in marriage, you wouldn't be getting married to anyone. You wouldn't be getting married at all." Then the line went dead.

Margaret hung up the telephone and sighed.

Fearing Tammy's ire, even in the ensuing days, she raised no protest. She suffered Tammy's glib remarks with a secret hurt. One week later, she was spending the afternoon with David when she overheard Tammy proclaim, "Yes, Girl. I'm sewing Margaret's dress," to a friend over the telephone.

Tammy added, "It's going to be beautiful." Then she pulled the phone closer to her mouth. "You know I'm trying to get along with those people, strange as that father of theirs is." She whispered into the receiver. "You know I saw that Jack Robinson outside the foundry again yesterday. He had that big ol' shiny car waiting outside. This time I think he even had a driver, and he was dressed to the nines too. You could just see money all over him. He moved like he owned the world. And not a smile on his face. Not a smile, not a scowl, not a hint of happiness, frustration, kindness, nothing. It's almost like that man has no spirit in him. Like he's made of clay or something. I done heard about people like that Jack Robinson. I done heard it said that people like him ain't got no conscience. That man could probably kill his own mother and watch her blood spill across the floor and not so much as bat an eye."

A f t e r  Tammy pulled the receiver closer to her mouth, Margaret heard her say, "Ain't no sense in walking around acting like we're living in a world that ain't got people without spirits living in them. Clay people. That's what I say they are. They are just plain

94

ol' evil clay people." She snorted. "And Lord of mercy, Girl, you ought to have seen that Ramsey Armstrong grinning all up in that man's face." She scowled. "And as if that ain't enough, as if that ain't plenty, my son has gone and forced me to have to be civil with that crazy man. Something just ain't right about that Ramsey Armstrong. Why is he always grinning at that Jack Robinson? Something is evil and sneaky about that Ramsey. He's one of them coward people. I can feel it." She released a deep breath. "Yes, Child. I'm praying. I'm trying to hold my peace, especially since that stupid son of mine's gone and decided to make that crazy family a part of ours. I told that boy and I told that boy." She released a deep breath. "My poor mother must be turning over in her grave. I'm so scared this all's gonna stir up a haunting." She shuddered and stared across the room at nothing in particular. "You and me, we're old time. We know how bad it is when spirits wake up."

It was strange. Although she only had to show up at Melinda's and Keith's wedding (she refused to do anything else -- Keith taking her baby from her), Tammy viewed David's and Margaret's wedding with an uncanny looking forward-to-ness.

It was for this reason that she made a decision.

Early the Monday morning that she designed the pattern to David's tuxedo, she changed her routine and drove down Tennessee Street on her way to Tilson's. As she'd hoped, she crossed paths with Ramsey and his only "friend", a guy named Tyrone. They were walking along the side of the road on their way to work at the foundry. Upon seeing the men, Tammy shifted the truck's gear from fourth to third, stuck her head out the window and waved to Ramsey, who nearly swallowed the gum that he was chewing while Tyrone and he, as they muddled along, exchanged conversation. He couldn't stop telling himself that Tammy was setting him up for a hard blow. What he was totally in the dark about was how much his colleague, Tyrone Walker, a nineteen-year-old father of two who lived closer to Mississippi than Memphis, knew about Jack Robinson and his past.

Tyrone was in Memphis not to gain employment as much as he was in the city to spy on Ramsey. He was the son of one of Tammy's second cousins. She'd hired him a month ago to chat with Ramsey at the foundry and deliver important information back to her. What he told her, she told Detective Cramer via cryptic notes that she dropped off at the police station. She didn't tell Philip. Yet, within a few weeks, her plan blew up, not with Philip, with Detective Cramer. The detective had been shopping at Tilson's Grocery Store when he let Tammy know that her cover was blown.

"Tammy, you lied," Detective Cramer had argued as he paid for his groceries at Tilson's Grocery Store. He scowled. "You haven't been getting the information that you've been passing to me from David or Margaret. I know why Tyrone's in town."

Peering up from the cash register at the grocery store, Tammy feigned ignorance. "What are you talking about?"

Detective Cramer leaned close to Tammy's ear and said, "And if I know why he's here, you can best believe Jack knows." He stood upright and withdrew his car keys from his pant pocket. "Drop it. You're way out of your league."

She waited until Detective Cramer left the store,

then she smirked. Two nights later, she was begging Tyrone not to leave Memphis. "But you've already found out that Jack has only placed two orders since he started coming to the foundry. That makes it clear that something else is going on between him and Ramsey." She gazed into Tyrone's eyes. "You can't leave now." She shouted. "Help me, Tyrone."

He hedged her off with truth. "Ever since I've been here someone's been following me. Think nobody knows it's odd that I'd come up from Mississippi and start working at the foundry and asking all kinds of questions out of the blue? Think nobody's thought about that? Last night when I went home, my wife and kids were hiding in our bedroom closet. Hiding in the closet, Cousin Tammy." He gawked at her. "Someone had broken in. Jimmied the window." He tossed his hand in the air. "Papers thrown all over the place. It ain't a secret no more, Cousin Tammy. Somebody knows." He turned away from her. "I'm out of this. I'm going home and I'm not coming back."

She'd pleaded with him to stay for all of five minutes. When she stopped talking loud and fast, he stared at her and let words come out of his mouth like heavy arrows pointing into the ground. "I. am.not. staying. here. to. get. killed."

Before he left Memphis that night, Tyrone handed Tammy a large envelope. As soon as she got home, she hurried up the stairs and ran into the bathroom. She locked the door and tore the envelope open.

*It is my recommendation that the minor, Jack Robinson, aged nine-years-old, be placed into the custody of the state until further observation. It is noted in the record that his mother has petitioned the court and the Department of Children's Affairs in this city of Chicago*

*to remove the boy from her home immediately.*
*Mother has repeatedly stated that she fears for her life*
*while in the company of her nine-year-old son.*

*Signed Dr. Andrew Poole on November 3, 1920.*

Tammy flipped the papers with such haste that half of the papers fell to the floor.

*I have tried numerous times to discipline my son. I read*
*to him, take him to the theatre and to visit museums. I*
*work desperately to engage him in conversations that*
*are light and gentle. His only interests are dark*
*subjects like death, murder, mutilation, strangulation,*
*abandonment and dying young. I am very worried for*
*my son and his future. He does not play with the*
*other children in the neighborhood. I cannot*
*remember the last time I even heard my son laugh. I*
*love my son, but I fear I am unable to tend to him*
*any longer. I do believe my son needs professional*
*care, and should receive such stated care*
*immediately. I can do this no longer. He is more than*
*a child. It is the whatever else he is that terrifies me.*
*I am seeking the help of the state. Ignore this plea*
*and I do believe, at some point in time, you will*
*deeply regret it. My conscience is clear. I have made*
*this matter known.*

*Jennifer Robinson, December 27, 1922*

Tammy shook her head.

*Deed of sale*
*5555 Ambrose Street to Jack Robinson August 27,*
*1932*

"Tammy. Honey, you in there?"

"Ah-just a minute, Philip. I'll be out in just a minute."

Philip knocked on the door. "Come on, now. I got a bad case of the runs. Hurry up."

"Ju-just a minute." Leaning over the toilet seat, she reached to the floor and grabbed the scattered papers. It wasn't until she was in bed that night, lying next to her husband that she stared up at the ceiling and reminded herself that, "5555 Ambrose Street is where my mother lived right before she died." She also couldn't stop thinking about several checks that she saw in the folder. They were all made out to The Home for Mentally Retarded Children, all in the name of BobbieLong.

"What," Tammy asked herself while she stared at the ceiling through the dark, "What would Jack Robinson be doing with a deed of sale for my mother's house and what on earth would he be doing making out checks to the Children's Home in Bobbie's memory?"

The following morning, she motioned David inside the kitchen to the corner most hid from living room view and offered, "I owe you an apology." She glanced around the corner.

A second later, she released a breath. Philip nor any of their other children witnessed her asking for David's pardon. "I've been hard on you over the years, even more after you started seeing that—" She bit her bottom lip. "--Margaret." She glanced around the corner again, then continued. "I feel bad. The last few nights, I've had trouble sleeping. Yes. Ramsey's weird—." She cleared her throat. "For years I saw those Armstrong children playing at the edge of school. I

99

knew they were all right. They can't help it that their father--"

She shook her head. "All those years, I shouldn't have been so mean. If-you—see- Ramsey tell him I said ah-ah I'd like to get to know him better. He has wonderful friends like ah, well, ah-Jack Robinson, a man who carries himself well. Mr. Robinson is very well thought of in the community. Ah-he's highly respected by everybody. Everybody likes Jack Robinson. Even pastor talks about how he helps out Coloured folk and all. So, I just shouldn't have been so mean."

It was that same unrelenting desire to "get to the bottom of Ramsey's and Jack's relationship" that took her to 542 Nettleton Avenue on September 1, 1945 at five-thirty in the evening. The sun was turning the sky into a golden, orange hue. Cars and trucks illuminated the avenue with their headlights. Heat was moving its way out of the day. The closer Tammy drove to the yellow, wood house, the more she noticed plants posted in windows of the homes lining the street. Moments later, a pair of gruff voices boomed behind her. When she turned in the truck parked in front of the yellow, woodhouse, she grinned like a fox at Ramsey who looked at her and smiled with an equal amount of nervousness.

Ramsey turned to head up the front walk. Just as he turned, Tammy called out, "May I come inside?"

The evening grew cool and dark. By the time what was five-thirty turned into six o'clock, Tammy, Ramsey and his wife, Rebecca, argued back and forth so long, their voices were hoarse.

Rebecca untied her apron from her waist and walked to the edge of the living room. "Tammy,

100

that'll be enough. I'm sure Ramsey didn't invite you in. Knowing you, you invited yourself in. So now, since you have made it clear that you don't have one good thing to say about my husband, me or our family, just keep walking right on back out the front door."

Tammy froze. "No. I'm going to finish saying my piece. I ain't going nowhere until I'm done."

Rebecca stepped toward Tammy and raised her hand. "Hold on one minute here, now. Just hold on one minute."

"No." Tammy shook her head and stiffened her resolve. "I didn't come over here to fight. I came over here to apologize for being mean to your kids all these years. Your kids can't help it that your husband has a sickness that's caused him to do goodness only knows what. Always grinning up in that Jack Robinson's face."

She pointed her narrowed brow at Ramsey and snarled, "Jack Robinson ain't got no spirit, you know." She pointed her words as if she could turn them into daggers to stab Ramsey with. "I can't count the times I've seen you and him huddled together at the foundry. Think nobody can see through those dirty windows at the foundry. How many well-to-do people do you know go visiting at a foundry? Ain't no rich White man ever took up being friendly with a Coloured unless that Coloured man was doing his dirt. I don't care nothing about what people going around saying about that Jack Robinson. He ain't nobody special to me. He's one of those clay people. He's a coward."

She glared at Ramsey. "Just like you. Don't think I ain't watching you. You play the innocent role, but I know better. You're into something evil real deep. I'm on to you, but," she lowered her voice, "It ain't your kids fault," she pointed at Ramsey, "That you're their father. I was going to apologize to your children. That's what I invited myself inside to do. But since you refuse to be neighborly or act like a Christian, I won't apologize. Now, that said, I will be leaving. And don't worry. I'll be sure to wipe the dirt that's all up in this house off my feet as soon as I get outside." She turned in a huff.

"Your gossip has hurt my family. Your lies," Rebecca shrieked, "Your made up stories are killing my family. Damn you," Rebecca called out the door. Tightening her jaw, she strangled back tears.

Standing outside the truck, Tammy shouted. "At least I ain't hiding nothing wicked behind my smile."

Less than twenty minutes later, Tammy hurried inside her own living room. Philip was sitting in his favorite lounge chair reading <u>Native Son</u> by Richard Wright. Engrossed in the book, he didn't acknowledge Tammy's presence until she threw her pocketbook atop the coffee table in front of the lounge chair. With his wife standing in front of him huffing, Philip knew that he couldn't resume reading undisturbed until he addressed her, and so, he lowered the novel to his lap and peered over the top of his horn-rimmed glasses. "What's the matter?"

Tammy huffed. "Went to see those Armstrongs. I hate those people." She shook her head. "They're a bunch of cowards. They are cursed. Mark my word. David going and marrying Margaret is going to bring something evil into our family. There's gonna be a haunting. David going and marrying us to those people is gonna wake something awful up, something evil."

Philip rolled his eyes. "I told you to let things be. We were getting along fine. I told you not to go digging up the past. Most folk can't deal with the pain from the past. You ought to know that as long as we've been dealing with all sorts of folk down at the store." He raised the novel an inch off his lap and pushed his reading glasses back on the bridge of his nose.

Tammy walked around the coffee table and sat on the sofa. "Maybe you're right a little bit." She bowed her head. "Philip?"

"Yea?" He sat the novel on his lap and pulled his glasses to the tip of his nose again.

"Go with me to the Armstrong's. If things don't change soon, Margaret's going to be our daughter-in-law in a few weeks. I want to set things straight. I know with you there beside me, I won't get mad. It'll be better afterward."

"Why're you so heavy on going to the Armstrong's?"

"Because the Good Book says you should ask forgiveness when you wrong someone and those Armstrong kids never did one thing to our family. I was wrong."

"Why are you really so big on apologizing to them?" He gazed at her. "Those kids are grown. They probably ain't even home and wouldn't care if you apologized now or never." He sat forward on the chair and looked at her. "You want to get back over there and do your own little investigating?"

Chapter Ten

Leonard Baxter stared at the stack of legal documents on the side of his desk. "How could you?" he asked while he buried his face in his hands. "After all I've given you." In one swipe, he wiped snot and tears off his face, then he stared at the wall on the opposite side of the room.

The ringing telephone forced him to postpone examining his marriage. "Hello?" he said, clearing his throat.

"Mr. Baxter? Mr. Leonard Baxter?"

Leonard was silent. He thought that he'd heard the voice before, but he wasn't sure.

"Leonard Baxter? Is this the law office of attorney Leonard Baxter?"

There was a pause then Leonard asked, "Who is this? Who am I speaking with? Who's on the other line? Identify yourself? Who are you?"

"Calm down," the man on the other line said. "This is Detective Cramer."

Leonard stopped and breathed in several deep breaths.

"Are you all right?" Detective Cramer asked.

"You were right." Leonard said.

Detective Cramer was silent.

"She had an affair."

Detective Cramer continued to be silent.

"I'm ready to go with you now." Leonard nodded while he stared at the receiver. "I don't care if she's not my daughter. I still love her." His voice cracked with emotion. "I always will. I have a right to see her. I want to meet my daughter's biological father. I want to know if she's with him. I want to know if she's okay. I have that right."

"Meet me outside Tilson's Grocery." He paused.

104

"You do know where Tilson's Grocery is, don't you?"

"Detective, just because I'm a White man doesn't mean I don't know anything about the Coloured side of town."

Detective Cramer laughed. "See you in half an hour."

"Half an hour." Leonard almost smiled when he hung up the telephone, but there was the stack of legal documents in front of him. He couldn't ignore the documents.

Reaching across the desk, he decided to start digging through the papers before he headed for Tilson's Grocery Store. "There might be something in here that could help Detective Cramer and me later today," he thought to himself while he pulled the stack of files toward him.

Twenty minutes later when the telephone rang again, he sat back in his high-back leather chair shaking his head at the facts hidden within two of the files. His wife had six affairs during their eight-year marriage. Three of the affairs resulted in pregnancies that had ended in abortions — except one.

Two photographs of a muscular, silver-haired man were at the bottom of the second file that Leonard leafed through. No date, no name, nothing was on the front or back of the first photograph that Leonard picked up. When he turned the second photograph over, he saw his wife's handwriting. *"I love you, Jack."*

Leonard stared at the words and asked himself why he didn't see that his precious, missing daughter Jocelyn looked nothing like him. She had none of his features and yet, when she ran up to him after he returned home from a hard day of working at the office or in the courtroom, he lifted her into his arms and said, "My precious little girl, my lovely daughter Jocelyn."

"Mr. Baxter," Leonard's assistant said after she knocked on his office door then slowly pushed the door open. "There's a Detective Cramer on the line for you."

Leonard leaped from his chair. "Oh. That's right. I forgot." He grabbed the two files that he'd looked through and shoved them inside his briefcase. "Thank you," he said to his assistant while he hurried through his office grabbing a pad, several pens, a camera, film, a tape recorder and his suit jacket. "Thank you," he said again when his assistant didn't move. When he stared at her, she turned and went back to her desk.

"Hello?" he spoke into the telephone. "My arms are full. I'm on my way now. I forgot. I've got some things I want you to see. Sorry, I lost track of time. I'm on my way now. Please stay put. I'll be right there."

He hurried toward the door. Normally when he left his office, he simply closed the door, but this time while he glanced over his shoulder at his assistant, he told himself to "lock the door."

"Where shall I say you've gone," his assistant asked while he walked away from his office and her desk and closer to the exit door. She stood from her desk and followed him down the corridor with her gaze. "In case Mrs. Baxter calls or stops by looking for you?"

"Tell her I'll be back in about an hour or so." He paused. "If she comes by." Then, he walked out the door.

Once inside his black Mercedes Benz, he sped across town to Tilson's Grocery Store. He pulled inside the parking lot. Before he started hunting for an empty parking spot, Detective Cramer drove up alongside the Benz.

Rolling down his window, Detective Cramer leaned

across his seat and said, "Follow me."

Leonard waited for Detective Cramer to steer his brown Ford pickup in front of his Mercedes Benz, then he rounded the parking lot corner and followed the pickup onto the street.

From where she stood ringing customer purchases at the front of the store, Tammy peered out the window and watched the two vehicles speed down the street.

Half an hour later, Detective Cramer pulled in front of a large colonial house and stopped his truck.

Leonard pulled up slowly behind him and turned off the ignition to his Benz. "Look at these," Leonard said as soon as he stepped out of his car and neared the side of Detective Cramer's truck.

"Come around to the passenger side," Detective Cramer said while he leaned across the seat and opened the passenger door.

Leonard handed him the files as soon as he got in the truck. "Look at these." A second later, he looked at the colonial house and asked, "Is this where he lives?"

"Where who lives?" Detective Cramer asked when he stopped looking at the files and glanced up at Leonard.

"My wife's lover?"

Detective Cramer shrugged.

"You know what I'm talking about?"

"Yes."

Leonard took the files out of Detective Cramer's hand. "Here. Look at this. See this picture? Is this him?"

Detective Cramer turned the photo over in his hand. He stared at the inscription on the back of the photograph, then he stared at the silver-haired man in the picture. When he faced Leonard, he was nodding. "I think this is him. I'm pretty sure that's him. That picture looks like it might be ten years old. He's older than that now. You can actually see the gray in his hair now."

"Is she still seeing him?"

"Mr. Baxter."

"Call me Leonard."

"Leonard, it doesn't matter now. I'm just trying to find your daughter. I'm not getting involved in your wife and your relationship."

"I understand that. I'm not asking you to get involved. I just wanted to know—" He nodded. "You're right. I shouldn't have asked you that. It wasn't fair. I'm sorry." He looked at Detective Cramer. "Are we going inside? Are you going to knock on the door?" He looked over his shoulder at his own car and thought about the tape recorder.

Detective Cramer looked at the picture one last time, then he opened his door, peered at Leonard and asked, "Ready?"

"Let's go."

"Follow me," Detective Cramer said while he walked toward the mansion.

Leonard and he stood on the porch knocking on the door for several minutes before they turned and looked at each other blankly.

Detective Cramer left the porch first. "He's not here. We don't have a warrant. We have to leave."

"Look," Leonard said when they reached the middle of the front walk. "A window's open. Look. Over there. The side of the house. There's a window open."

Detective Cramer laughed. "What do you think we ought to do, climb through the window?" He enjoyed another burst of laughter.

Leonard wore a straight face. "Yes. That's exactly

what we should do. I even brought a camera with me."

"You're kidding."

"No. I'm not. What if she's in there?"

"All by herself?"

"Yes. All by herself."

Detective Cramer shook his head. "We can't. It's against the law, and even if we could, Jack would make us pay. We'd both lose our jobs, our homes, everything, by the time he finished with us."

"Then drive away. Pretend you were never here. Pretend you never showed me how to get here. I'm going in."

"How do you know he's not in there sleeping?"

"Something tells me he doesn't do a lot of walking, Detective. Look in the driveway. His car's not here. If his car's not here, he's not here."

Detective Cramer stopped walking toward his truck. He looked up at the windows of the other mansions lining the quiet street. He laughed when he faced Leonard again. "I'm surprised you wouldn't already know where he lived. Both of you are rich men who enjoy the quiet comforts of your wealthy homes."

"But you see, we aren't similar. He has my daughter and I don't."

"Tell you what," Detective Cramer said. "Let me see if we can bring him in for questioning. If he won't come in, we'll use what's in those files to see if we can get a search warrant. How's that?"

Leonard raised his voice. "What if my daughter is in there?"

"He's not going to hurt her."

"No. Of course not. He just kidnaps her in the middle of the day, but he's not the type of guy to hurt someone."

"Okay. Okay. Shadow me down to the station—"

Leonard grabbed Detective Cramer by the arm. "Is that him? Coming around the corner. The BMW down there, at the end of the street?"

"We gotta get out of here," Detective Cramer said while he ran toward his truck. "If he sees us, he'll know we're on to him, and we'll blow our cover. Hurry. Hurry," he added while he climbed inside his truck.


It didn't happen that night. It happened two days later. The police department issued a search warrant for Jack Robinson's residence at 62 Madison Avenue. Leonard followed Detective Cramer, a locksmith and another cop on this trip, but he didn't come inside.

"Stay in the car when you get to the house," Detective Cramer had told him when they spoke over the telephone that morning. "The other officer can't even know that you're there. You cannot come in. It's against the law. Stay in the car."

Three hours later, Detective Cramer, the other police officer and the locksmith pulled up to Jack's mansion.

Moments after they arrived, Leonard pulled onto the street that Jack lived on. He parked five houses behind Jack's mansion, too far away from the house to hear Detective Cramer advise the locksmith to, "Stay out here on the porch."

As soon as his colleague and he entered the house, Detective Cramer thought, "Look how sterile this place is. Does this man re- paint the walls every week? I've never seen a house so clean, so sterile."

He hurried through the rooms of the house taking photos. Finally, he stood in front of a little girl's picture that was placed in a frame next to Jack's bed. He held the picture up to the light so that he could see the picture better.

"Is that her?" the other officer asked.

Detective Cramer shook his head. "I don't know. I don't think so." After he examined the photo longer, he shook his head and said, "No. That's not Jocelyn."

"Jack Robinson has other children?"

Detective Cramer shook his head again. "Not from what I read in the files. He can't have anymore children. He's lucky to have—"

"This is awful, Man. Her folks have got to be torn over this. I could only imagine what I'd feel like if my little girl turned up missing. And what do you say, we hurry and we get out of here? I'mstarting to get a bad feeling. We've gone through every room in the house. Not only is no one here, but neither is anything a little girl would own. No clothes, nothing. It's time we left. We better be going."

Detective Cramer took a picture of the photo then they hurried out the front door. After the locksmith secured the door, Leonard followed them as they drove down the street. Leonard was half a block from the house when he saw a man with silvery-gray hair climb out of a BMW. He carried two large children's store shopping bags in his free hand.

Chapter Eleven

After Ramsey and Rebecca picked their two
youngest children up from their aunt's and uncle's in
Atlanta, they drove to the Memphis International
Airport. The car in front of them drove around long
curves in the road at a snail's pace.

Finally, Ramsey pressed the brake to slow the truck
and pulled behind the car that he'd followed into the
airport. After he pulled the truck inside an empty
parking space, he saw the red, white and blue banners,
American flags, tee- tottering children, and smiling
women and men who stood with their hands buried
deep in their pant pockets. They filled the fenced off
parking lot next to the main runway.

Ramsey turned off the ignition and, raising his
voice, said, "Everybody out. We're here."

While his family climbed out of the truck, Ramsey
busied himself by glancing in short intervals at a red-
haired woman sitting in a Chevy that was parked next
to the truck.

Rebecca stood outside the truck's passenger door.
"Pops, you coming?" She didn't wait for him to answer.
"I'm going to get some fresh air." Then she pulled her
pocketbook against her hip and walked away.

Ramsey's pressure lowered when he realized that
he was alone. He pulled the key from the ignition and
pushed it inside his pant pocket. He smiled when the
woman—she didn't look eighteen— swung her infant
daughter toward the Chevy's ceiling. The baby girl,
with barrettes fastened to her pigtails, balled her legs
close to her buttocks then screeched and laughed each
time that her mother lifted her in the air and swung her
toward the ceiling.

While he watched the woman play with her
daughter, Ramsey recalled the words that Jack spoke to

him the day before Jocelyn Baxter disappeared. "Her mother doesn't love her. She never loved anyone, and that man is not her father, so how could he possibly love her? They leave it to her nanny to raise her. She actually thinks that her nanny is her aunt even though her nanny is Coloured and she's White." Jack said flatly. "Keeping her quiet won't be hard. I don't want her growing up like that. I'm not going to let her well-to-do parents go on with their lives while she stands silently to the side."

Jack's face was so devoid of emotion, Ramsey shuddered. "I'm going to take her, Ramsey, and I don't need you to do much. Sure. Her folks'll put on a performance, act like they really care that she's missing. Can you imagine? How in the world can you ever miss a child you don't love enough to spend five minutes a day with? I'm not going to let her grow up the way I did. I'm not." He stared at Ramsey with eyes that reminded Ramsey of death. Ramsey called them "graveyard eyes".


Shaking his head, Ramsey forced himself to stop thinking about Jack and the missing girl. He buried his head in his hands and told himself that he was innocent.

Half an hour later, after she watched her brother Alex's father-in-law walk away from her own dad, Margaret approached the truck. The wind ruffled her hair while she peered at her father out of the corners of her eyes. The day, clear and shaded in hues of blue and yellow, was beautiful. She craned her neck and looked into the sky before she stuck her head inside the truck. Ramsey's breath warmed her forehead and the tip of her nose. She watched him lean forward over the steering wheel. It didn't escape her that this was the closest that she'd been to her father since she was a small child. She wondered if her father loved her. Even now, he didn't speak to her. After several moments of silence, she asked, "Why do you talk to him?"

Ramsey stared out the windshield. "Who?"

Margaret almost laughed out loud. "Sharieffa's father, Dad. He was the only other person here."

Ramsey didn't turn or flinch, and yet Margaret felt the hair on the nape of her neck rise. She'd crossed a line, and she knew it. She swallowed hard and played with the ends of her hair. "I'm sorry."

Silence.

"Dad, I'm sorry."

Silence.

She arched her shoulders. "I only asked because everybody knows he beats his wife. Even Sharieffa knows. It's why she goes around saying if Alex ever laid a hand on her, she'd leave him lickety-split."

Tossing his head back, Ramsey let out a roar of laughter.

Margaret stared at the ground. When she peered up at the side of her father's head again, she mumbled, "Said she would."

Ramsey turned slowly and faced his daughter. "Just because he hits her?"

"Dad, it's wrong for a man to hit a woman. It's not right."

"It ain't right, but it ain't no reason for a good wife to leave her husband." Then, he turned and gazed out the front windshield.

"Dad. It's not right."

He laughed.

"What would you do if David hit me?"

"After you get married, you're moving out of your

mother and my house."

She swallowed hard. "I know that."

"Whatever happens in your home is no business of mine."

Margaret stood outside the truck imagining how she could hurt her father ... deeply ... just to make him feel. After five tortuous moments of silence passed between them, she said, "I'm going to join Mama, Dave and everyone else. If you want to get a spot and be able to see the planes land, you better come on."

She asked herself a question while she moved away from him. "How long has Dad had that deep cut on the side of his face?" She peered over her shoulder at him and stared at the cut. When she turned back around, she almost ran away from her father.

Ramsey opened the truck door. The young red-haired mother and her daughter were gone. "Probably down by the fence," he guessed. He was alone. He looked at the ground and thought, "Every child has a mother and a father. Every child has someone who wants them to come back home."

The words were like a mantra. He'd spoken them to Jack last year. He'd pleaded with Jack not to hurt the little Baxter girl until beads of sweat broke out on his face like large wet pimples. "Take her back home, Jack. Take her back home. It's almost suppertime. Just drop her off in front of her house. Her parents won't know any better. You'll never be found out. They'll just think their daughter was outside playing. Take the little girl back, Jack."

"I'm never going to get caught," was Jack's response as he spoke in his soft, nasal voice. He winked at Ramsey. "No one even thinks I know the girl. Who in this town is going to stop me?" He glared at Ramsey. "Who? You?" He laughed in Ramsey's face until Ramsey felt spit spray his nose. "No. Not you. You're a coward."


When Ramsey looked up, it startled him how far away from everyone he was. His three-year-old grandson, Karl, was first to see him approaching. He stood on his toes and pinched the side of Sharieffa's calf. "Mama, Pops. Mama, look." His shirt rolled up his stomach while he clapped his hands overhead and waved to Ramsey. "Pops. Pops."

This time Sharieffa turned and stopped buttoning her youngest son, Michael's, sweater and looked up. Across from her, Rebecca smiled. "Hi, Girl."

Sharieffa bade Rebecca to walk inside her arms, then she embraced her. "How's my mama-in-law?"

Rebecca pecked Sharieffa's cheek. Bright red lipstick left a mark of the kiss. "Glad to see you, and come here, Karl and Michael."

"Watch out now." Sharieffa stepped back and gave Rebecca room to stoop and open her arms. The boys raced inside. "They're heavy."

Rebecca nearly lost her balance trying to pick her grandsons into her arms simultaneously. "Too late for that. These boys sure have grown, Girl. Look at you, Karl, so big. Mmmm, boy. Give me some sugar. Ewww, that's some good sugar. Come here, Michael baby."

Sticking two fingers inside his mouth and leaning back against Rebecca's heavy bosom, one-year old Michael bounced, pointed and called out, "Pops. Pops."

Rebecca stopped playing with his small, soft fingers long enough to look up at her husband of twenty-eight years. "Yeah, and you know what?" She sang to her grandson. "Pop's first name is Ramsey just like your middle name is Ramsey."

Michael shook his head and smiled into her face. She was his favorite person. Whenever she saw him, she made certain that he had what he asked for. He always enjoyed visiting her and "Pops" and spending nights over their house.

"Yes, it is. I know," she told him. "That's my husband."

"Pops?"

"Yes, Sir."

Ramsey tipped his head at his grandson and wife, before he turned toward Sharieffa and asked, "Where did your folks go, Sharrie?"

"They're around here somewhere."

He withdrew his hands from his pant pockets and stared at Sharieffa. "You been doing okay, Girl?"

"Since I got news that my man's coming home, I have been."Before she had time to say more, a loud noise of rushing wind echoed across the airfield.

Sharieffa turned to see what caused the noise. All around her, fingers pointed while banners and miniature American flags waved beneath the noonday sun.

Everyone watched the airplane bump the runway. Next to Sharieffa, Ramsey, Rebecca and Margaret inched forward and pushed the fence until it curved and fit the shapes of their stomachs. Of the trio, only Ramsey spotted the woman who owned the Chevy. He smiled when she lifted her daughter into her arms and raised her high so that she could see her father exit one of the incoming 747s.

David propped Michael on the nape of his neck and crooned, "Daddy's coming home today on one of those big airplanes," when Michael inquired the cause of the commotion.

Upon hearing the news, Michael leaned his chin atop David's head and started chanting, "Da-de."

Sharieffa's mother massaged Sharieffa's shoulders. A second later, she felt her own lower chin break into long, nervous spasms as she watched her daughter twist the ends of her hair. She stopped massaging her daughter's shoulders and held her hand.

General Davidson, first to depart the airplane, tipped his cover at the crowd. Then, he smiled and waved as he bound down the ramp. Two captains followed him to the microphone placed atop a podium in the center of the parking lot.

Ramsey swallowed hard and stepped close to Sharieffa and Rebecca who held Sharieffa's other hand.

"Hello!" General Davidson's deep voice boomed. He stepped back from the microphone and awaited the crowd's response.

"Hello!" Hundreds of voices called back.

Margaret bit her bottom lip. She was always first in the Armstrong family to break emotionally. A tear went down her cheek. Fearing that she would be judged as being too emotional, she turned and looked over her shoulder. She searched for her father.

General Davidson stepped close to the microphone and spoke in a stentorian voice. "War, in and of itself, is not noble. Yet, to preserve this great nation, what she stands for, what she believes in, we must be willing and ready to go to war." He paused and surveyed the crowd. "Fathers, mothers, wives, brothers, sisters and children become a part of war when fathers, husbands, brothers and sons fight the cause of a nation." He reiterated. "It is not noble, but at times, it is necessary. America, Memphis, Tennessee, these men, your men, your husbands, sons, brothers, fathers and your friends — our heroes —have done a most noble thing. They have gone to war to help preserve our great nation so that you and I may continue to be free. I know that you, like I, am proud of their noble deed. I know that you will welcome them — heroes, they are — nobly during this homecoming, their homecoming. And I trust that the God who has sustained our great nation and these great men and women will stir something up in all of us, Dear God, so that these men and women, no man, no woman, will have to march off to war again."

Cheers and fevered applause erupted when General Davidson stepped away from the microphone.

The woman who owned the Chevy ran one hand over her head, relaxing her Shirley Temple curls. A fat woman wiggled her way to the front of the crowd and stuck her head between the shoulders of two tall men.

The first soldier to exit the plane leaned on a cane. During the war, shrapnel was thrown inside his partner and his foxhole and tore off the side of his thigh, and though each time he took a step he felt sharp pain knife his leg, he chose to walk instead of push a wheelchair.

Newspaper and magazine reporters scurried to the spot the first serviceman to exit the plane, his wife, and their son gathered in. Camera bulbs flashed and captured the man kissing his wife. Rows of reporters, with their microphones and tape recorders, raced toward General Davidson, the captains and the exiting servicemen and servicewomen.

Across the parking lot from them, Sharieffa inhaled her answer with a deep, noisy breath. Her hands no longer inside her mother's and mother-in-law's grasps, her jaw clenched and she made tight fists. Alex had betrayed her in his recent letters. He would never run with Karl. Promises that he'd made to push

Michael while he learned to ride his first bicycle, the hour long softball games and walks through nearby parks ... they were lies, for on February 3, 1945, Alex and his foxhole partner met a piece of shrapnel. If not for his partner's heroism, Alex would be dead.

Sharieffa wondered how Alex "forgot" to tell her that he had been crippled in the war. She wondered how he forgot to tell her that his legs were twisted into a permanent state of fixed helplessness. He couldn't move his legs if he wanted to. She wrung her hands while she waited for him to cross the runway and reach her side. She realized that she was caught between her fears and her desires.

Her hands lowered but did not open and, her eyes dim, she watched Alex push the two big wheels at the sides of the wheelchair round and round while she worked to steady her hands. She was young, but she knew how to suffer.

A man would never touch her until she burned with desire again. She would never again feel safe just because her husband was home. She felt as crippled as she saw her husband to be, pushed into a fixed state of misery, forced to live a life that she clearly did not want. She hailed herself a heroine as she stood, shoulders tall, head erect, gaze focused directly in front of her, and spine straight, and watched her man come home to her.

Six hours later, Sharieffa still had not begun to learn to grieve. She looked at the kitchen counter and saw that the only remaining food from the "Welcome Home, Alex" celebration that she had to find room for in the refrigerator was the cole slaw.

Her hands shook when she lifted the glass bowl

120

filled with cole slaw, "Calm down," she told herself.

She laid the bowl on the counter again and took two deep breaths. A moment later, she walked to the refrigerator and rearranged two gallons of milk, a plate of deviled eggs, a pan of roast beef, a sweet potato pie and a cheese ball.

Finished, she pushed the bowl of cole slaw onto the second rung. When she closed the refrigerator door, she knew that the only chore remaining was to finish sweeping the floor.

She moved slowly while she pushed the broom across the piles of dirt lining the kitchen floor. "It's not Al's fault. He nearly died in that bloody war. It's not like he wanted to come home paralyzed," she talked out loud to herself. "It's not his fault."

She choked back tears. "None of our dreams'll come true. Every day'll just be marking off time, waiting until we die and don't have to live this tortured life anymore." She shook her head and stared at the floor while she continued to push the broom. "Al can't hold me in his arms. He's struggling so hard just to control his own hands. It's almost like his body's not his own anymore. It belongs to the war."

She swallowed hard. "We won't be intimate, ever again." The broom scraped the floor. "I can barely stand to look at him. It just hurts. He didn't have to go into the Army. Daddy said they don't draft family men. He didn't have to go."

She pushed the broom and shook her head. "Oh, Sharrie! Why didn't you tell yourself your husband had been shot up after you saw the first soldier get off the plane? Why did you expect something better?"

She pushed the broom until she felt the urgency of the last two years that she'd raised Karl and Michael as a single parent suffocate every thread of hope that she'd desperately clung to. Alex more than provided financially (the boys and she never went without), but money wasn't company on a lonely night, a father to Karl and Michael to spend their youngest days with, or the love of a strong and gentle man to feed her inner longings.

She'd been scared living alone with the boys. With stories of a child missing, her fears for her sons had increased. Sometimes she found herself afraid to let them play in the front yard while she was working in the living room with the curtains fully open. She feared turning her back and Karl leaving their property and getting lost in the woods or sauntering off to the railroad tracks.

Alex was in Europe three months the night that she lay in bed reading a Frederick Douglass essay. Outside it was raining. Fifteen pages into the essay, she heard footsteps around the back of the house. She listened. Nothing. Seconds later, she scolded herself for unleashing her fears, and pulled the small book close to her chest.

When she turned the page, her neighbor's boxer barked, growled and yanked on his chain. Moments later when the dog stopped barking, Sharieffa pushed the book inches below her nose and, brushing the thought of a stranger lurking outside the back of the house from her mind, quickly read another paragraph.

Rain and wind pricked the hair on the nape of her neck. It startled her to find the bedroom window open when she turned and looked behind herself until she remembered that she'd opened the window after she'd fried liver and onions for dinner.

She gazed across the hall. Karl and Michael slept soundly. The rain tapered and drummed the windowpane at a steady pace. She scooted down in the bed—the book resting atop her chest—and allowed herself to become drowsy. Her eyes closed as slowly as the rain fell against the windowpane. As tired as she was, she'd managed to hear the back door squeak on its hinges.

She sat up and retraced her "lock-up" steps. She'd locked the front and back doors after she cleaned the kitchen after the boys and she ate dinner. She'd secured the windows downstairs moments after she cleaned the kitchen. She'd even checked to make sure that the window in the basement, though it was too small for an adult to climb through, was secure. She'd noted that besides the chimney, there was no other entrance to the house.

Then, she'd thought about the gun. Alex gave her the gun before he left for the war in Europe. Afraid that the boys would find the weapon and think that it was a toy, she'd put it in a box in the attic.

She laid the book on top of the bed and pulled on her robe. In the hall, she froze and listened. She heard feet rustling through the kitchen. "Dear God, let my ears be playing tricks on me."

She heard footsteps again.

She'd cursed Alex for not being home when she heard glass shatter against the kitchen floor. She knew she had to move. She would have to pass through her sons' bedroom to reach the door inside the closet that Alex had paid a friend to disguise with a mural because he didn't want to swap bedrooms with the boys due to silly ghost stories.

The door led to the attic. By the time Karl and Michael were old enough to decipher truth from fantasy, Alex trusted that they'd no longer be afraid of the attic.

After she'd pulled the covers over her bed so that it would look like she wasn't home, she raced into her sons' bedroom. She'd lifted Karl off his twin bed. Next, she'd lifted Michael out of his crib. With her sons cradled in her arms, she hurried. The stairs creaked behind her, and she wished that she could dab at the sweat racing down her forehead so it wouldn't sting her eyes. "Be quiet. Be quiet." She'd kept telling herself to, "Be quiet."

Karl's head had rolled to the center of her arm. Her back ached, but she kept walking. She squinted into the dark. She didn't want to stumble and bump a piece of furniture.

At the top of the stairs, the intruder had stopped and examined the empty corridor.

Fighting tears, Sharieffa had opened the inner closet door and, using a raised knee for support, she'd shifted Karl and Michael in her arms to keep them from falling.

At the foot of the ladder that reached into the attic, she'd heard someone breathing outside the closet door. She'd let out a long, slow breath and dropped the latch that opened the closet door inside her robe pocket. Turning, she began her ascent. "Dear God, in the name of sweet Jesus, don't let me and my boys die tonight," she'd prayed.

At the top of the ladder, she'd laid the boys in a crate. An old sofa covering lay on the attic floor beside the crate. She'd lifted the sofa covering off the floor and spread it over her sons. Shame had chilled her conscience but, her boys safe, she'd turned and looked for the semi-automatic.

On the house's third floor, the intruder had studied the closet mural curiously. He'd leaned against the painted door and ran his thick hands along

124

the door and wall. He'd pushed at the door with both his hands, then with his shoulder.

Having searched every corner of the attic and not finding the gun, Sharieffa had crawled to a space on the floor beside her sons and squeezed her shoulders. Above her head was a shelf. She massaged her neck. When she did, the tip of her elbow bumped the bottom of the shelf. The gun fell into her lap.

Perspiring and exhausted, she'd listened. Ten minutes later she said, "Thank you, Jesus," as she heard the intruder go back down the stairs.

Crawling across the attic floor, she'd went to the small attic window. She ran her hand in circles across the window until dirt moved away and she could peer out the window. She heard the back door open and close.

"They ain't there," she'd heard a tall man holler into the night. "Must have gone over her folks."

She'd shook her head. She didn't recognize the two men standing at the edge of the back yard, but their voices -- she'd heard their voices before.

"They ain't in there," the man who'd forced his way into her home said again while he turned and stared up at the house. When the man looked toward the attic, Sharieffa ducked.

An hour passed before Sharieffa gathered enough courage to leave the attic with her two boys and return to her bedroom. She'd put her sons into bed with her, put chairs in front of every door in the house and, slipping the gun into her nightstand drawer, sat on the edge of her bed. She'd picked up the telephone and called two people, her mother and Tammy.

Her mother had told her that she'd send her father over right away to check the house, but Sharieffa kept telling her, "No." She'd kept saying, "I'll be all right,

Mama. I'll be all right."

When she'd called Tammy, she said, "Someone was outside the house tonight, not too long ago. Me and my boys hid in the closet. I could have died tonight, Mrs. Tilson. Me and my boys, we could have died tonight."

"Did you see who it was?" Tammy had asked.

"No."

"Did the intruders say or do anything that made you know who it was?"

"I've heard their voices before. After the guy who came inside left the house, I heard him outside talking to two other men. Think they work for Jack Robinson doing construction. I've heard their voices around construction work sites before. They helped put that extra room on at the cleaners a few weeks ago."

"Jack sent them there to send Ramsey a message. That coward."

"Mrs. Tilson, Ramsey's my father-in-law."

Tammy had sighed.

"Well, he is."

"Sugar, I know." Tammy had sighed. "But I know that's the reason those men came to your house. They know Alex is far away, and if you ask me, Jack saw you as an easy target to send Ramsey a message through. He's going to keep Ramsey in line." She paused. "Have you called the Armstrongs?"

"No."

After an award silence, Tammy had said, "If you need anything, call me. Call me at home. Call me at the store. I don't care where I am, just call me. And," she'd added, "Be careful. You and the boys be careful."

That was a year ago. Today Alex came home.

Pulling a chair away from the kitchen table, Sharieffa sat. She tried to relax. "I'd still have to run if those men came back."

She folded her arms and laid them on the table. "The only difference would be, this time I'd have to save Al too--."

"Coming to bed?"

She jumped. "What?"

Alex pushed the wheelchair to her side and pecked her cheek. "Baby, I know it's hard for you."

She steeled her nerves. "It is." A second later, she looked into her husband's eyes, buried her head against his chest and wept.

"I know it, Sharrie. You've got every right to be mad."

"It hurts so much." She clutched his shoulders.

"I'm gone for over two years, then I come home paralyzed from the waist down." He paused. "I can't tell you how guilty I feel. I gotta find my way through this, but you. Sharrie, I'm a cripple. I would've told you when I called, but I couldn't bring myself to tell you. I just couldn't. I didn't want to hurt you. 1 don't want to hurt you, Sharrie. I can't do much but sit in this chair all day, but I still think that's better than being dead. But you, Sharrie, you're not paralyzed. I am. You can walk away from all this now if you want to. I mean. I know we're married, but you ain't gotta stay. You've stuck by me, Sharrie. You've always been there for me, even before the war. You stayed right with me. We were partners. Hey. I know during the war we both doubted sometimes. But hey, Baby, we made it this far. We made it."

127

"I know."

He cupped her chin in his palm. "Somehow saying it makes me feel better." Then he pursed his lips to kiss her, but she pulled away. His hazel eyes dimmed. He wanted to hold her, all her fears, all her pain, all her disappointments, all her strengths -- all of her. He reached for the sides of her face.

She leaned toward him. Her breasts fell against his chest. As they did, his shoulders and chest began to tingle. Suddenly he remembered how much time had elapsed since they had held each other. Her breasts were tender, warm and full. He tried to pull her closer, but he only managed to brush his lips across hers.

The heat from her body rushed inside his mouth. He caressed her back. Her hair flowed through his fingers. He buried his head against her hair and squeezed her shoulders.

She wept softly.

"Sharrie," he began, her hair muffling his voice.

She sniffed hard. "What, Baby?"

"You don't ... "

Her tears quickened.

"No, Baby. Don't cry." He tightened his fingers and her hair bunched inside his hands. "Let me say this, because I love you. I love you, Sharrie. I love you so much. You don't have to stay. You don't have to go through this with me."

She raised her head and looked into his eyes. "A1, if you have to deal with it, I have to deal with it."

He shook his head. "Please, please listen, Sharrie." He tightened his fingers around her hair. "You don't have to go through this. It didn't happen to you. You do have to go on with your life, though. You just don't have to carry the burden of my being paralyzed with me."

"Al, what are you saying?"

"You've been like a warrior, living here by yourself, taking that job at the cleaners, watching after the boys alone. You never left me. I always had your support. You wrote so many letters. I needed all of them."

"I needed to write all of them."

"Because of you, while I was ditched in that foxhole, I never felt all alone. I wonder if I could have made it without you. Sharrie. I love you."

She leaned her head against his. Tears went slowly down her chin, down the sides of his face and into his lap. "I love you too, Al."

"Still, Baby, you don't have to go through this. You've been through enough." Her tears warmed his face. On their way into his lap, where they disappeared and became bits and pieces of a memory, he almost licked them.

"You keep saying that."

"Because it's true."

"What are you talking about?"

"I'm talking about us."

She caressed the side of his face. "Baby, please."

"No, Sharrie. This didn't happen to you. You've been through enough."

"Sweetheart, I will go through this and anything else with you. I didn't realize it until now, but I'm a stronger woman than I was when you left. We both grew from this. Somehow, we did. I want to love you, Al. I'll have to work through the anger and sorrow and I will."

"We may never be sexually intimate again."

'She held her breath.

"Look at me. Can you be celibate for the rest of your life?" He jerked his shoulders and shook her hands free. "Look at me. Please, Sharrie."

"You're more than sex to me, Al. Don't you think I can deal with this? Don't you think I can still be your wife? Still love you? Don't you think we can be happy together? I don't want to be with another man. I want to be with you. I love you, Alex. I love you and I always will."

He tightened his fingers around her hair. He talked between tears. "You really are willing to deal with this?"

"I'm in love, Alex Armstrong. That's what it is. I love you. I love you so much."

Chapter Twelve

Ominous clouds cast a dark shadow over the earth. If it rained, it would be the third day this week that Johnnie Dee, WBEJ's weather forecaster, had predicted the weather wrong. Yet, at noon, despite sounds of thunder and lightning pealing the sky, Johnnie pushed his mouth over the radio station's microphone and issued to all of Greasy Plank, "No rain for the afternoon and evening. Clouds —but no rain."

Dry, brittle grass swayed in the wind. It was a brutal ninety-three degrees. Rain evaded Memphis for two weeks. Parched soil, high temperatures, high humidity and relentless winds posed major concerns for the city. As usual for two o clock, ice cream trucks rang their way down Greasy Plank streets and avenues. Voices belonging to happy school-aged children could be heard throughout the town. "Mama! Daddy! The ice cream truck is coming! Can I have a nickel, so I can get a cone?" these same school-aged children screamed into opened house windows. In back yards, toddlers wobbled in and out of laundry pinned to clotheslines. Due to the gusty wind, the tall wooden poles, pushed into the ground at each end of the clotheslines, weakened. Some clothes blew in the wind and scraped the ground.

Back yard gardens were scant. Mostly weeds grew were collard greens, corn, peas and tomatoes once flourished. Ant mounds filled cracks in sidewalks. Paint peeled and chipped on houses, garages and barns.

To offset the misery that the high temperatures brought Greasy Plank, not only had hundreds of servicemen and servicewomen returned home, the Tennessee Valley Authority, signed into implementation on May 18, 1933 by President Franklin D. Roosevelt, was a huge financial and economic success. Effects from the depression of 1929 were slowly becoming memory.

Women replaced men as clerk typists and secretaries, some women were even becoming doctors and lawyers and sitting on school boards. The fight to free nine Coloured men who'd traveled from Chattanooga to Memphis on a freight train on March 25, 1931, and were later accused of raping an unsavory woman on the train, continued. The Harlem Renaissance thrived. Marion Anderson stunned the world with her soprano solos in New York City accompanied by the Metropolitan Opera Company. Richard Wright, Zora Neale Hurston and Langston Hughes continued to take the lead in the literary world. Duke Ellington, Billie Holliday, Cab Calloway, Ella Fitzgerald and Nat King Cole were musical favorites. 1945 was a pivotal time for Greasy Plank, Memphis and America. 1945 was also a pivotal time for the Tilson and Armstrong families.

Rebecca zipped the back of Margaret's gown. "Turn around so I can see you."

Margaret turned slowly from the long mirror. She gathered the hem of the white-laced gown in her hands and spread the bottom of the gown for her mother to see.

"Oh, Baby! You are beautiful!"

Margaret peered at her mother. "Really?"

"Really! I must admit Tammy did a fine job designing and sewing your wedding gown. You look beautiful."

Margaret smiled. "Thanks, Mama."

"This is a very special, day, Margaret. I

remember when I got married." She waved. "You don't want to hear about it."

Margaret released the gown's hem. "Yes, I do, Mama. Plus, I'm scared. Hearing you talk will help calm me down." She sat on a corner of her bed and patted the empty space next to her. "Mama, come sit on the bed with me and tell me about Dad and your wedding day."

"Okay." Rebecca answered with a raised finger. "Just a minute. I don't want you to be late for your own wedding." She neared the bedroom door and called down the stairs. "Ramsey!"

Ramsey jumped. He peered up the cellar stairs, but he didn't answer. If he did, he knew the echo in his voice would cause Rebecca to know his whereabouts.

Rebecca raised her voice, "Ramsey!"

He dabbed at the sweat on his forehead.

Ire and concern found its way into Rebecca's voice. "Ramsey!"

Closing and locking the closet door at the back of the cellar, Ramsey pushed away dead, clingy spiders and dry cobwebs and tiptoed up the stairs. He'd built the closet five years ago, board against board, day after day whenever he was in the house alone. It was a small closet hidden behind a thick slab of cement. Only Ramsey knew about the closet; only Ramsey had the key to the thin hole in the cellar wall.

In the secret closet that he tiptoed away from, papers bundled with string and thick rubber bands filled the top shelf. The papers were drawings of street maps and house layouts — a project of Jack Robinson's that Jack began undertaking after long evenings of socializing with the city's wealthiest residents.

The bottom shelf of the closet was filled with letters to and from attorneys and psychiatrists. Jack had asked Ramsey to keep the letters.

Ramsey hung his head and looked sheepishly at Jack each time that he was met with the requests. He hated keeping secrets, and yet he felt that he had no choice. Jack Robinson was a powerful man, and though he never uttered it - not once - Ramsey was terrified of Jack. To him, Jack was like a quiet disease that never revealed itself until it was too late to fight back and win.

Ramsey didn't call out, "Yea!" until he reached the center of the kitchen. He went to the sink and washed his hands and face and brushed his shirt and pants free of dirt. The small bits of human bone that stuck to his clothes he flushed down the sink. Once clean, he returned his attention to icing cakes.

"What time is it, Honey?"

"Ah . . . one-fifty . . . it's two o'clock."

"Is everything ready?"

"Yea! I'm almost finished icing the last cake!"

"Alright! We'll be down in a minute."

"Okay," he called up the stairs, then he licked icing off his hand. He flinched when his tongue ran over deep cuts on his finger.

Upstairs, Rebecca walked to the bed and sat next to Margaret.

"Look at me," Margaret giggled. "I'm shaking."

Rebecca placed her hands gently atop her daughter's. "Calm down, Child. Relax."

"It's hard."

Rebecca winked at Margaret. "You're blushing."

134

Margaret raised then lowered her shoulders. She smiled until her face glistened. "So, tell me about Dad and your wedding day."

"I was seventeen and your father was eighteen. We thought we were grown. I loved your father's family, especially his mama. I was crazy about your dad's mama. You know I love your father so, on our wedding day, I was on pins and needles. Your father — he was cool as a cucumber. You know how your father is. He ain't changed since the day I met him. Never gets upset or worried about anything. Always got everything under control. Anyways, my mama got me ready. Ramsey's mama wanted to help, but my mama said 'no'. She said whenever women get together, they get in one another's way and try to boss each other around. When your dad and I got married twenty-eight years ago, I was as scared as you are now, if not more. My mama kept talking to me trying to get me to calm down. I never did until two weeks after our wedding."

Rebecca stood and walked toward the long dresser with the mirror nailed to its back. When she looked into the mirror, more than her reflection peered back at her. Scenes from the past rushed to greet her. She began to talk. "You should have seen us. My mama and me ran around that little brick house like two headless chickens. Mama didn't like my hem; she thought it was too short. So, she took it down. Then, she thought it was too long. So, she took it up a bit."

"After three tries, she was satisfied. Me. I was tired of lifting and dropping the bottom of my wedding dress. I didn't have a gown. Our wedding wasn't big. Not as big as your's and Dave's." She stared into the mirror at her own reflection.

135

"Everybody can't have the kind of money and power like Jack and the Tilsons." She chuckled. "Well, not even the Tilsons have the power Jack has." She turned and faced her daughter. "Our family owes a lot to Mr. Robinson, Sweetheart."

"Don't tell that Tammy Tilson, but he helped pay for a lot of David's and your wedding. I can't tell you what all that man's done for our folks. He's the reason the recreation club for kids in Greasy Plank went up. He has given more money to scholarships for Coloured folks' kids to go to college. I can't count how much money he's given to put somebody's child through school." She shook her head. "A lot of people jealous of Jack's power, but when you think about how that man's mother just put him in a home and turned and walked away from him—" She shook her head. "It's amazing. Jack Robinson is a miracle. God has truly blessed that man, and we're so blessed to have him in our lives. Look how Greasy Plank has changed since he came here. Jack Robinson doesn't mind helping Coloured folks."

"He's a very important man, Honey. He's on big company boards and knows all the high-to-do folk in town. Everybody respects him." She nodded, "And everybody should. But we can't all have power. Shoot. It's hard enough just keeping our churches running." She turned and faced her daughter. "You. You've got a good head on your shoulders, Margaret. Your daddy and I are proud of you. We want the best, the very best, for you."

She pulled on the back of her duster and wiggled her hips until the duster loosened around her buttocks. "You didn't ask me to go on and on. You asked me about my wedding day." She turned away from the mirror. "It was hot the day your dad and I married, real hot, like it is today. I don't know if it was a record high or not, but it was hot."

She chuckled. "Whenever I get mad at your dad, I tell him it's because we got married on such a hot day." She gazed at the floor. "It was almost like there was a madness in that heat." Peering up at her daughter, she added, "You know. The kind of heat that sticks to you?" She chuckled. "It was a beautiful day though, just like today. Just crazy hot. I can't tell you a story about something terrible happening, because nothing terrible happened. No one got mad at no one. We all had a high time that day. Sometimes I remember it crystal clear. Sometimes I only remember bits and pieces of my wedding day. Whatever, I'm glad I married your dad." She nodded. "I am. We've been good for one another. That's what I want for you, Baby. With the Tilsons owning the grocery store, and it does so well, you'll have better than I did, and your kids will have better than you and Dave. I'm glad about that."

A second later, she twisted her mouth. "Never mind that Tammy decided she didn't want to contribute one cent to Dave's and your honeymoon after your dad and I insisted upon having the wedding at Mount Zion." She laughed. "Guess that Tammy Tilson thought she could stop Dave's and your wedding if she didn't give a dime toward it." She laughed again. "Your father just got right on the phone and called Jack. I was sitting in the living room when he called him." She nodded. "Sure was."

"Mr. Robinson took care of everything. It all came together after he heard word about how that Tammy was acting." She pursed her lips. "But I sure wish you and Dave could have gone somewhere nice for your honeymoon. Be different from me and your dad." She raised her voice. "Despite his mother's ways, I like Dave. He's a good young man. He's a hard worker." She wrapped her arm around her daughter's shoulders. "I love you, Baby."

Margaret wrapped her arm around her mother's waist. "I love you too, Mama, and don't worry about the honeymoon. Dave and I are happy to spend it with our family and friends."

She kissed Margaret. "We better get cracking or you'll be late for your own wedding."


Further into town, David ran his long fingers over his suit coat. He stood in front of the bedroom mirror that he shared with his brother for sixteen years and peered down at his newly shined shoes.

Early in the morning, before the day became hot and humid, before Charlie's Ice Cream Truck started ringing up and down Greasy Plank streets and avenues, Tammy woke. With her house robe still on, she went through the back door, off the porch and into the flower garden beside the shed. She broke a blue and white carnation off at its stem.

With the hem of her housecoat bunched in her thick hands, she returned to the house, climbed the noisy stairs, and pinned the flower to the right breast pocket of David's tuxedo, the tuxedo that she'd finished sewing three nights ago. Besides that one carnation, alone and against David's chest, she assembled a bouquet of carnations in the center of the dining room table.

All wedding preparations were finished; the family only had to dress and drive to the church. It was as Tammy desired. All last week, she'd stood at the cash register at the grocery store ringing customer purchases and talking about the wedding. The entire previous week, while she was at home, while she shook rugs, pushed clothes up and down the laundry board and stirred food, she thought about the wedding. She kept saying, "These wedding going on's are gonna be done by the close of this week, God willing. I'm not gonna be running around here like a chicken with its head cut off trying to get things in order at the last minute. I'm not gonna."

Because he didn't want to rush either, and tired of hearing his wife repeat her vow to be ready, Philip washed and shined the truck yesterday. He took his moth ball ridden suit to the cleaners, telephoned meat and produce vendors Wednesday instead of Friday and placed the following week's order. Unlike his oldest son, Philip owned no newly shined shoes. So, while Tammy talked about things that David did when he was a child, Philip fumbled through the bedroom closet searching for his worn down dress shoes.

"Margaret's probably the only child that could turn David's head. What do you think, Honey?"

Philip tossed one of his boots against the side of the closet wall and cleared his throat. "Yea."

"Reminds me of that Ramsey, if you ask me."

At that, Philip stopped tossing shoes and boots inside the closet and stood upright. David was his son, born of his flesh and blood, and yet he was closer to the man who would soon be his father-in-law. Ramsey and David, in their quietness and willingness to do "woman's work" if it would benefit their family, were akin.

Philip envied their relationship. He wished that David would realize that it pained him to listen to him throw a "See you later, Pop. I'm going fishing with Dad Armstrong," over his shoulder seconds before he went out the front door. The pain deepened when David returned home and Philip questioned the content of his day. The most that David did was shrug and comment, "My day was all right." Then he turned and climbed the stairs to his bedroom and closed the door.

Tammy stopped pushing her high-heeled shoe onto her foot and, arching her brow, she narrowed her gaze and leaned forward on the bed. "Honey?"

Philip almost jumped. He forgot that he wasn't in the bedroom alone. "Yea?"

She tried to see inside the closet, but from where she sat on the bed, she wasn't able. "You all right?"

Bending at the waist until his hands touched the closet floor, he began tossing shoes and boots again, "Yea."

While her father rummaged through his closet, Janice lay curled on her side in bed wiping salty tears off her face. For the first time in her life, she lied to her sister. Last night, she did go out looking for the missing Baxter girl. She waited until nightfall.

Certain that her parents were asleep, she hurried into the back yard and untied the family dog, Buster. Then, she ran toward the railroad tracks. Dark went like a thick curtain over Greasy Plank. Even when she pulled her hand inches from her face, Janice saw nothing but dark. Her eyes were set in a fixed protruding state. She felt blood coursing through her veins. Her heart pounded in her throat. Her breathing was labored.

At her side, Buster moved silently through the night. The dog didn't bark until Janice climbed up on the ridge below the tracks. Her foot slipped and she fell down the ridge onto the riverbank. Her ankle turned and she winced in pain. When she found her footing, Buster was gone. "Buster," she'd whispered while she limped forward and squinted into the night. "Come here, Buster." She'd started to cry. It was as though not seeing anyone, she felt she was in a crowded space and had to be silent.

Climbing back up the ridge, she'd stopped at an opening in the earth. Buster yelped twice, then he leaped onto her chest and she fell. After she caught her breath, she kissed him and told him to, "Come on. Let's hurry and get out of here. Let's leave this God forsaken place right now." She looked over her shoulder. "Right now." It wasn't until they got home, under the light coming off the back porch lamp that she saw the change in the color of Buster's hair.

Running her hand across the dog's spine, she'd stepped back and shook. Her hand had went over her mouth. She'd choked a scream. Blonde hair, strands of thin blonde hair spotted Buster's coat.


Unaware of his sister's haunting, David fastened the top button on his shirt. His eyes were strained and red. He slept only two hours last night. He looked at his suit pants and scolded himself for having doubts about his forthcoming wedding. He longed for Margaret and he, unlike many couples that he knew, to love one another as long as their parents had. He listened to his parents get dressed in their bedroom down the hall knowing that they were ignorant of his admiration of their marriage.

It occurred to him that Margaret and he not once worked to bring each other embarrassment or any other discomfort during their courtship. It was only due to his fears that so many years had passed prior to this, their wedding day.

Convinced that they shared a love only death had

the power to part, he straightened his tie and recalled the day that he met his future wife.

Her family had just moved to town. He didn't like her. In her T-shirt and blue jeans, with a single braid reaching beyond her shoulders, with her "a woman can do anything a man can do" attitude, she was too brazen for him. Yet, it was that same assertiveness that drew him to her and caused him to ask if he could see her again.

It wasn't until one year ago that he realized that, as it was with Ramsey and Rebecca, with him, it was Margaret's openness and assertiveness that filled the emptiness that he felt within.

**********

Chatter created a loud noise as wedding guests gathered on the wooden pews of Mount Zion First Baptist Church. Outside, rain drummed the tops of cars and trucks and spilled onto the street at a steady, rapid pace. Tied to the outer pews were bouquets of red and white carnations. In the center aisle, Margaret's flower girls stood stiffly in their sky-blue, ruffled, ankle-length dresses. They shook with nerves. They held a bouquet of assorted flowers close to their chests.

David stood with his hands clasped together. He refused to face his wedding guests, particularly his parents and future mother-in-law. Instead, he stared at the church's entrance doors. To his right and, equally nervous, stood his best man, Jonathan.

David stared at the church's entrance and watched the wind try to push the two wooden doors ajar.

All at once, no one moved. Chatter ceased inside the small church. At the rear of the sanctuary, Margaret cuffed the hem of her gown between her forefinger and thumb and prepared to walk through the doors that she'd traipsed through no later than nine-thirty every Sunday morning for the last seven years.

At her side, Ramsey stood tall, proud. Rebecca applied an extra layer of starch to his garments this morning. He looked regal as he extended his foot and took his first step.

Margaret followed.

They strolled arm in arm toward the pulpit. Unlike Ramsey, who practiced this altar march numerous times in his dreams, Margaret's steps were slow and cautious. While she walked slowly toward the man who would soon be her husband, she thought about the word 'forever'.

At once, there was something about the word that frightened her. She loved David dearly. She'd endured verbal and emotional abuses her soon to be mother-in-law had heaped upon her just so that she could be close to David. Yet, there was something about living 'forever' with David that sent such a fear inside her that it caused her hands and her knees to quake.

Thunder cracked the sky.

Margaret jumped.

Ramsey didn't flinch.

Lightning glistened through the stained glass windows.

David stared at the church doors. He saw the doors jerk and sway. When he glanced at the first two rows, his gaze fell upon Sharieffa's father. He recalled words that the older man had spoken at the airport, the day that Alex came home from the war. Recalling the words, he couldn't help thinking that it was storming on his wedding day.

Margaret and Ramsey reached the altar. After they did, Ramsey stepped alongside David and heightened his shoulders. He glanced at his daughter and wondered where the time had gone. It seemed like it was just yesterday that she was a little girl playing at his knee, begging for his attention. He wondered why he never told her that he loved her, not once. His gaze fell across her face. He thought she was beautiful. He did love her, and he missed her already.

"And do you, Margaret Armstrong, take David Tilson as your lawfully wedded husband? To love, honor, support, respect, cherish, and to stand by, through sickness or health, rich or poor, for better or worse, all the days of your life, so help you God?"

Margaret almost turned and looked at her mother before she answered, "I do."

"Now we will exchange rings," the pastor announced.

David slid the fitted ring up Margaret's finger until it stopped at her hand. A second later, the pastor, in a loud voice, turned, faced the wedding guests and boomed, "By the power invested in me, I now pronounce you man and wife." Then, he nodded toward David. "You may kiss the bride."

Cheers, applause and shouts of well wishes erupted when David lifted the veil off Margaret's face.

Midway into the church, and leaning toward the center aisle, Donna looked at Evelyn and hollered, "Throw the bouquet."

Instead of throwing the bouquet, Evelyn watched David greet Margaret and his wedding guests. She tried to forget the fact that over a year ago when she was walking home from the mill where her mother had sent her after two strips of lumber, she saw David looking through the woods. She didn't stop asking herself what he was looking for until she neared the railroad tracks.

The wind had nudged her back and she'd quickened her pace. Moments later, a familiar poignant odor rushed up her nose. For the first time in weeks, she gave the odor a name. "death," she told herself while she'd started to run. The gusts in the wind thickened her breath. She looked back to make certain that she was alone.

She didn't look up again until she was flat on the ground. She cursed the rock behind her feet. One of the strips of lumber had broken in two. She thought about her mother and tears welled in her eyes. When she pushed to her feet, her hands dug into a mound of dirt.

Seconds later, she was back on her hands and knees digging further into the ground. She didn't stop digging until she came away with a wallet. Her heart pounded in her chest when she opened the wallet. "David," was all that she said as she grabbed the lumber, hurried to her feet and raced home as fast as her legs would carry her.


Today, back at the church, Evelyn watched Donna raise herself up on her toes and shout, "Evelyn, throw the bouquet."

The flowers soared toward the ceiling and separated before they sunk into the tops of newly pressed and clipped hairdos. One by one, people turned and looked at Evelyn while they brushed flower pedals from their heads.

Evelyn stepped back alongside Donna and buried her blushing face inside her cupped hands.

David's and Margaret's wedding reception was held at Donna's parents' large, spacious home. People danced, laughed, played cards and told jokes for hours. At the end of the celebration, Ramsey raked in the final deck of cards and said, "This here is more than a wedding. It's a great coming together." When he looked up, he smiled and winked at Tammy.

Chapter Thirteen

"Meet me at the bar on Beale Street. Now. You know which bar I'm talking about."

Leonard didn't need to ask who the caller was. Over the months, he had come to recognize Detective Cramer's voice. He grabbed his suit jacket and ran out of his office door.

"Mr. Baxter," his assistant called as he raced down the corridor. "Mr. Baxter?"

He looked over his shoulder. "What?"

"Your appointment. You have a client coming."

"Please tell the client that I had to reschedule. Something came up." He hurried away from his assistant, then ran down the hall and out the door to his car.

Five minutes later, his assistant sat at her desk looking into the face of a stocky, silvery-gray haired man. "I'm sorry," she told the man. "Mr. Baxter had to leave on an urgent matter. I'll be sure and tell him that you stopped by. I had you penned in on his calendar." She shook her head. "I really am sorry. It's just that something urgent came up."

The man shifted his weight onto his cane. He smiled warmly at the assistant. "Not to worry."

When the man turned to leave, the assistant raised her voice and said, "I'm sorry. I never got your name. When you called yesterday you said that you were the owner of JR Construction, but I never got your name."

He stopped walking down the corridor and faced her again. His brow was tight, a sign to her that he was annoyed with her question. "My business is located in Louisville, Kentucky. I'll call and reschedule. Don't worry about it." Then, he left.

"I drove here as fast as I could without getting pulled over by a cop," Leonard said as soon as he entered the bar.

Detective Cramer laughed. "They don't ticket that much in this area. A little tip."

Leonard chuckled. "Thanks." H e nodded and added,"You asked me to get down here in a hurry. What came up?"

"For starters, the client you were scheduled to see moments after I called you is none other than Jack Robinson."

Leonard sat back in his chair stunned. When the bartender approached him and asked what he wanted to drink, he said, "Tequila. On the rocks." He waited for the bartender to leave the area before he asked Detective Cramer, "How did you know?"

"I did some checking. For the past few weeks, when you kept telling me you couldn't meet with me at noon on Wednesdays like we normally do then would call back and say your emergency noon appointment had cancelled, I knew something was up. I checked it out. That's how I found out who your important, emergency client was."

"I wonder what made him show up today." He shrugged. "If he did show up." After a pause, he continued with, "I mean, why would he reschedule those other times if he never really meant to keep the appointments then finally show up today?" He shrugged again, "If he did, in fact, show up at my office today."

"Who knows. Maybe he realized he couldn't stop us from meeting so he thought he'd come see you for himself, see what he could dig out of you." He shook his head. "That Jack Robinson. He's a slick one."

"Do you think I'm in danger?"

Detective Cramer took a swig of his soda. "I don't know. But it never hurts to be careful."

"But I really don't know anything. Why would he think I knew something?"

"We went through the man's house, Leonard."

"And got absolutely nothing. And how would he know we were in his house?"

Detective Cramer arched his shoulders. "I don't know." He took another swig of his soda. "Maybe he saw us leaving his house when he was turning the corner that day. I mean. You said you saw him with those shopping bags. Maybe he saw us too. It's hard to tell about these things."

"Yea. I suppose you're right. Now are you going to tell me the other reason why you called and told me to get down here right away?"

"A neighbor of Jack's said she thought she heard a little girl talking at Jack's house a few days ago."

"How long have you known this?"

"The woman called today."

"Wh-why didn't she call sooner?"

"Leonard, if I knew the answers to those types of questions—"

"--You're right. I apologize. You wouldn't know. This has just been very trying. Sometimes I don't think we've gotten anywhere. I want to find my little girl. I'm ready to elevate this to a higher level. If the local police department can't find Jocelyn, then I've got to take this above the local police."

"You and I both know that's not a good idea."

The bartender approached, carrying Leonard's drink. He smiled and nodded at both men after he placed the drink on the counter in front of Leonard. Then, he turned and stepped away from the men, walking to the other side of the bar.

"We can't keep pulling for straws, Detective," Leonard said as soon as they were alone at the counter again. He stared at the posters on the wall; they advertised expensive liquor brands. "Let's go by there." He took a sip of his drink "Now."

When Leonard stood to leave, Detective Cramer placed his hand on his shoulder and pushed him back down onto the barstool. "She's not there anymore."

"Detective—"

Detective Cramer raised his voice. "She's not there anymore."

A few of the bar customers glanced in their direction. When they did, Detective Cramer took another swig of his soda and looked at the glass door. "She's not there anymore," he whispered a third time to Leonard.

"Well, where—"

"She was seen with—" He released a deep breath. "She was seen with Ramsey Armstrong—"

"Who's Ramsey Armstrong?"

"Lower your voice. There's a reason we're meeting here instead of out in the middle of the street. Remember?"

"Okay. Okay." Leonard whispered, "Who's RamseyArmstrong?"

"He moved his family here from Louisville, Kentucky about seven years ago. He keeps to himself. No one knows much about him. His record is clean. He could just be eccentric. I don't think he'd hurt any—"

"This is my daughter we're talking about."

"I realize that, Leonard. Ramsey works at a foundry. Jack probably asked-- I don't know." He bowed his head, then he sighed. "Maybe Jack asked Ramsey and his wife, Rebecca, to watch the child while he went away on business."

"How could that be?" Leonard snarled. "That's impossible. Jack Robinson was just at my office. Out of town. Are you kidding me? I want to know who this guy Ramsey Armstrong is. I want to meet him. I want to talk to him, see what he knows."

Detective Cramer turned the soda can back and forth. He looked at the liquor ads on the wall for several seconds before he turned and said, "Leonard, we have to back off this case."

"We've come this far and you tell me we've got to quit?"

After a heavy sigh, Detective Cramer said, "I never had the support of the department to pursue this case. I pursued it on my own. Yesterday someone made a phone call to my boss. If I want to keep my job, I have to drop this case."

"But you told me the case was still open."

Detective Cramer chuckled. "In an open-closed kinda way. Nobody's officially assigned to the case. It's really closed. They do that to keep people off their backs." He shook his head. "You're not the only one. Believe me. It happens."

"Who made the phone call?"

"I don't know."

"Who do you think made the phone call?"

"The same person you think made the call."

"Look, Detective, I appreciate everything that you've done. I really do. I know you've had a lot at stake going after this case. I know that, and I do appreciate what you've done. I'll never forget what you've done, but I have got to find my little girl, and I need yourhelp to do that."

"Look on the good side, at least you know your daughter's fine."

"You don't know if that little girl some anonymous

151

caller telephoned the station about is Jocelyn. You've never seen Jocelyn in person. You've only seen those pictures of her that used to be plastered on posters across town." He drank his Tequila. "They even took those posters down. How long does a town get to mourn the loss of a little girl, a month?"

"Come on, Leonard."

"No."

"What do you want to do?"

"I want you to either show me where Ramsey Armstrong lives or take me to meet him?"

"You're not the only one who wants to get to the bottom of this case. Tammy Tilson." He chuckled. "She even sent a cousin of hers up from Mississippi to try to bust this case wide open. Paid him to snoop around for her. Even set it up so he got a job working at the foundry with Ramsey." He laughed. "Somebody ran her cousin out of town, scared out of his wits."

"Who are all these people?"

"You know the Tilsons. The grocery store in Greasy Plank."

"Ah, yes. What interest would she have in the case?"

"Ramsey Armstrong. His daughter is the wife of Tammy's oldest son. They got married not too long ago. Tammy did everything she could to try to stop that wedding. She doesn't like theArmstrongs, doesn't trust them."

Leonard sat on the barstool in silence. "I really am glad I came down here today."

"Yea."

"So, where does Ramsey Armstrong live, somewhere in Greasy Plank?"

"Yea."

"Where?"

"We're in over our heads, Leonard. Without the help of the department, we can't win against Jack. No way. And," he said, looking over his shoulder. "Let's get out of here. I don't even feel comfortable whispering. There could be ears, if you know what I mean. I just have a creepy feeling right now."

They paid for their drinks then walked to Leonard's car and got inside. "So?" Leonard said as soon as Detective Cramer closed the passenger door.

"Jack's connected, Leonard. He's more connected than you or me. We'd need the entire department backing us to win this case. This isn't theatre. This is real life. We're in way over our heads."

"Why are you really pulling back now? Somebody threaten you?"

"Let's just say I have come to believe that Jack's got friends in the department as well as politicians from downtown on his payroll, high level friends. Very high level." He paused. "Not to mention the fact that Jack found the two bugs I left in his house that day we paid him a visit."

"You bugged his house?"

Detective Cramer nodded.

"Nothing ever came of it?"

"Let's just say if it did, someone on Jack's side at the department intercepted it. I can't tell you how much trouble I got in over that. Eleven years of hard detective work almost went right down the drain." He snapped his fingers. "Nearly ended my career just-like-that over that incident."

"Tell me where Ramsey Armstrong lives and I'll never bother you again."

Detective Cramer laughed.

"Well, we both know I'll bother you again, but not for awhile."

Detective Cramer laughed again. "Two days."

This time both men laughed.

"542 Nettleton Avenue. And when you get there, you don't know me."



Rebecca answered the door after Leonard pulled in front of the house, stepped out of his car and started knocking.

"Is this the Armstrong residence?" Leonard asked.

Rebecca wiped her hands on her apron. "Excuse me, Sir. I was making biscuits for dinner. May I ask who you are?"

Leonard tried to look inside the house, see if he could spot any sign of a child. "Yes." He reached inside his suit jacket. "My name's Leonard Johnson." He flashed his business card at her then he quickly pulled it back and returned it to the pocket inside his suit jacket. "Is your husband home?"

"No. He's at work at the foundry." She smiled. "Gives me time to get something nice together for supper without having to rush."

"Yes. Certainly. Ah. You look awfully mature and wise to have children who are still in school."

Rebecca arched her brow.

"I could have sworn that I saw a little girl playing out back when I pulled up."

Rebecca shook her head. "No. All of Ramsey's and my children are grown. There's no child here."

"I must have been seeing things."

"You had to have been seeing things." She laughed. "We're finished raising children. Our oldest daughter just got married a few weeks ago. None of our children are in school. They're all grown."

"Grandchild, maybe?"

"No. They're not here today. Maybe you got our yard confused with our neighbors' yard."

"Maybe." He turned to leave.

"Do you want me to have my husband call you when he comes in?"

Leonard shook his head. "No. I'll stop by the foundry. Sorry to bother you. Thank you for your help."

"I'm not even a good llar," Leonard said to himself while he walked to his car. "Neither one of us believed that bit about me seeing a kid in her backyard." A second later, he whispered, "Jocelyn, where are you?"

He didn't go to the foundry. Instead, he drove to the railroad tracks, the last place that police said his daughter was spotted before they stopped searching for her. A boy had called in anonymously and said that he saw something that night. He'd been out drinking with a friend. He refused to give his name, just kept saying that he saw a group of men and a little girl up on the railroad tracks.

Leonard didn't know why he expected to find something different this time. He'd driven to the railroad tracks at least four times since Jocelyn turned up missing. And Detective Cramer just told him that one of Jack's neighbors said that they heard a little girl talking inside Jack's house and someone else said they saw a little girl with Ramsey Armstrong. And yet he went to the railroad tracks.

He got out and searched the tracks, the wooded area close to the tracks and the riverbank. As he expected, there was nothing, not a hint of foul play. No blood. No clothing. Not a strand of hair. Nothing. An hour and a half later when he returned to his car, he buried his head in his hands and cried for a long time.

While Leonard wept, Ramsey stood in the living room assuring Rebecca that everything was fine.

"But who was that man who came by here today and why are you always going off into a corner whispering whenever you talk to Jack? It's like nothing the two of you say to each other can be heard by anyone else, not even me. I'm your wife, Ramsey. I want to know what's going on."

"Look," Ramsey said while he ran his hand across his face. "I've been working all day. I'm tired. Nothing is going on. Jack and I do business together. You know that. Why do you keep asking me what's going on between the two of us? We're businessmen doing business together. We don't want to bore you with the details of our business affairs. That's all." He spread his hands. "That's all."

"He looked like a detective, Ramsey. You should have seen him. He even showed me his card. He's not from around here. That much, I know."

"What are you talking about?"

"I just want to make sure nothing is going on, that's all."

"If you're talking about those rumors Tammy started about me knowing something about that missing girl, you can forget that. It's over. Nothing's going on. That case has been closed. There is nothing to worry about. I have done nothing wrong. Now, if you don't mind, I'd like to eat dinner."

When she stood in front of him staring at the floor, he kissed her forehead, massaged her back and said, "Everything's okay, Rebecca. Everything's okay."

Part III

Chapter Fourteen

Margaret hobbled onto the front porch and pressed her knee against the screen door. Three bags of groceries filled her arms.

While inhaling and exhaling deep breaths, she unlocked the front door and held it ajar with her foot. Two of the grocery bags fell to the living room floor. Never minding the fallen bags, she mused, "I wonder what Dave would like for dinner," while she walked inside the kitchen. After placing one bag on the kitchen table, she turned and walked into the living room again, and opened the mail shoot.

Five pieces of mail fell inside her hand: the utility bill, the telephone bill, a letter from Sharieffa, a card from her favorite aunt and a letter from the district attorney's office.

Sharieffa and Margaret started corresponding two months after Margaret's and David's wedding. In her last letter, Sharieffa told Margaret, *"Through prayer, fasting and faith in God, Alex finally believes I love him just as he is. I couldn't have taken much more. It had gotten to the point where no matter what I did, Alex didn't trust me and thought I was staying with him out of pity. I don't care what he says. He was starting to hate me. I was scared around him a lot. I never knew what would set him off. He was real mean to me sometimes. Sometimes he would go days without talking to me. I tell you, Margaret. Trying to convince someone you love them when they are having a hard time loving their own self is one of the hardest things anybody will ever do. I wouldn't wish it on my worst enemy."*

Margaret, a profuse letter writer, pushed

Sharieffa's letter and her aunt's card in front of the utility and telephone bills. She shoved the letter from the district attorney's office inside her bra.

There was a knock on the front door. When Margaret looked through the small window at the top of the door, she was surprised to find Melinda, Janice and their husband's, Keith and Greg, standing on the porch.

"Hi, come in," she beamed after she opened the door.

Melinda shouted, "Girl. What are you doing throwing your groceries on the floor?"

Margaret dabbed her forehead with the back of her hand. "They fell. I was so loaded down. Now I'm tired."

Melinda looked at the bags. "I guess you are."

Margaret laughed. "Where's your baby, Melinda?"

"With Mama."

Margaret smiled. She could almost see the little girl's pigtails bouncing in the wind. "How old is that pretty girl now?"

"Almost two."

"Keith's baby girl, right?" Margaret asked, turning in a circle. "Where did Keith go?"

"I don't know." Melinda answered before she craned her neck and peered inside the kitchen. "He's in the kitchen putting away your groceries. Do you need him?"

Margaret walked inside the kitchen. "Keith?"

He pushed two cans of sweet peas to the back of the cupboard. Then, he grabbed two boxes of yellow cake mix and pushed them inside the cupboard next to a box of rice. "Yes?"

"Here. Catch." She tossed him a can of creamed

corn. "What are you doing putting these groceries away?"

"You look like you could have your and Dave's baby at any second."

As if the words bore a mystical effect, Margaret ran her hand over her round stomach. "I feel like I could too."

Keith turned long enough to tip the crown of his head. "Well, sit down."

Margaret quickly obliged him. "Thanks."

He resumed shelving the groceries. "You feel all right?"

"Sure," she gasped. "Just tired."

"Well." It was Melinda again. "Girl, go sit down on the sofa."

"That sounds good." When Margaret pushed up from the kitchen chair, her arms quaked.

Janice and Melinda raced to her side. "Let us help you."

Margaret leaned into their arms and tried to stop her eyes from rolling while she released a deep breath.

"Margaret, when are you supposed to have the baby?" Janice asked.

"In ... oh ... in about a couple of ... days," Margaret answered.

"Melinda," Janice said, peering at Margaret. "We better call her doctor. She doesn't look good."

"I know," Melinda agreed. "Come on, Margaret. Take it easy. Okay?"

"Okay." Margaret sat on the sofa and leaned back. She exhaled in deep breaths. "I don't know what happened. I was fine when I came home, and then the baby moved so suddenly. I just feel different."

"Margaret?"

"Yes, Janice?"

"I know you're tired, but are you okay?"

"Yes," Margaret nodded. "I'm okay."

"Then, why are you frowning like that?"

"Because my back hurts."

"Okay. We're going to lay you down. All right, Sis?"

Margaret blew out another quick breath. "Sure, Melinda."

"Janice, I'm glad we came over," Melinda told her sister.

Margaret almost laughed. "I am too."

Melinda dabbed beads of sweat from Margaret's forehead while Janice brushed her hand over Margaret's stomach. Together they lowered Margaret's back to the sofa. "Just take it easy and try to relax," Melinda said.

"I will, and thanks." Margaret paused and looked around the livingroom, "Thank you to all of you." Before she took her gaze off Keith, the front door opened and closed.

David stood motionless.

Melinda raised her hand in effort to quiet David's fears. "Now, don't go panicking. She's fine, thank the good Lord. You do need to call the doctor though. I was going to call, but then you came."

"All right," David said, unbuttoning his jacket and tossing it across the arm of the side chair. "Thanks. Dr. Glasner thought she wasn't going to have the baby for three to four days." He walked to the edge of the dining room and picked up the telephone. "Dr. Glasner, please."

Melinda massaged Margaret's hands and created small talk. "What do you want, Margaret?"

"A healthy baby. That's blessing plenty for me."

"I know what you mean. I was so happy when I

saw my baby and that she was all right."

"Janice, you and Greg are next," Margaret smiled.

"I hope so. You know I had two miscarriages a year ago."

"You're gonna have a baby. Watch and see," Margaret smiled.

"I've been praying," Janice said.

"Dave and I have been praying for you and Greg too. We know how much you want a child and, besides, don't forget — you can always adopt."

On the other side of the room, David spoke into the telephone receiver, saying, "Yes. Dr. Glasner. Yes. Ah, this is David Tilson. My wife, Margaret's breathing is labored and her back's hurting her. Un-hunh. She's laying down. Okay. Sir?" After a pause, he said, "Her labor pains are." Turning toward the sofa, he asked, "How far apart are Margaret's labor pains, Melinda?" Before Melinda could answer, David returned his attention to the telephone and said, "Bring her to the hospital? Okay. Well, what do you think? Alright," he nodded. "Thanks. Bye. Sure. Bye."

"What did he say?" Margaret asked.

David raced to the side chair and grabbed his jacket. "Keith, I've got to get my wife to the hospital."

Keith followed David. "We'll go with you."

"Thanks, Man. God knows what I'd do without you."

They were at the door when Margaret blurted, "Wait." She wobbled across the room to her purse. "I have to do something." She reached inside her bra and pushed the district attorney's letter to the bottom of her purse. Then, she covered the letter with make-up, her wallet, address book and a ball of tissues.

# Part IV

## Chapter Fifteen

Like a deep-rooted tree that bends, then straightens only to yield and bend again, time saw Greasy Plank shift. The town's population had grown from five thousand to eight thousand people. There were twice as many restaurants in town than there were a decade ago. More than half of the town's Negro population owned their own farm or another business, with the more popular companies operating in beauty, education, fashion or construction industries. Throughout the changes, Tilson's Grocery Store remained a community staple, increasing its revenues by more than six hundred percent over the past thirteen years. Evidence that Greasy Plank's changes were uncontainable, saw larger Memphis add another Negro to its law enforcement department, increasing its number of Negro police officers to two, a meager shift, as if change frightened the police force. What hadn't transformed beneath the winds of change created a stain, left ugly scars on the town. One event in particular continued to scare adults and children, causing a shadow where safety and trust was intended to be. The shadow was darkening especially for Leonard Baxter, taking on an ominous hue, a ghastly impression.

After thirteen years of searching, praying and waiting, Leonard told himself, "Jocelyn's gone forever." Detective Cramer had stopped returning his weekly telephone calls. He said that he didn't have any more time to devote to a missing person's case that was more than a decade old. "If anything turns up, I'll do what I can to see where it leads," he'd told Leonard. "But for now, I have to stop working this case. Altogether. Totally. I'm falling behind on other cases, murder cases, other missing persons' cases. Unless new evidence turns up, I have to put an end to this."

Leonard wondered how Detective Cramer could push his daughter's disappearance to the back of a file, turn his back on her, say because no solid evidence had turned up on her, that she was no longer as important as she had been on the first day that she was discovered missing. In so many ways, Leonard tried to keep her close to him. He didn't want her memory to fade. He wanted to be able to recall her image with clarity, as if thirteen years hadn't passed since he'd last seen her, as if he'd just been with her yesterday.

While out shopping downtown or at a grocery store, Leonard smiled softly at little girls who met his probing glance. As he smiled at the girls, he told himself that he was smiling at Jocelyn. "I apologize," he'd end up whispering as a girl ran to her mother, seeking safety.

Jocelyn was missing for two years when Leonard decided to avoid stores except at night, a time when little girls were safely tucked in their beds at home. When he shopped at department stores, he went to the girls' clothing section, picking up the latest outfits, holding them against his chest.

Flipping through magazines, he whispered "I love you, Jocelyn" as he stared at pictures of blonde-haired girls with beautiful sea-blue eyes. But it wasn't enough. After thirteen years, Leonard couldn't forget the little girl who'd spent all her life calling him, "Daddy."

He worked twelve to sixteen hours a day to reduce his free time, arresting his thoughts from obsessing about Jocelyn, wondering where she was and if she was dead or alive. It kept him sane. Working long hours also kept him away from his wife, Stephanie. He'd never revealed to Stephanie that he knew about her affairs. He knew if he did, she would emasculate him.

They hadn't been intimate in years. They didn't even sleep in the same bed anymore. Worrying about how others perceived them is what locked them into their dreary marriage.

Leonard remembered the day that Stephanie looked right at him, not so much as blinking, and told him, "I'm pregnant." Months later, his mind filled with great expectation, he'd bought the large, colonial house on Monroe Avenue. He'd hired Lenora, their live-in maid and nanny. He'd telephoned a local home decor company and had their unborn child's room decorated with pastels, popular cartoon characters and musical trinkets.

At the same time and although Stephanie more-often-than-not told him that she was "too tired" for sex, it never occurred to him to take a test to confirm that he was Jocelyn's biological father. He just believed his wife. He was in love. Now, he realized that he'd merely been a lonely, married man. When he was younger and heard older men complain about being "married and lonely" while nursing a bottle of whiskey, he wondered how they could be both at the same time — married and lonely.

Now he knew, and yet he didn't have the courage to leave Stephanie. She had become like a wall fixture. He'd grown so accustomed to seeing her every morning when he left for work and every night when he came home, he thought he'd be lost without her. After years of marriage, her voice had become like a familiar song. What he was accustomed to, what he was familiar with day in and day out, was killing him slowly, he told himself.

He sat at his long wooden office desk reviewing evidence to use in an upcoming court case. A woman had shot her husband in a crime of passion. She'd come upon her husband and his lover naked in their bed. Their two sons, ages nine and eleven years old, were outside playing in the backyard. Before the woman knew it, she had a gun in her hand and her husband and his lover were dead. "I didn't mean to do it," she kept saying.

Leonard had sat across from the woman on the first day that they'd met, nodded at her and said, "I know. I understand." And he did, so much so that he was thinking about abandoning the case. It reminded him too much of home.

## Chapter Sixteen

Across town from Leonard's office, in the hallway of the home that she shared with her husband, David, and their four children, Margaret glanced into the mirror on her way downstairs. The last decade had been good to her. Her father was right. The investigations did stop. It was as if the universe was being kind to her family for the first time in as long as she could remember. At night, her subconscious brought her deepest longings to the surface and she dreamed about marching over to the Tilson's and making it unmistakably clear to her mother-in-law that she was wrong. Her father was not a coward. He was not one of those spiritless "clay people" as Tammy so eloquently put it. If she would so much as give her father a chance, Margaret knew that Tammy would come to respect him.

He'd been through a lot since his father died when he was a mere twelve years old. Twelve was too soon to carry a full- time job and take on the role of man of the house, but it had been Ramsey's lot in life. He did the best that he could.

Admittedly, until her mother told her how her father had become "the man of the house" at twelve years old, Margaret had looked at her father with suspicion too. She'd wondered if he loved anyone except her mother. Now, she wanted Tammy to get to know her father, to give him a chance to reveal his true nature to her before she formed hard opinions about him.

After David's and her oldest child, Richard, was born eleven years ago, Ramsey started visiting. Sometimes he even stopped by without Rebecca. He spoke to Margaret when he saw her; he even hugged her a few times. He adored his grandson, Richard. He

166

took him camping and on fishing trips. Richard did for Ramsey what no one else could. He made him feel that he belonged.

As if that was not enough, marriage proved one of the most rewarding and joy-bringing events in Margaret's life. David surprised her with home cooked, candlelit dinners. He showed up unannounced at her job and took her out to lunch. He paid their neighbor to baby-sit so that he could take Margaret to the theatre or wine and dine her at one of the finer restaurants on Monroe Avenue.

Being with David made Margaret realize why her mother never left her father, even after the investigations, both in Memphis and Kentucky. Outsiders' opinions didn't matter. It took Margaret nearly thirty years to realize that fact. Her father was good to her mother. He loved her, and that was enough.

Margaret pulled down on the back of her skirt and laughed. She felt that heaven had heard her pleas for mercy. Her family was finally winning; they were overcoming their foes. When she and her mother spoke two days ago, Rebecca told her that Ramsey had started communicating with his therapist from Kentucky again and that his therapist had said that he would look around and find an affordable psychiatrist in Memphis who Ramsey could visit.

Then, Rebecca had laughed and told Margaret, "Your father and I have started going out again. Just last weekend, your father took me to a dance Jack Robinson put together for the men at the foundry and for the men at his construction firm. And I can't tell you how much Ramsey loves Richard. He talks about that boy what seems like all the time. Your son has pushed life inside your father. Just the other night, your father was talking about Richard. Couldn't have been a second later that he said he didn't care what people said or thought about him, he was going to start enjoying life again, and all because of your precious son." She'd chuckled. "Imagine that," She'd laughed. "Richard reminds me so much of Ramsey. The older he gets, the more he does."

Margaret reached the bottom of the steps. The house was empty. She could hear her children playing outside. As she listened to the sound of their deepening voices, she marveled at how they had grown and how their personalities were developing. Richard was eleven. Carolyn was ten. Ruth was nine, and Arthur was seven.

Despite Carolyn's fault finding and bossiness, Ruth's tattle-telling, Richard's aloofness and Arthur's mimicking, the siblings fared well together, this despite their differences.

Carolyn hated being criticized, never mind how subtle or gently it was meted out. On the other hand, intelligent beyond her years, she was first to point out others' faults.

All through elementary school, Carolyn had made Honor Roll. Math and science were her favorite subjects. Richard lost count of how many spelling bees Carolyn had won. Because of her smarts, Greasy Plank adults extended her a similar respect that they normally reserved for elders. It was her fault finding that extinguished even her best friends' patience. "It's one thing to constantly criticize other people with your thoughts, but to speak on it is the worst. Stop telling people everything you notice that's wrong about them," Margaret told Carolyn so often that the words seemed a mantra. Carolyn nodded at her mother, but she didn't take the advice to heart.

Richard, on the other hand, paid close attention to what his mother told his sister, Carolyn. Whether he had to tiptoe up the stairs, ease out of the bathroom and around the corner or crack the door to Arthur and his bedroom and stick his head out, Richard found a way to eavesdrop on the tongue lashings his parents gave his sister, Carolyn.

Listening to the verbal discipline, Richard knew that had he not been silent the times Carolyn turned up her nose and told him, "You're a coward. You don't know how to box your way through whatever it is you're afraid of," he could have spared her the bedroom meetings.

He often reflected on how his sister sized him up by telling him, "You worry too much what others think of you. You'll never be a self- made man. You'll be a puppet."

The words stung and yet he continued to think about what his sister thought of him. "You flunk school because you're lazy. If you weren't afraid of hard work, you'd be a straight A student."

Carolyn was loud while dispensing her judgments. Even adults in the neighborhood wagged their heads and arched their brows each time Carolyn voiced her strong opinions.

Carolyn was also active in the community. She gave her favorite clothes that she outgrew to children from needy families. Years passed and her cousin Missy, Alex's and Sharieffa's six-year-old daughter, grew tall. It was at that time that Carolyn gave Missy most of her hand-me-downs. Carolyn also tutored middle and high school students.

Introspective, insightful and bright, her parents and siblings often caught her sitting on the edge of Ruth's and her double bed with her head buried between her hands. As they quietly went down the hall, they knew that Carolyn was daydreaming or praying.

It was Carolyn who filled the bathtub until sudsy water lined the rim, then sat for half an hour in the warm water daydreaming about how she could come to the aid of suffering people living in Greasy Plank. Major holidays and family birthdays, when their grandparents, aunts and uncles filled the living room and began talking in raised voices, Carolyn would listen to family talk. She seemed to know when they were discussing a community member who was enduring financial, marital, child raising or spiritual problems. She would listen more intently after she heard her grandmother, Rebecca, excitedly exclaim something like, "Why, the president of the motherboard over at Star Hope Baptist Church's health has been failing fast. I heard one of the church faithful's telling a sister from over at First Baptist that the president of the motherboard ain't been to church or prayer meeting in weeks. Her health's failing on her so fast."

That said, Carolyn would start praying. Her prayers were always answered. Even Richard admitted that there was something to his sister's prayer life. Throughout Greasy Plank, Carolyn came to be viewed as "the blessed one". Elders in the community called her "inyanga". In other circles, she was viewed as equal to the local soothsayer or root doctor. Folk came to her for a variety of pains and ills.

Only ten years old, Carolyn rarely talked about the visions that haunted her. The one time that she did, she was visiting her Aunt Janice. They were alone, sitting on the living room sofa at Janice's and Greg's home.

"Aunt Melinda said you used to see a little girl running until she went into fire," Carolyn said matter-of-factly while she looked at her Aunt Janice on that

170

lazy, late afternoon.

"Aunt Melinda told you that?" Janice looked at her niece and asked.

"She said you went down to the river at nighttime once."

Janice turned away from Carolyn and snapped, "Aunt Melinda was talking too much whenever it was she told you all this."

"When did you start seeing a little girl running?" Carolyn wanted to know.

Janice's mouth tightened before she said, "Carolyn, there used to be bad things happening in Greasy Plank."

"Like what?"

"It's all stopped now." Janice shook her head. "It's best to leave it in the past."

"Do you still see the little girl?"

"Carolyn please—"

"--What does she look like?"

"Slow down, Carolyn. This isn't something people should go digging up. It was a very bad time."

"What happened to the little girl? Why did you start seeing her?" Carolyn asked as she moved close to her aunt.

"Carolyn, Honey, we shouldn't be talking about this. I know you have a gift. I know you know when spirits rest it's best not to waken them."

"But, Aunt Janice—"

Janice raised her voice. "--Carolyn, I'm sleeping at night for the first time in years. Right after Aunt Melinda got married, I started being home by myself a lot. It was then that the little girl started haunting me. It was almost like she knew I was alone. Even to this day, sometimes I wonder if she was waiting for Aunt Melinda to leave so she could find an outlet through me."

"An outlet for what? What did the little girl look like, Aunt Janice?"

"She was clear, a gray color." She turned away from Carolyn. "Now stop." She shook her head. "No more questions. We've talked about this enough."

"They say there's a little girl's ghost up by the barn. You know, up by Lenox's."

"That's an old story."

"But stories don't start out of nothing, Aunt Janice."

"Rumors do."

"You think the ghost up by Lenox's is all a rumor?"

"Carolyn, please." Janice begged, wringing her hands.

"I see little girls," Carolyn continued, unwilling to abandon the discussion. "It happens when I'm sleeping. I wake up and remember the girls."

Janice was quiet for a long time before she asked, "Carolyn, how long have you been having these dreams?"

"They're not dreams. They're faces."

"What do they say?"

"Nothing. I just see them. Why? Did your little girl talk to you?"

"She wasn't my little girl."

"How do you know? Every time you got pregnant you were having a little girl."

"Carolyn."

"Aunt Janice, none of them ever lived."

Janice pulled her hands between her legs so that Carolyn wouldn't see them shaking. "Carolyn, you are reading too much into this. I had miscarriages, simple miscarriages."

"That little girl was trying to come through you."

"Carolyn," Janice screamed.

"She looked different than we do, didn't she?"

"Carolyn—" Janice said between clinched teeth.

"--The little girl you saw didn't look like us. I know it. I know she looked different than we do. She was White and somebody killed her."

"Carolyn, stop or I'm going to have to take you home to your mom and dad."

"You don't have to take me home, Aunt Janice. I'll walk if you want me to leave, but I know what you know. We both know that little girl was killed. She came to you for help, Aunt Janice, and you didn't help her."

Janice stared at her hands. When she looked up, her lips were trembling. "I put my life in danger thirteen years ago, and more than once. I took Buster out to the railroad tracks. It was late at night. Every time I went up there, I took Buster with me. The first time I fell and Buster got away from me." She gazed across the room. "When I found him, I went right back home. I was scared. I've never been that scared. I got back home and the porch light went over Buster's coat. You should have seen the hair on Buster. It was blonde."

"How long was it before you went back?"

"Two days. I had to be careful. I couldn't let Mama and Dad know what I was doing. They'd of had a fit. There were a lot of bad things going on in Greasy Plank back then, a lot of bad things."

"What happened the second time you went up on the railroad tracks?"

Janice shook her head. "Nothing. I even took a flashlight with me that time. Flashed it all in that hole in the earth. Nothing was in there."

"So where did the blonde hair on Buster come from?"

"Carolyn, stop," Janice stammered. "I appreciate

173

your inquisitiveness, but you can be a hardheaded little something when you want to be. Now I'm asking you to stop talking about this. I don't want to talk about it anymore—"

"--What if she comes back?"

"It's over, Carolyn. Ain't nothing happened around here since your brother, Richard, was born. It's over."

"You're not going to ever have any kids, Aunt Janice." Carolyn said matter-of-factly.

"Little Miss."

Carolyn shook her head. "You're not." Her face drew down. Her eyes were full, yet sad. "You're not, because you won't let that little girl come through. She wants you to find her, Aunt Janice, but you keep being scared."

"That's enough—"

"--She's blocked your womb."

"Stop it—"

Carolyn sat across from Janice staring at her as if she was looking right through her. "Aunt Janice?"

"Yes."

"I only have my visions on nights when Grandpa Ramsey visits."


**\*\*\*\*\*\*\*\*\***

The root of Carolyn's spiritual transformation went back to stories that her grandmother Tammy and her parents shared with her.

When she was very young, Tammy would lift Carolyn into her lap, smile and tell her, "When I was a little girl, not much older than you are now, my mama would sit me on her lap and talk to me about root. She'd tell me how important it was to have good root in our family. She'd say, 'Tammy, everything on a family tree

174

springs right from its root.' She sure would. That's what she'd say, Sweetie."

Then Tammy would pull her granddaughter, Carolyn, close and hugging her, tell her, "Mama said you would come." Then, she'd kiss Carolyn's small forehead and said, "Inyanga."

But it wasn't just Tammy. When their children were toddlers, Margaret and David called them around the kitchen table once a week and, vividly rehashing scripture, told them about a man named Jesus. Sitting across the table from her parents, Carolyn allowed every word to infuse her being.

A week after the first story telling episode, Richard passed Ruth's and Carolyn's bedroom and overheard Carolyn praying to Jesus. She was praying for one of the Henrik girls because she had the flu. Four years later, Carolyn realized as seemingly powerful as her prayers were, she wasn't self-sufficient, and that she needed to be saved.

After reading John 14:13-14, she came to realize that as a child of God, she was to pray directly to God in Jesus' name. From that day forward, her prayers gained incredible power. She was blessed with the insight and wisdom of an old sage and the faith of a little child. She never outgrew either.

Whereas Carolyn was highly respected in the community, Ruth was better liked. School also came easily for Ruth. Her favorite subject was English. She talked as much as Carolyn -- only faster. With two headstrong sisters conversing on their favorite topic, it was difficult for Arthur or Richard to get a word in edgewise.

Besides being talkative and studious, Ruth served as family tattletale. "Mama—Dad. Mama—Dad," she would limp through the house whining while she groped the front of her leg, "Carolyn kicked me." Her favorite complaint was, "Mama—Dad. Mama—Dad, Carolyn said she was going to beat me up after everybody went to bed and was asleep."

Margaret and David always sided with Ruth.

Arthur was the baby in the family. Outside his mimicking and shadowing Richard, the brothers got along fine. Cause of that was the fact that, for nearly all of Arthur's young life, Richard and he had shared separate ends of a queen sized bed for their sleeping place each night.

Still, Richard had a group of cronies and the image they created of him to fulfill. Arthur's shadow was embarrassing. Richard turned and yelled, "Go back home!" at Arthur when he found him walking in his footsteps. Had Richard not, his friends would have sought someone else for their hero. Whenever Richard's cronies asked him why Arthur clung to him, ire burned inside Richard. If he yelled too fiercely and ordered Arthur out of his sight, Arthur, like Ruth, would race and tell their parents. Upon Richard's arrival home, he would be meted out a punishment and strictly enjoined not to leave the house for a week except to walk to and from school.

Of the four children, it was Richard who caused his parents the most sleepless nights and tested their patience the severest. He spent the early part of his adolescence telephoning neighbors and church parishioners pretending to be a concerned police officer or a worried physician. He also took apart every birthday and Christmas toy that family and friends gave him just so that he could put the toy back together again — his own way. In school, he did just enough to keep from getting put back, not a bit more.

It was David who told Richard that he was only six years old when he began to paint. As a child, Richard had climbed the stairs to the attic, found his way through the dust, and tugged on the bottom edge of his mother's favorite oil painting. With the painting in hand, he'd crawled to the attic floor, took his water color pack from his back pant pocket and. in one long slow stroke after another, painted over the mother holding her son in the original oil painting until the two faces blended and became a sad faced clown.

When David climbed up the attic stairs and discovered what six-year-old Richard had done, he threw his hands over his mouth and gasped. One breath later, he stuffed the painting in an old toolbox shoved in a corner of the attic. He kneeled close to Richard's ear and whispered,"I won't tell your mama."

That May, when Margaret started her spring cleaning, she stopped in the living room, drew her hands down toward her hips and, letting out a deep sigh, decided to rearrange the furniture and hang the oil painting above wherever she decided the sofa's new location would be. Richard listened intently while she shouted, "shucks and doggone-its" and searched the attic. While he sat on the edge of his bed listening to his mother rummaging through the attic, he could almost see her head turning from wall to wall, her gaze darting over the empty cardboard boxes, the dust, the cobwebs and the toolbox.

Seventeen years would pass before his father would tell him that the oil painting was given to his grandmother Tammy as a Christmas gift in 1923, the year that his father, David, was born. It was a gift to Tammy from her mother. The painting cost Tammy's mother five hundred dollars, a sweet mint back in the late eighteen hundreds," David told Richard. "Your

Great-Grandma had a feeling her daughter, Grandma Tammy, was going to give birth to a baby boy — which turned out to be me - the first time she found herself in the 'motherly way' and, sensing my mother would be a part of something historical and unforgettable, she bought the painting of the mother holding her son."

"When your mom and I got married," David told Richard, "I gave the painting to your mom as a gift. She fell in love with it."

Two years passed after Richard repainted his mother's favorite oil painting before he touched paint again. He drew pictures with crayons, but he avoided paint. His grandparents bought him stacks of coloring books. He was eight years old when he started oil painting. A year later, Ramsey bought him a chalkboard and his own portfolio paper. Each time he needed drawing pencils or a box of chalk, Ramsey saw that he got it. At first, Richard drew mainly clowns, houses and kids, then he began drawing landscapes, farmhouses, all the lines in an old woman's sagging face, scenes of little children playing in Meeman-Shelby park and in their front and back yards on the chalkboard. On paper, he drew pictures of little girls with scars and bruises on their hands, arms and faces and rope tied around their throats. At eight years old, he knew to hide the pictures of the little girls, so he stuffed them in his pant pockets and pushed the pants to the bottom of his dresser drawers.

Chapter Seventeen

"Carolyn," Margaret called up the stairs.

Jogging halfway down the stairs, Carolyn answered, "Mama?"

"Aunt Janice wants you on the telephone."

Walking to the edge of the dining room, Carolyn took the receiver from her mother. "Aunt Janice."

"If your mother is within earshot," Janice began, "Say 'one'."

"One."

"Okay, just listen. Every few seconds say something like 'yes' and 'okay', and throw a few 'yes, Ma'ams' in there too."

Carolyn chuckled. "Yes, Ma'am."

"I thought about what you said when you visited last week."

"Okay."

"About the haunting, about the little girl. I'm going back. Aunt Melinda is going with me. If you want to go, say 'yes'."

"Yes."

"Okay. Put your mother back on the phone. I'm going to ask her if you can go to the mall with Aunt Melinda and me. I'll tell her we're going to look for a surprise birthday present for your sister Ruth and afterwards we're going to get dinner and maybe catch a movie. I know she'll go for it. Make sure you're ready to go by six o'clock tonight. We'll head to the tracks as soon as it gets dark. We'll have you home by nine-thirty or ten o'clock so your mom and dad don't start asking questions. Okay?"

"Yes, Ma'am."

Carolyn spent the next few hours playing marbles and freeze tag with her friends. At five o'clock, she went into Ruth and her bedroom and shut the door. She secured the windows and closed her eyes. She sat still and repeated, "Come to me. We're trying to help you. Come. Go with us, tonight. I know you know. Meet us down by the railroad tracks. Meet us tonight. Let us tell your story. Let us tell what happened to you, so you can go free. So we can all be free. Come. Come to me. We're trying to help you. Go with us tonight. I know you know. Meet us down by the railroad tracks. Meet us tonight. Let us tell your story. Let us tell what happened to you, so you can go free. So we can all be free. Come. Come to me. We're trying to help you." Nearly an hour passed.

Nothing.

Carolyn trusted that she would get connected. She didn't open her eyes. She didn't move. She breathed deeply, evenly.

Not another moment passed before she felt the hair stand erect on her arms and on the nape of her neck. Seconds later, she felt a strong breeze moving through the room. She opened her eyes and smiled.

"Carolyn," Margaret called up the stairs.

Before Carolyn opened the bedroom door and left the room, she looked over her bed at a quote that she'd scribbled out of a book during English class last year. She read the quote out loud, "Two roads divulged in a wood, and I — I took the one less traveled by. And that has made all the difference." She smiled and said, "Thank you, Robert Frost." Then she opened her bedroom door and went downstairs.

Janice and Melinda did take Carolyn to the mall in the city. They did buy birthday presents for Ruth, but it was mainly an exercise in time passage. After they finished shopping, they sat in a mall cafe and waited for the sun to go down.

"Let's go," Janice said, reaching for her purse. "We'll drive to the tracks in Greasy Plank, the ones over by the ridge. As soon as we get there, I'll get flashlights out of the trunk and then we can head down the ridge."

It took half an hour for them to drive from the mall to the railroad tracks. Carolyn could scarcely see her hands in front of her face when she stepped out of the car.

"Hold my hand," Janice said reaching for Carolyn while she and Melinda began their descent down the ridge. "I fell the first time I came up here."

"Your hand feels like fire, Aunt Janice," Carolyn said as she took small, careful steps to the bottom of the ridge.

Janice chuckled. "I know, Honey. I get like that sometimes when I've been thinking real hard."

"Where was the hole you saw all those years ago, Janice?" Melinda asked.

Janice moved her flashlight back and forth over the base of the ridge. "Over here, Melinda. This way."

Carolyn and Melinda followed her.

"Over here," Janice kept saying. "It was over here."They walked for half an hour.

"We're going in circles," Melinda said. "We've been at this exact spot at least five times already. Janice, are you sure the hole wasn't further down? Was it closer to the river?"

"I don't know. All I know is I was up on the tracks. I decided to look down on the ridge. I fell close-to—" After a pause, she said, "You're right, Melinda. Now I remember. I fell down onto the edge of the river. When I got up, I was wet and Buster was gone. Buster's the one who found the hole. There must have been a lot of dirt or something in front of the hole,

181

because the cops never found it and I didn't see it at first either. Maybe Buster smelled something and started digging. I don't know. All I remember is, I got up to go find Buster so we could go home. I was scared something awful. I had this bad-awful-feeling, like something horrible was going to happen if I stayed down there. When I climbed up to the top of the ridge again, all of a sudden, Buster leaped on my chest. If I would have been older than I am now, I think I would have had a heart attack—"

They stopped.

Melinda whispered, "Did you both hear that?"

"Probably a possum or a rat," Janice said. "Come on. Let's hurry. I don't plan on staying down here much longer. I'm starting to get that creepy feeling I had the first time I came down here."

"And Buster's returned to the earth. He can't help lead the way," Melinda said.

Carolyn looked at her Aunt Melinda, "I think we should split up. Stay within earshot and eyesight of each other. Just go in different directions. First one to find the hole calls to the other two and we all continue our hunt together."

Melinda and Janice nodded.

While she walked, Carolyn whispered, "Come to me. We're trying to help you. Come. Guide us. I know you know we're here. Meet us where we are. Let us tell your story. Let us tell what happened to you, so you can go free. So we can all be free. Come. Come to us. We're trying to help you. Come to us right now. I know you know we're here. Meet us where we are. Come—" A second later, she turned and called over her shoulder, "Aunt Janice. Aunt Melinda." Behind her, she heard footsteps.

Janice ran until she caught up to Carolyn.

"Where's Aunt Melinda?" Carolyn asked.

"She went back to the car. She got scared. She only came out here because I asked her to. Melinda's had no visions. She's had no dreams. The little girl never called out to her. Aunt Melinda doesn't understand why we're out here. I mean. She knows we're looking for evidence that'll lead us to the girl's killer, but why we're so sure we're supposed to be here, that she doesn't understand."

"Look," Carolyn said, pointing. "There's the hole. You can tell somebody dug it. It's not too big. We'd have to get down on our hands and knees and crawl just to get in there and, even then, we might not be able to fit. Buster must have dug that hole, and I bet you over the years the rain has made the hole a little bigger, but just a little." Carolyn pointed her flashlight into the small opening.

"The hair's probably gone," Janice said. "It was thirteen years ago when I came down here and saw the blonde hair."

"I wonder how far in the hole Buster went before he turned around and came back out." Carolyn said. Pausing she added, "And I wonder why he leaped on you when he came out of here. Something must have spooked him."

Janice stared at Carolyn. "You're right. Something must have spooked Buster or else he wouldn't have come running and leaping out of here like he did."

All at once, Carolyn froze. When she did, Janice walked into her heels. Then, she looked down and followed Carolyn's gaze.

Carolyn bent and started digging into the ground, faster and faster. Dirt caked beneath her fingernails, but she kept digging. "Look," she said after minutes of digging. "Looks like a bone. Could be an animal bone, but it could be—" She looked up at her Aunt Janice.

"How could the cops have missed this? They swore they went over every inch of land down here several times."

"Nothing but time allowed us to see it, Aunt Janice. Time and rain," Carolyn said. "Over the years, the rain washed away the dirt they covered that little girl with."She paused and stared at the bone. "If this is her." She turned the bone in her hand. She started squinting. "I don't know what this bone is to."

"I still don't see how the cops didn't find anything, and how can you hold that-that bone like that?" She recoiled in disbelief. "Aren't you scared?"

Carolyn looked into her aunt's eyes. "She's not going to hurt you, Aunt Janice. She knows we've come here to help her." She looked at the bone again, "And stray animals come down here. Could belong to a fox or a wolf or a raccoon. It's so small. I don't know. But," she looked closer at the bone while she held it beneath the flashlight. "Look. You can tell it's been broken." She turned and faced the pile of dirt that she'd dug through to find the bone. "Maybe there's more."

"No." Janice shook her head. "I'm not staying. Let's get out of here."

"Maybe the cops didn't come down here," Carolyn suggested.

"They said they did. And," Janice stared up at the sky, then she turned and looked at the river. "All the newspaper reports said someone threw the girl into the river. They even dug in the river. But how could

184

someone say they saw men dump a body in the river and the girl's bones be over here?"

"Aunt Janice, we don't even know what this is—"

"It's her, Carolyn. I came down here with Buster. This is where he was." She clinched her teeth. "Those are her bones."

"Who said they saw men -- and what men -- throw a bodyinto the river?"

"I don't know. An anonymous caller told the cops that."

"They didn't get any information on the caller, nothing?"

"Papers said it was a boy. That's all they said."

"What about the men? Does anybody know who the men were?"

When Janice turned away from the river, she was shaking her head. "No."

"Aunt Janice, we have to get this to the police."

Janice kept shaking her head. She started backing away from the hole.

Carolyn followed her aunt away from the hole.

Janice started to run. "No."

Carolyn ran after her. "What is it?"

"She was alive," Janice said as she moved away from the hole.

"What?"

"How could Buster have hair on him if she wasn't alive?"

Before Carolyn could respond, a chilling scream came from the road above the ridge.

Janice and Carolyn started running. They sprinted up the ridge until they felt their hearts pounding in their chests. When they reached the top of the ridge, they saw Melinda sitting in the car. She was rocking back and forth and honking the horn.

185

"I saw a man," she said when Janice unlocked the door. "His face. You should have seen him. You should have seen his face." She started to cry.

Carolyn jumped onto the back seat and shouted, "Let's go. It's not safe." She shook her head. "It's not safe anymore. Drive. Drive fast."

Janice pulled away from the ridge so fast, the car's tires spun and squealed, grinding up dirt at the back of the car. "We have to go to the police station. We have to tell them about the bone."

Melinda leaned against the passenger door and wept.

Janice sped through the night streets and avenues until she reached the police station. Melinda, Carolyn and she stayed at the police station for an hour, pleading with the officers to, "At least come with us to the hole below the ridge."

Janice pleaded at the police station, "Come and see where we found the bone." None of the officers budging, she said, "It may be nothing, but how will you know unless you come and look? This could be the key to the case. Something's down there. We got this bone from down there."

One of the officers looked at Melinda. "And where were you when all this was going on again?"

"I was on the ridge with them. Then, I heard something behind me. I got this feeling that we weren't alone and I turned and went back up the ridge to the car. I locked the door and sat and prayed for my sister and niece to come back soon so we could leave. Before they reached the car, I saw the man."

The officers laughed, outright knee slapping laughter.

Across from them, Carolyn clenched her jaw and

her fists. "An old man down by the railroad tracks this late at night?"

One of the officers looked over his shoulder and snickered to his colleague, then he burst out laughing again. "Who ever heard of such a thing. What would an old man be doing at this time of night in Greasy Plank?" He roared. "Next you're gonna tell me you were followed. Somebody tapping your phone? Are you a private eye? Who'd be following you?" H e s m i r k e d . He stopped laughing and shook his head."It makes no sense. Don't you see? Why would an old man just show up at the railroad tracks at night, and what on earth would he want with you?" He shook his head. "It makes no sense. Nothing you all are saying makes sense."

Melinda nodded.

The officers laughed in her face.

After five more minutes of pleading, one of the officers leaned across the desk and said, "Let's go have a look."

At Carolyn's insistence Melinda, Janice and she didn't ride in the squad car. Instead, they followed two officers back to the ridge in Janice's car.

"They know who did it," Carolyn said as soon as they climbed in Janice's car and locked the doors.

Back at the ridge, Melinda, Janice and Carolyn stayed close to each other. While they led the officers to the hole beneath the ridge, Melinda kept turning and looking over her shoulder.

When they climbed down the ridge and reached the hole, the officers peered at each other. Then, they turned and faced Carolyn and Janice and asked, "Where's the hole you supposedly found the bone in? Look at this place," they said, waving their hands over a mound of dirt. "There's nothing. Nobody's even dug here. We went over every inch of this area years ago. There's nothing here. I don't even see the hole you claim to have dug." He pursed his lips and shook his head. "You're all nuts. Don't pull this prank again."

Chapter Eighteen

Ramsey parked his truck behind the office complex and waited. When half an hour passed and he was still sitting alone in the dark, he started cursing and sweating. "I don't have to do another thing I don't want to do. I've got demands coming at me from Rebecca, the kids, the job and that damned Jack."

He stared up at the name engraved in the top of the building - JR Construction. "I could just drive away from here, just start driving and never stop. Get the hell out of this no good town."

He forgot that Jack was the reason that he'd packed up his family and left Louisville to come to Memphis in the first place. Moving someplace else wouldn't rid him of Jack. Not now.

Jack had become an appendage, like a malignant tumor. He was not going away. Ramsey owed him too much. In a way, the two men complemented each other. Jack paid off Ramsey's debts and got him out of legal trouble. He helped to create the illusion that Ramsey was a good husband. Ramsey disposed of Jack's victim, born of his flesh and blood. He stepped in when people in Greasy Plank started asking too many questions. People were sure the girl was dead. It didn't matter how many times the cops rattled other men's front doors or rang their telephones pointing the finger of guilt in their direction. They knew. Everyone knew the girl was dead. But they didn't know who the killer was. They just knew it wasn't someone from Greasy Plank.

On the other hand, White people in Memphis had no doubt that a Negro man had taken the little girl from Monroe Avenue and killed her in cold blood. When people from both sides of town happened upon one another while shopping on Beale Street or visiting an uptown theatre, they glared at each other and cut and rolled their eyes. They hated one another more with each passing day.


"Ramsey?"

He faced the window.

"Roll down the window."

After he rolled down the window, he said, "What did you call me out here for at this time of night? My wife gave me a fit when I told her I had to go out. I lied and told her something happened at the foundry and I had to go and check it out."

"I thought you said Tammy had backed off?"

Ramsey clinched his teeth. "She did."

Jack smirked. "Her daughter—" he began. After a pause, he added, "Are you going to invite me in or are you going to make me stand out here for the rest of the night?"

Ramsey reached across the seat and unlocked the passenger door. He waited for Jack to walk around the truck and slide across the seat. "Tammy's not up to anything," he told Jack.

"Her daughters were down by the tracks. And her granddaughter, that mouthy one."

"Carolyn?"

"Yes. Her. You wouldn't know what they were doing down there, would you?"

"What were you doing down at the tracks?" Ramsey asked. " There's no reason to go—"

"--I go down there to remember, to think."

"You murdered your own daughter, Jack."

"Damn it, Ramsey, how many times do I have to

go over this with you? Are you that stupid? Do you think I could let her go? She'd seen me. She would have identified me if I let her go." He scowled. "I am not going to go over this with you again. Ever. We've gone over this enough damned times. I did what I had to do. Nobody regrets it more than I do. Nobody. Think I don't miss her? Think I'm not haunted by thoughts of her? She was my baby girl, damn it. I loved her, Ramsey. I don't need you reminding me of what happened."

"I told you to take her back home."

"You are so dumb, Ramsey. You are an idiot. Just take her back home. You're dumber than I thought you were. Take her back home, she fingers me and then what do I do?"

They sat in silence.

"Just what did you do back in Illinois and Kentucky, Jack?"

Light rain started to fall against the truck.

Ramsey stared up at the moon and the stars. "You killed your own daughter."

Jack listened to the sound of the falling rain.

"She didn't even have to see you. She wouldn't have known it was you who ordered the kidnapping. You're the one who demanded to see her, to be with her. And as soon as people found out she was your daughter, they would have understood. With all the money you've got, you could have paid your way out of the mess. You were her father, Jack. Her father. Who would have put you in jail for spending time with your own daughter? Why did you kill her, Jack?"

"Shut up. That's it. I don't want to hear another word out of you. You're a moron. Her father's a brilliant attorney, you idiot. He would have investigated me until they found out about the other four--" He cleared his throat. "--You told me Tammy was no longer hunting for answers, looking for clues. Then I go down to the railroad tracks to visit my little girl and who do I see?" He shouted. "Tammy's daughters and that loud mouthed hussy granddaughter of hers."

Ramsey turned the heat in the truck on 'low'. He spoke in a whisper. "I'm sorry, Jack. But I really thought and I still think the Tilsons don't know anything about what really happened. If anything, Tammy might ask around about Bobbie Long every now and then, but that's it."

Cool air blew through the front passenger window, but Jack didn't roll the window up. "Who's Bobbie Long?"

"I don't know. People talk about a ghost, a little Negro girl's ghost up by an old barn. I've been hearing that story off and on since I moved my family here." He waved his hand. "Probably just an old wives' tale."

"Never heard of the ghost before," Jack said. "Wonder why I never heard the story before."

"It's just a story old women in Greasy Plank keep going," Ramsey shrugged. "That's all."

"But why would Tammy care?"

"I don't know," Ramsey shrugged. "Maybe she knew the little girl."

"What happened to the little girl?" Jack asked.

"People say somebody killed her and dumped her body in the river by the railroad tracks, the tracks by the old barn."

"Oh, you mean the Lenox barn?"

"Yes."

Jack gazed into the sky. "Amazing how many stars are out tonight. It's raining. Most nights when stars are out like this, the weather is clear, not a cloud

192

in the sky."

"It's just talk," Ramsey said.

"Just talk. And now what are we going to do about these Tilsons? That granddaughter actually found something down there by the tracks tonight. I don't know what, but she had something. They went to the cops with it."

"Nothing's going to come of it, Jack. The body's gone. We disposed of it." He swallowed rising vomit. "No one knows anything. I certainly didn't tell anyone anything." He looked over his shoulder at Jack.

Jack laughed.

"I'm not going down for this," Ramsey said.

"Neither am I, so you better find a way to shut those Tilsons up."

Ramsey started to shout. "They can't tell what they don't know, and I have told them nothing."

"I left one of the bones done there."

Ramsey stared blankly at Jack.

"I had to. I had to keep something back."

Ramsey continued to stare blankly at Jack.

"And it doesn't matter if you didn't say anything. Your daughter is married to one of them."

"My daughter doesn't know anything."

"So, the Tilson girls just show up at the tracks tonight?"

"Jack, I don't know everything those people think. My daughter knows nothing. The Tilsons know nothing."

"Talk about Bobbie Long, those girls coming to the tracks tonight. Your daughter married to one of those Tilsons. Something's going on." Jack shook his head. "I can't risk this, Ramsey. T his could open into a world of trouble for both of us. You obviously don't know what the Tilsons know. You didn't even know they were heading for the tracks tonight—"

"--Jack, I—

Jack raised his voice. "If it wasn't for me going to the tracks at the last minute, we wouldn't even know they'd been down there. I almost didn't go to the tracks tonight." He gazed into his lap. "I've been trying to stop going down there. I've been trying, but every now and then I just gotta go down there, but I'm trying hard to stop."

"There wouldn't be anything there to find if you had given me every shred of evidence. And even then, everything happened thirteen years ago. There is nothing to point to us."

"One of those Tilson girls saw me."

"It's dark out. She didn't recognize you."

An insect flew inside the opened window. "She saw me. I thought I could get out of there. She was sitting in a car when I went to cross the road to go to my car. She turned on those damn headlights and started honking that damn car horn." He watched the insect crawl across the dashboard. "She saw me. If she goes back and starts talking to her mother, this thing is going to open up. I am not going to prison."

"If you knew taking your daughter would bring all this on, why did you take her?"

Jack lunged across the seat. His hand went around Ramsey's throat, and he squeezed. When he sat back in his own seat again, he opened his fist and wiped the fluid that had oozed out of the insect that he'd just killed across his pant leg.

While Ramsey massaged his throat, he asked, "What do you want me to do?"

"We've got to take another girl. We've got to do it," he said, shaking his head. "Tell you what. I'll send a release to the papers that I'm organizing a charity event out of town. I'll leave town and then you can take the girl. You'll bring her to a vacant lot that my firm's been contracted to build a motel on. It's out in the middle of nowhere. No one will see you. I'll take her from there."

"Jack."

"You tell me, you just tell me what other possible way we can throw the Tilsons off. You tell me how we're going to keep this thing from blowing up?"

"Taking another girl is certainly not the answer." Ramsey lowered and shook his head. "Jack, I'm not going to do it. I'm not. I'm not."

"You. Will. Do. What. Ever. I. Tell. You. To. Do."

"Jack."

"The police will work on this case and forget all about Joycelyn. If the Tilsons start talking, no one will believe them. They might even start to think that the Tilsons are hiding something. This'll work, Ramsey." He shook his head. "If we do it right, it will."

Ramsey buried his face in his hands. "Jack, please."

"I wish we didn't have to, but this is the only way."

"And what if this doesn't stop the Tilsons from trying to get to the bottom of things?"

"You better hope it does." Jack watched rain fall against the truck's front windshield.

Next to him, Ramsey choked back tears. "Jack, we really shouldn't do this." He stared up at the stars in the sky. "What else do you want me to do, kill the Tilsons?"

## Chapter Nineteen

Leonard reached for the telephone so fast that he knocked his Rolodex watch and his eyeglasses off the corner of his home office desk. He dialed fast, his fingers hurrying around the holes in the telephone number panel. As soon as he heard the other line pick up, he asked, "Is this the Cramer residence?"

Evelyn looked into the kitchen at her mother who was mashing potatoes. "Yes. Who's calling?"

"My name is Leonard Baxter. I'm a friend of your father's. May I speak with him, please?"

"Mama?"

Mrs. Cramer wiped her hands on her apron and hurried into the dining room. She took the telephone from her daughter. "Hello? Whom am I speaking with?"

"Leonard Baxter. I'm an attorney."

"Baxter."

"Yes, Ma'am."

"Baxter?"

"Yes."

"Ah. My husband's not home right now. May I take a message?"

"It is very important that I speak with him. Is there a way to reach him?"

"Leave a number and I'll have him call you. He stepped out. He'll be back in a moment or so." After she took the number and hung the telephone up, she lifted the receiver out of its cradle again. She dialed Tilson's Grocery Store. "Tammy, Girl," she began, "You're working late tonight. I didn't think you'd pick up."

"I was heading home when you called."

"Well, I'm not going to keep you. Is Robert still down there?"

"You know those men are in the back room watching sports on that small black and white TV."

"Will you go get him, please? It's important."

"Girl, you alright?"

"Yes. I just need to get him a message right away."

"Hang on."

While Tammy went to get her husband, Mrs. Cramer stood by the telephone trying to remember when she'd heard the name Baxter before. A few minutes later, she heard her husband's voice on the line.

"Honey?" he said.

"Robert, Sweetheart, a man named Leonard Baxter called here looking for you. He said it's important. He wanted to speak with you right away."

"He didn't say what he wanted?"

"No. He just said it was important."

"I'm on my way home. I'm coming home now."

Before he hung up, Mrs. Cramer heard Tammy ask, "Everything alright, Cramer? Need Philip to come with you?"

Dinner was still warm when Robert pulled up to the house. He went straight to the dining room phone. He dialed fast. "Leonard?" he said, his voice breathy.

"Who is this?"

"I'm sorry, I thought I had the Baxter residence."

"This is the Baxter residence. You're speaking with Mrs. Baxter. Who is this?"

"I'm a good friend of your husband's."

"Leonard," Stephanie shouted up the stairs.

A second later, Leonard called, "I've got it," back downstairs. He waited until he heard Stephanie hang up the downstairs phone before he said, "Hello?"

"Leonard?"

"Hang on a second." He went to his bedroom door and listened. When he didn't hear anything, he returned to the telephone. "Call me on my work number. I don't trust this line."

"But—"

"--Just call me there, please."

Seconds later, the telephone on the desk in Leonard's home office rang. "Robert."

"Yes."

"Thank you. I didn't want to take a chance on my wife listening in on the call."

"I understand. My wife said it was important. What is it?"

"You'll never believe what I got in the mail today."

"What?"

"A copy of Jocelyn's birth certificate."

"What?"

"I couldn't let it rest. I c o u l d n ' t . The hospital finally sent me a copy."

"Wait a minute. You weren't her biological father. You didn't have legal custody papers. Why would they do that?"

"Let's just say, they did."

"Alright."

"You were right," Leonard said, glancing at his closed office door. He lowered his voice to a whisper before he said, "A man named Jack Robinson was her father."

Robert released a sigh of frustration. "We knew that."

"That's not all."

Robert looked at the meal at the center of the kitchen table. His wife stared at him, begging him to hurry so they could eat. "Let's hope not," Robert said, his voice lower. He turned away from his wife's prying gaze.

"Jack Robinson is a psychopath," Leonard said.

"What?" Robert stepped back and asked. Then, he said, "Hang on, Leonard." He looked into the kitchen at his wife. "You and Evelyn go ahead and eat. Don't wait on me. As soon as I get off the phone, I'll be right in."

Mrs. Cramer left the kitchen and walked to the edge of the dining room. She crossed her arms and smiled softly at Robert. "Do you want to take this upstairs in our bedroom, so you can have some privacy?"

He winked at her and handed her the receiver. It wasn't long before she heard. "Thanks, Baby. I've got it. You can hang up now."

While Evelyn and her mother put the dinner in the oven, so it would stay hot until Robert returned downstairs, Robert sat on the edge of the bed talking to Leonard. "A psychopath?"

"A cold blooded killer."

"Are you kidding me?"

"I wish I was."

"What do you have that proves that?"

"If you saw the stack of psychiatrist papers sitting on my desk, you wouldn't doubt it for a minute. That guy Ramsey Armstrong you were telling me about."

"Yea."

"He's got serious head problems too."

"Psychiatrist papers. Leonard, what have you done?"

"Jack's a killer, Robert. I think they both are. All these tests and treatments and recommendations and confidential memos and letters, notes from Jack's mom to the court, notes from criminal court clerks to Jack's mom. An expunged police record on Ramsey. Mental health records on Ramsey involving serious, and I do mean serious psychological issues." He shook his head. "There's a lot here, Robert, a whole lot."

"Alright. Ah—"

"--I can make copies. You can take them to the precinct first thing Monday morning."

"Let's keep this quiet for now. I'll meet you Sunday after church and look through the papers." He shook his head. "You really fooled me, Man. I thought you had put this behind you. You've probably been playing private eye this whole time."

"I tried to let it go. I really did. Taking up different hobbies, working until my eyes were bloodshot. Hell. I even started fishing."

Robert laughed.

"Anything to keep my mind off Jocelyn, just so I wouldn't think about her all-the-time. I was doing pretty good, then last Christmas when I was in the cellar getting the decorations out of a box, I came across Jocelyn's first coloring book." He chuckled. "Can you believe that? It was under the box the decorations were in. One of the China ornaments rolled to the back of the box. When I went to move the box, I found the coloring book. Every other year, except this one, I used the decorations in the garage."

"Garage?"

"Yea. The wife doesn't like clutter in the house."

Robert laughed.

"I don't know what made me go to the cellar this past Christmas. After I saw that coloring book, I couldn't pretend Jocelyn wasn't the most important person in the world to me anymore. I just couldn't."

"So you started investigating on your own?"

"Yea. This time I told myself to check places I hadn't checked before. First thing, I wanted to be sure that Jack Robinson was Jocelyn's father." He stood, walked to the office door, and peered into the hallway. After he saw that the hallway was empty, he closed the door and sat down behind his desk. "Then I started digging for information on Jack and Ramsey."

"Good work, Man." He chuckled. "What can I say? Good work. Want to come work at the department with me?" Robert smiled.

"Nah. We attorneys do as much digging for information as you detectives do. We do a lot of the same work."

Robert released a deep breath. "No evidence that Jack or Ramsey has killed though?"

"Nah. None."

"Just psychiatrists' and court letters, memos and other documentation and correspondence?"

"Exactly."

"I don't know, Leonard. That's not much to go on."

"Can't the department at least re-open the case?"

"With the paperwork that you have that you just told me about — I mean — I doubt it."

"Will you try?"

Robert sighed. "Leonard, let me see the papers first. I can't promise anything, Man. If I take those papers to my supervisor, you know what the first question he's going to ask me is going to be."

"How did you get the papers."

"Bingo."

"Shit."

Part V

<u>Chapter Twenty</u>

The Tilson children and their friends spent Saturday, May 15, 1959 playing in the park. The wind danced through their hair. Above their bobbing heads, their brightly colored kites zigged and zagged against the backdrop of a clear, blue sky. Their hearts stirred under the power of their laughter which chorused, rang and echoed its way over the park as they ran up and down the steep, grassy hills with their skinny kite strings securely fastened around their hands.

Earlier in the day, the Tilson children's friends walked in one large group to David's and Margaret's house. Richard, Carolyn, Ruth and Arthur knew that they were coming. The night before, Carolyn asked their parents if they could go to the park. Margaret looked over her shoulder at David and told him that the children had to clean their rooms, dust the living room furniture and scrub the bathroom before they left. David nodded at her, and she turned from looking at him, smiled and nodded into each of her children's faces.

It took them two hours to finish their chores. No sooner were they finished, did their friends crowd their way onto the porch and begin to rap the wood of the front door. David opened the door and called up the stairs. "Wash your hands first."

Water splashed over the bathroom sink and dripped to the floor as Carolyn, Richard, Arthur and Ruth washed their hands and hurried to join their friends outside.

While they walked to the park with their friends, they pretended to be eighteenth century Robin Hoods. All of the children tied the paper lunch bags that their mothers had filled with food to skinny tree branches that they picked off the ground and toted the bags over their shoulders.

The day was hot and muggy. Only the wind and the shade of the trees provided relief from the sun. The journey to the park left the kids' throats parched. They headed for the park benches. There were so many of them at the park that some of them had to sit on the ground.

Carolyn opened her lunch bag first. The rest of the children looked on in suspense while she peered inside her bag. When she lifted her head and smiled, her friends unrolled the tops of their bags and looked inside and smiled. Working holes in the bottom of each of the children's bag was a juicy orange.

Carolyn squeezed and rolled her orange in her hand the way that she always did until the fruit warmed her palms. She plunged her teeth into the orange's navel once before she began to peel away the skin.

Her brother, Richard, watched her peel her orange and hoped that his would be as juicy. Pulling his feet against the back of the park bench, he opened his bag again, pulling out his orange.

Moments later with their oranges eaten, the children reached inside the other bag that they had carried and withdrew their kites, which they quickly assembled. They dashed off the grassy hill as a single unit. Richard looked over his shoulder while he ran. The kites dazzled the sky, their different colors, shapes and designs blending until they looked like ornaments in a parade.

Three quarters of the way through the park and deep into the late afternoon, Ruth's best friend dug her foot in the ground and grinned.

Richard watched the girl's back disappear as she sprinted down the long hill shouting, "Last one down is a rotten egg!"

All the children chased the girl down the hill.

Carolyn swung her arms and extended her legs. She felt a freedom that she hadn't felt in so long, while she ran, the feeling, its power liberating, seemed foreign to her. She wished that she could run forever. In front of her, Ruth's best friend ran with all her might to win the race to the bottom of the hill. Seconds later, the girl leaned and fell onto her hands as she reached the bottom of the hill ahead of the other children.

Moments later, while the children walked home, they swapped stories. Arthur re-enacted two cartoons that he'd watched on television early in the morning. Carolyn, Ruth and their friends skipped alongside one another. They sang an old rhythm and blues tune as they skipped.

The girls' voices blended agreeably, and the song came to have a calming effect on all the children.

Richard leaped to the top of the wood fence that they walked alongside. He extended his arms and walked teeter-totter on the fence top. While he walked, he listened to a friend telling corny jokes. Finally, the fence ended, and one of the friends hollered, "See ya later!"

"Bye." The children answered as a group.

"Bye! See you in school on Monday," the friend called in return.

Further into town, Richard walked backwards, away from his friends and his grandparents' store.

"See you, Carolyn," a girl cupped her hands around the corners of her mouth and called out. "The kids have to sing in church tomorrow."

Arthur turned his hand down, dismissing everyone.

He was hungry and ready to go home. "We'll be there."


Family filled David's and Margaret's house by the time the kids got home from the park. Some of the family sat on the sofa. Others sat on living and dining room chairs.

Richard's eyes opened wide as soon as he saw his family.

Ruth skipped further inside the house. Arthur followed her. He grinned while he moved closer to the kitchen where he was certain that a delicious hot meal was.

Carolyn examined the faces in the living room, the worry in her family's eyes. She listened to the long silence that filled the house. Then, she started an immediate search for her grandfather, Ramsey.

Another girl was missing. Of that, Carolyn was certain. It showed on her grandfather's face. And he had fear in his eyes. The past had come back. Carolyn knew. Several nights ago, she had woke up sweating and screaming, "She's alive. A kitchen. A basement. Cellar. A cellar. Dirt. A pipe. A pipe. A pipe."

No one came to soothe her fears. She lay back down and cried herself to sleep.

During the last few weeks, even though her mother ushered her to her room, she'd heard detectives questioning her mother about her grandfather's mental history. She heard her mother lie for the first time, lie again and again. Her grandfather was what people called "crazy." Carolyn pieced that together from the gossip that she'd heard around town, a poem and two letters from the district attorney's office that she'd opened late one afternoon after she picked open the small lock box that she saw her mother hide in the lower portion of her sewing machine. Her parents had been dining at Smother's, a downtown fish and spaghetti restaurant. Carolyn read the poem slowly.

*Little girls running from the past*
*Hurry into a frightening future*
*Trusted men meet into their lives*
*Until the little girls running are met with*
*A quick end*
*Inyanga knows*
*Inyanga*

"Who's been at this dining room table?" Margaret asked when David and she returned home from Smother's.

Carolyn sat on the edge of her bed with her ear toward the door. She scowled when her mother asked the question.

Seconds later, Margaret went through the house calling out, "Carolyn, Ruth, Arthur, Richard!"

Carolyn listened intently while her mother made her way up the stairs. She called out, "Carolyn, Ruth, Arthur, Richard!" while she climbed the stairs.

Carolyn didn't answer.

Certain that the children were outdoors playing, Margaret walked completely passed Carolyn's and Ruth's bedroom and into her own. A moment passed before she returned to the hallway and inched alongside Carolyn's and Ruth's bedroom door.

When Carolyn looked up, she saw her mother standing in the doorway.

"Why didn't you answer me? Didn't you hear me calling you?"

Carolyn tapped the two letters from the district

attorney's office and the poem into the palm of her hand. Then, she slowly raised her gaze and lifted the letters so that her mother could see them. "Mama, why do you keep lying for Grandpa Armstrong?" She raised the poem. "And who wrote this?"

Margaret snatched the letters out of Carolyn's hand. "Give me those." S h e raised her open palm and readied to slap her daughter across the face. She took in a deep breath. "A woman named Donna Lane wrote the poem years ago. We were all teenagers when she wrote it. When she told me about it, I paid her ten dollars for it." She chuckled. "You have no idea how happy she was. Her first sale." She chuckled again. "I bought her first poem." She stared at the floor. "I couldn't let it get out. I couldn't let anyone else read that poem. I had to buy it. I had to get it."

"Where's Donna Lane now?"

"She left Memphis about nine years ago. She got married and moved to Chicago. No one's heard from her since."

Carolyn shook her head. "This poem is a story. It's telling something."

Margaret stretched forth her hand. "Give me the poem, Carolyn. The letters and the poem belong to me. They are not yours and you are to never, ever, ever speak of these a day out of your life."

She wept when she turned to leave her daughters' bedroom, grateful that she hadn't slapped her child, sad that she felt obligated to continue to conceal her father's secrets.

Carolyn listened while her mother went slowly back down the steps. Then, she lowered her head between the locks of her shoulders and wept softly herself.

In addition to her mother's demand that she keep

the poem and letters a secret, the past few weeks, children at school had begun teasing the Tilson children. "Your grandfather's a pervert. You aren't good people. You think you're better than us because your family owns a grocery store, but you're no better than us. You're worse. Your grandfather steals little girls and throws them in ditches."

Except for her closest friends, the last few weeks Carolyn saw little, if any, reprieve from the taunting. Ruth usually cried when classmates teased her. Arthur raced to Richard and followed him around in school.

Richard waited until he got home to deal with the accusations. Once there, he hurried to his easel, grabbed blank sheets of paper and started drawing pictures of a little girl with rope around her neck.

Carolyn retraced each of her family member's steps, especially her grandfather Ramsey's. She tried to bring order to the crisis. She focused on resolution. Without it, she disallowed herself one uninterrupted night of sleep.

From listening to older folk talk around town, she'd already figured that the last time a little girl turned up missing, a wealthy elderly man had visited the foundry a lot.

"But he's always down here," Carolyn told Ramsey the last time that she was at the foundry. "Grandpa, you know rich folks don't hang around a foundry. Why is he always down here?"

Ramsey had smiled softly at her, rubbed the top of her head and said, "It's okay, Sweetheart. He's a nice man. Mr. Robinson's different. That's all."

"But people are mad at us. People are saying mean things about you. And I heard people are looking for a reason to hurt us." She raised her brow. "Grandpa?"

"What, Sweetheart?"

"Are you telling the truth?"

Ramsey had looked at her for a long time. Then he'd told her to hurry home before it got dark outside.

That was a week ago. Until she saw her family sitting in her parents' living room, Carolyn had forgotten the discussion. Playing at the park with her friends then singing her way home alongside her siblings and friends had been like a doorway, leading her out of her troubles. Now, she was home staring in her mother's troubled face, wishing that she was back at the park.

"Where have you been?" Margaret asked.

"Flying kites with our friends at the park, Mama," Arthur answered. "Can I have a cookie?"

Margaret told him, "Sure."

"Me too?" Ruth asked.

"Sure, and you too, Carolyn and Richard."

Carolyn tapped the top of her mother's head while she strode toward the kitchen, "Thanks, Mama." She made a point of staring at Ramsey when she passed him. When he winked at her, she turned away from him and tightened her brow.

"You're welcome, Baby," Margaret said. "Don't forget to wash your hands."

"We won't, Mama." A second later, Carolyn looked down at her hands. They were shaking. She knew her mother and her grandparents were hiding something. She felt it in her heart. From where they sat around the kitchen table, Richard, Carolyn, Ruth and Arthur listened to the grownups talk in the living room.

They heard their Aunt Janice ask, "Where are Melinda, Keith and the girls? Melinda called and said they'd be here over an hour ago, and they only live fifteen minutes from here. Where are they?"

Rebecca pulled down on her skirt's hem. "Maybe they stopped by the store."

"David already checked there, remember?" Tammy said.

Next to her, Philip stared at the television screen.

"What are we going to do, just sit here?" Janice asked.

Rebecca peered at Janice. "Let's wait awhile longer." She pursed her lips. "They probably stopped by the store after David went by there." She cut her eyes at Ramsey. "Let's wait awhile longer, see what happens."

Guilt clung to Margaret's thoughts. Just this once she told herself to say what was really on her mind. She felt doing so, just once, would make up for all the times that she'd held her tongue when she should have spoken up, lied when she should have told the truth.

"We can't wait forever, Mama." Margaret stared into her mother's eyes, the same eyes that had brought her comfort, taking away her fears when she was a little girl.

Tammy looked at Margaret, a woman who had all of her children under the roof of her home, a woman who had not to ponder one of her children's whereabouts. Her voice was cold, her words sharp. "Well, what else do you suggest we do? We've called friends and Keith's folks looking for them. Philip's driven to Keith's and Melinda's twice already." She looked from Margaret to Rebecca. "David looked at the store for them twice. So, what else? What now?"

Margaret said, "Call the police."

Philip laughed. "The police. They won't help.

210

They'll tell us to wait too. They're probably in on it. Coming around asking us questions about another missing girl. They can't find a criminal, so they harass the hell out of us. The police," he laughed.

After she rustled the hem of her dress, Rebecca snapped, "Let's change the subject."

Ramsey sat stoically in his chair. He wondered how Philip knew another girl was missing. He'd abducted the girl from a sliding board earlier in the day. When he looked at Philip, he told himself that Philip was lying. His own grandchildren had just come home from playing at the park. The abducted girl's parents were probably just starting to look for her. No way could Philip already know that another girl was missing. It was impossible.

While the family discussed where Keith, Melinda and their daughters could be, Ramsey wondered if the talk that he'd had with one of the men from JR Construction had paid off. "I can't keep it to myself anymore," he'd told the man when he met with him at a bar on Beale Street a few days ago, after he got off work at the foundry. "I know they're family, but you and some of the other guys were right. The Tilsons had something to do with that Baxter girl turning up missing."

He sipped his beer. "They've always known. Now, I'm not saying they did it, but they've been hiding information since day one. They've held this whole thing up from the start. They've got this crazy idea that somebody killed Bobbie Long, and they loved her. I guess it's their way of getting back at the town for not investigating Bobbie's death more. I don't know," he shrugged. "I just know they know who took that Baxter girl and they've been protecting them. They're always trying to divide people in this town. Anyone who's not with them, they try to destroy. Sure wish it was different, but—" He watched the man's brow tighten. "I couldn't keep it to myself anymore. I thought you'd want to know."

"How do I know you're telling the truth, boy? I know you and the Tilsons don't get along. How do I know you're not just making this up?" The man tightened his grip on the neck of the beer bottle that he held in his hand. "And why are you telling me this now, after all this time?"

Ramsey looked around the bar to see who was watching. When he saw the bartender glancing in their direction, he took a deep breath. "I couldn't deal with it any longer. It was eating me up. I couldn't keep it a secret anymore."

"Why should I trust you?"

"I had to tell somebody and I know how much folk around here look up to you and your people on a count of the fact that you all don't stand for no foolishness."

The man placed the beer bottle on the counter. "So, you're saying the Tilsons know who killed that little girl?"

Ramsey nodded.

"If you know they know, then you must know too. So why don't you just tell me who did it?"

Ramsey glanced at the bartender who peered back at him. "I don't know who did it," Ramsey told the man. "From conversations I've walked up on, I can tell the Tilsons know, but I don't know who did it."

"People talk, boy," the man said. "Just what all have they said that makes you so sure they know who the killer is? You playing with me, boy?"

"No. I'm telling you the gosh awful truth. It's things at their houses. Things their grandson's done.

I'm telling you, they know. They all know, especially that Melinda."

"Melinda? Thought you were talking about Tammy and Philip?"

"Melinda's their daughter. She knows."

"Why in hell would she keep it a secret?"

"I told you. They think somebody from around here killed Bobbie Long and the cops never did investigate that case right, so they're protecting this killer to get even."

The man stared at Ramsey, then he spun in a circle and laughed. When he faced Ramsey again, he had the beer bottle in his hand. "If you're playing with me, boy, you will be sorry."

Ramsey watched the man saunter out the door. "Would I have kept it a secret all these years if I was playing games, if I onlywanted to hurt the Tilsons?"

Since Ramsey met with the man at the bar, anonymous callers had been contacting the Tilsons at the grocery store and at home, shouting obscenities and threatening them. The last time that Melinda came down to the grocery store, she went into the back room with Tammy and told her, "Somebody's been following me. Seems like every time I get in the car and drive somewhere, when I look in my rearview mirror, I see a car or truck behind me. I turn left, they turn left. I turn right, they turn right. I even went down a few dead-end roads and the driver followed me then too."

"Did you recognize the drivers?" Tammy had asked.

"No, but one time when Sharieffa, Janice and me were going shopping, Sharieffa said something about a man breaking into Alex's and her house while Alex was at war." She looked at Tammy. "Did you know a man broke into their house back then?"

"I know, Honey. Sharieffa called me the night it happened."

"Well, Sharieffa said that something about one of the men who's been following me reminded her of the guy who'd broke into Alex's and her house that night."

"Those men were just trying to scare Sharieffa, trying to keep that coward Ramsey in line. He must have mouthed off to that Jack Robinson and Jack figured he'd scare that coward Ramsey by putting fear in his own son's wife. Those cowards. They ain't nothing but clay people. They don't have no spirit in them."

"But why would the men be following me?" Melinda asked Tammy.

That night when Melinda went home, she told her husband what Tammy said. "Those men are still following me," she also told him.

He'd held her in his arms and said, "I'm going to call some of my friends and ask your dad to get in touch with men in town, so we can make sure our women are safe. You won't be harassed anymore. I'll put a stop to it. If they want to harass somebody, they can harass me, not my woman."


Arthur, Carolyn, Ruth and Richard left their places in the kitchen and went into the dining room. They saw their Aunt Janice's husband, Greg, leaning forward in his chair. His arm was extended and, reaching around Tammy, he squeezed one of her hands. "Keep the faith, Mrs. Tilson. I know it's hard, but try to keep the faith." He pulled his hand back and sat against the spine of his chair. "I know it's hard."

Philip bit down on his words. Anger made his voice shake. "Why now? We've been living in this town all our lives. We've always had enemies, jealous, ignorant, racist thinking cowards, but nothing like this. Why all this confusion now? We haven't done anything wrong or hurtful to anybody."

Janice listened to the sound of the grandfather clock as its pendulum swung back and forth. "This isn't about us. No," she said. "This isn't even about color. This is about that little girl." The pendulum went back and forth. "This is about that little Baxter girl."

David sat in the chair across from the front door. He thought back to the night when he was on the railroad tracks drinking. Days later, Evelyn came to their house and returned him his wallet.

On that day, his wallet became a gift. He wanted to embrace Evelyn and thank her over and over, but he didn't. He just nodded at her and said "Thanks" once. After she left, he went to his bedroom and sat on the edge of his bed. He ran his fingers back and forth over the wallet. He opened it and looked at the pictures inside: a picture of his mother and his father, pictures of his sisters and brother and a picture of Margaret. He'd raised the wallet to his nose and breathed deeply. He felt that the wallet, his wallet, had given him his life back. He held the wallet in his hands and pressed it against his chest and allowed himself to cry.


That was years ago. Now, as he sat in his own living room, the sunken feeling that he'd had the night he'd been drinking up on the railroad tracks with the boy from Chicago crept over him again, made him feel tired and heavy.

In the three hours since Melinda had telephoned Margaret and told her, "Yes, Keith, the girls and I are coming to your and Dave's get together. We'll be over in a bit," no information concerning Keith, Melinda and their daughters' whereabouts had interrupted the conversations.

David started the family get-togethers at Margaret's and his home the year that Richard was born, because, as he had explained, "Our family doesn't get together like we used to, and if we don't do something about it now, we're going to drift apart."

For years, the get togethers had proved like a reward, inviting laughter, connection and fun inside David's and Margaret's home. Not once had David thought that the get togethers would bring regret. Sitting in the living room, he wished that he'd called his relatives and told them not to come to the house this evening.

As if family not being at the house would work a magic, ensuring Melinda's, Keith's and their daughters' safety, David blamed himself for Melinda's, Keith's and their daughters' absence, a disappearance that had pushed urgency into the family.

Half an hour ago, Sharieffa's parents had telephoned and said that they planned to stop by.

Looking out the living room window, Sharieffa feared for her parents' safety. "I'm going to call Mama and Dad and tell them not to come. Besides," she said, "They can always visit some other time." She let the phone at her parents' house ring ten times. There was no answer.

While Sharieffa waited for her parents to pick up the telephone, credits to a comedy program inched up David's and Margaret's black and white television screen. What was to Richard the most feared and regrettably true program on television, the evening news, aired next. When company wasn't visiting during late spring and summer, Carolyn, Ruth, Arthur and Richard leaped from their places on the living room floor and dashed outdoors to play if Margaret failed to stop them in time when the evening news aired. They dreaded laying in bed at night reliving the terror of the retelling of the day's latest most unfortunate events.

Tonight, the newscaster, wearing a gray suit and maroon tie, discussed the nation's economy. Alex listened intently.

As Carolyn watched Alex's focused eyes widen, she thought about her grandfather, Ramsey. It was Ramsey who held to the belief that "everyone with good sense reads the daily newspaper and listens to the evening news on television." In fact, while she watched her grandfather flip the pages of the newspaper with intent and haste, she wondered if he wasn't hunting for a particular story.

Sunday's edition, with its slick, brightly colored department store ads and folds of the Funnies, was the only circulation that interested Richard. He climbed out of bed before his mother on Sundays. Once out of bed, he raced for the newspaper after he heard it thump against the porch. After he toted the heavy newspaper inside, he pulled out the Funnies, stretched them across the living room floor in front of the television set and, while laying on his stomach, sometimes spent as long as half an hour reading the Funnies. His stomach jiggled and bounced against the floor when he laughed.

As sweet as it was, that mirth was gone tonight. In its place was a knotty dread.

Richard glanced at the television, observing a sportscaster's face as it flashed across the screen after the newscaster ended his discussion of the nation's economy. Richard found it surprising that Sonny Liston wasn't the focus of the sportscaster's attention. Tonight, instead of Sonny Liston, Richard heard the familiar name of a celebrated woman athlete from Tennessee, Wilma Rudolph.

Before Richard turned a deaf ear to the television set, he heard the sportscaster say, "The University of Memphis expects great things out of Joseph Rogers who signed with the school's football team last year."

As if offering relief to the day's heat, wind gusts pushed against the front door and pressed until the door's hinges squeaked. Rain splashed the roof and sides of the house. Richard figured that the rainwater was rushing down the corners of the avenue, searching for nearby sewer holes.

"And now to local news," the newscaster said, taking over where the sportscaster had left off. "A fire has just been reported in Shelby County. The fire is reported to have happened on Davidson Street in Greasy Plank. Officials are not releasing the names of the residents until they contact the next of kin. It is believed that there are no known survivors. Officials also have not yet determined the cause of the fire."

Everyone in the living room stared at the television while the wind pushed at the house. Richard was first to hear the knock at the door. He turned and faced his father.

Tammy and Philip stared at the door.

The wind pushed the door with so much force, the knocker lost their balance. The last knock on the door was quietest of all.

Carolyn sprang toward the front door. When she opened the door, the wind blowing tree limbs until they leaned toward the ground, uprooting clothesline poles and chasing stray cats and dogs beneath parked cars, pushed its way inside the house.

Tammy folded her arms across her chest.

The wind brushed Richard's shoulders and combed his body with a coolness that made him shake.

Sharieffa's father followed his wife inside the house. He placed his hand on Philip's shoulder and shook his head. Tears streaked his face.

Philip buried his head in his hands.

Margaret rushed her children upstairs into their bedrooms. There they were instructed to remain until summoned, until a bit of pain had removed itself from the house. On her way up the stairs, Carolyn looked at Janice and mouthed, "He saw her. The man from the ridge. Aunt Melinda didn't just see him. He saw her too."

A crisis had entered the family, and it was too late for Tammy to change her ways toward her son-in-law. She sat in the chair by the window and listened as the wind whistled loudly. It sounded like a speeding train. It seeped between the window and the ledge and pushed its way inside the living room.

"Philip, I'm so sorry!" Sharieffa's father said.

"Tammy," Philip said, reaching for his wife's hand. They fell inside each other's arms.

Margaret stood inside the kitchen bending and twisting plastic ice trays and filling a silver mixing bowl with ice and water. She kept her head down. Despite the certainty covering Sharieffa's parents' faces, she hoped that Melinda, Keith and their daughters had survived.

She'd told her mother that she didn't want to be a part of the secrets, but Rebecca had wept and begged her to keep silent. After her children were born, Margaret started lying to investigators and hiding letters that her mother gave her. It turned into a long deception. Margaret almost asked herself if the very events that her mother and she feared most had come upon them after all.

She abandoned her thoughts when Janice's husband asked for a towel to dab his wife's forehead with.

Rebecca left her place on the sofa and helped Margaret in the kitchen. "It'll be all right," she whispered to Margaret, leaning close to Margaret's shoulder.

Inside the living room, Ramsey turned from the television and met Sharieffa's father's gaze "What happened?"

Everyone looked at Sharieffa's parents.

Sharieffa's mother jammed her hands to the bottom of her raincoat pockets. "We thought we'd go see how the new room to Keith's and Melinda's house was coming along before we came over here." She pulled one of her hands from her coat pocket and dabbed the corners of her eyes with a Kleenex. "We figured they'd be here, so we only planned to drive by and see the outside of the new room. We were so excited about it and all, and we knew they'd do a good job. You know? The way they did a good job building the rest of their home." Her brow tightened. "About half a mile from their house, we saw the road to their house was blocked." She looked around the room. "Didn't you see it on the news?"

Janice wiped tears from her eyes. "They mentioned a fire on the news, but they didn't say how it started or if anyone survived."

Tammy found strength in her anger. "Go on."

"We sat for about ten minutes. Finally, we turned

220

around and took a back road not too many people know about. We still couldn't get all the way to the house, but we did get closer. Smoke was all over the sky."

"Go on," Tammy said.

"The fire was out of control. You could see people in the street and standing on their porches watching the house burn."

Fifteen miles from where the family sat, people who knew Keith, Melinda and their two daughters watched the fire pop and snake through the sky. People who'd dined with Melinda and Keith stared into the sky at the moving fire. People who'd picnicked with Melinda and Keith at Church's Park when they were all only children, people who'd swam with them at the community pool, these same people gossiped until they felt that they knew why the house burned.

People who had passed Keith and Melinda on their way to and from work and church, people who had passed them as they shopped at Tilson's Grocery Store wondered out loud about what had created the fire. These people stood outside their car and truck doors, on the edges of their porches and in the center of front and back lawns, staring into the sky while beneath the smoke and the flames, Keith's and Melinda's house burned to the ground.

Tammy sat in the high back chair opposite David. She felt empty. Light from the moon shone through the sheer curtains going from the ceiling to the floor across from the chair that she sat in. She knew that she would no longer gird her hips inside one of her cotton, summer wrap-around skirts, the ones with printed flowers decorating their fronts, come noontime and drive up the road to her daughter's and son-in-law's house. Her two granddaughters would never again burst through the front door of the wood house that Keith had built right from the earth with his strong hands. They wouldn't rush up the front walk with bright eyes and wide smiles blanketing their faces to leap into her opened arms.

Tammy's jaw trembled. It was as if she had just left from visiting with Melinda, Keith and the girls and returned to Philip and her house. It was as if, after unlocking the door and, finding herself alone, she'd gone to her favorite chair in the living room of her own home.

But she wasn't home. Sitting across from the picture window at David's and Margaret's house, Tammy began to feel isolated from the world, as if she was suffocating.

Keith had been a great help to her all the years that he was married to Melinda. Though heavily provoked, not once had he spoken an unkind word to her. Not once had he betrayed her. He'd proved to be a man large in stature and warm in heart, a believer in hard work. He managed to take the smallest income and build the piece of property that Melinda, their two daughters and he had spent their lives in. With coveralls on and a bandanna wrapped about his head, he'd tilled the land that his family had lived on until enough crops had pushed from the earth to feed their family year after year. What remained, he'd divided between giving to the hungry and selling to Tilson's Grocery Store cheap.

Old and unpleasant habits needled Tammy. She wished that she hadn't treated Keith so badly. Sitting in the high back chair facing the permanent gulf that death had created between the living and the dead, she realized that she loved him.

Next to her, Philip kept running his hand back and forth across his forehead. Already he missed Melinda's high, pitched laugh. He missed watching her face light up whenever Janice and she happened upon one another. He missed how warm his body felt when she hugged him and kissed the side of his face each time when she visited. He missed the way that she would stop by the house and listen to him tell old stories. He missed the way that she laughed at his corny jokes. He missed his daughter, his baby girl.

Chapter Twenty-One

It was nearly ten o'clock in the morning. Churchgoers, out-of-town relatives and the curious followed ushers to empty pews.

New Mount Holly Baptist Church filled with mourners. Outside it was raining. It hadn't stopped raining since last Saturday, the day Melinda, Keith and their two daughters died in the house fire.

Rain fell at a slow, steady pace. Richard listened to its drumming sound while he watched deacons stand from their seats on the front pew. They clapped their hands and sang in unison. "O talking with Jesus makes it right, all right. Talking with Jesus makes it right, all right." Their voices were joined by other voices ringing out from the congregation. "My friend, I used to be so lost. I tried and I prayed, but still I was lost. Living in this world, taking this unseen journey, brings trials and troubles for me and you."

A member of the motherboard waved a flowery, laced handkerchief and said, "Amen," as the deacons continued to sing, "My brother and my sister, I'm sure you've had troubles and trials here too as you try to do what's right, as you walk with the Lord. But keep trusting the Lord. The Lord knows just what to do."

The song finished, one of the deacons opened a large Bible. Its pages were upturned at the corners. He read Psalms 12:8. "Help, Lord, for the godly man ceaseth; for the faithful fail from among the children of men. They speak vanity every one with his neighbor: with flattering lips and with a double heart do they speak. The Lord shall cut off flattering lips, and the tongue that speaketh proud things:who have said, with our tongue will we prevail; our lips are our own: who is lord over us? For the oppression of the poor, for the sighing of the needy, now will I arise, saith the Lord; I

224

will set him in safety from him that puffeth at him. The words of the Lord are pure words: as silver tried in the furnace of earth, purified seven times. Thou shalt keep them, O Lord, thou shalt preserve them from this generation forever. The wicked walk on every side, when the vilest men are exalted.'"

The deacon closed the Bible. "God has already blessed the reading and hearing of his holy word."

A unified "amen" sounded throughout the church.

The oldest deacon, a tall, narrow man with an afro full of gray, knelt on one knee, "Let us pray." He bowed his head. "Oh, wise and heavenly Father, thank you for this, another Lord's day. Thank you for the roof over our heads, the food you gave us for breakfast, and the loved ones that surround us. God, we need you this morning." He shook his head. "We need you this morning, God. Please bless the bereaved Tilson and Brown families right now, Lord. Wipe the tears from their eyes. Let them know your eye is on the sparrow and that you are watching over them."

**\*\*\*\*\*\*\*\*\***

Miles away from the church, a parade of police cars followed Jack Robinson as he drove to David's and Margaret's house. When the police cars stopped, Jack turned off the ignition to his BMW. He stepped outside his car and pointed at David's and Margaret's home, daffodils and tulips swaying beneath the wind and falling rain. "They're in there," Jack said flatly. "I'm not sure where they're hid, but the boy's grandfather told me. The older son, Richard, has picture after picture of the little girl that was taken this past Saturday, rope about her neck." He turned and faced the cops. "Hopefully, you got the search warrant. You'll find the pictures, all of them in there." He pointed at the house again.

While Jack stood with cops outside David's and Margaret's home, Ramsey crawled through the cellar of his own house. He dragged a girl's body behind him. Stench from her bloodied body pushed up his nose. He almost turned back. It took him forty minutes of frantic digging, but he finally sat against a wall of the cellar.

He breathed deeply. Fast. The girl was buried and the stink was gone. It nagged his conscience that he'd lied to Rebecca again. "Go on. Ride with Margaret and David. They'll run you to the church. I'm gonna stay back and figure why our truck's not starting. Won't take me long to get it started. I'll be along to the church soon." When she looked at him with an arched brow, he added, "I'll be at the church before Reverend Cleveland gets up and starts preaching." She didn't move, so he grinned at her and said, "Watch and see."

**********

The church's oldest deacon stood and, in his usual soft, nasal congested tone, he faced the congregation and said, "Thank you for joining in devotion. And now we'll turn the rest of the service over tothe pastor."

Reverend Cleveland, a tall, stout man, stood and stretched forth his hand. "Congregation, please stand as the choir marches in."

**********

Search warrant in hand, the cops walked around the house until they found a ready entrance, a window cracked open with a stick. They pushed up the first floor window and climbed inside. Although he had never been inside the house before, Jack knew where to move, which corners to round, which closet to open, the exact box the drawings were in. "Odd," was all the cops said while they stared at the drawings and looked at each other. "Odd indeed," the last cop to leave Richard's room said with a snicker. "I always knew those Tilsons had something to hide." He tucked the box that held the drawings in the crease of his arm and followed his colleagues down the house steps and back out the opened window.

**********

New Mount Holly's pianist sang lead while he sat at the piano placed at the front of the choir chamber. He watched the choir sway in their crimson robes as they made their way to the front of the sanctuary. "Promised the Lord that I would walk with him all the way, and I'm going to do just that. No matter how hard things in this world get, I will not turn back."

**********

Less than half an hour later, Ramsey stopped the truck half a block away from the church. Jack pulled his shiny BMW alongside the truck.

The two men rolled their windows down and exchanged brief words before Jack, pressed the BMW's accelerator and sped down the street.

Jack gone down the street, Ramsey stepped out of his truck, pulled down on the hem to his suit coat and bowed his head. When he lifted his head, he didn't see Rebecca standing on the porch of the church. She watched her husband move passed the line of cars and trucks at the front of the church, passed the three hearses, closer to the church, closer to her.

Inside the church, the pianist tossed his head back and opened his mouth wide. "I've seen victories and hardships too. But I won't turn back. Promised the Lord that I would go all the way with him, and that's just what I'm going to do."

\*\*\*\*\*\*\*\*\*\*

Detective Cramer stared across the room. He threw the pictures on his desk. "The drawings aren't much to go on, but these—" Picking the pictures up again, he shook his head, "These pictures. It looks like the kid had to have been there."

"Detective," one of the officers began. "There's hair on one of the pictures. Brunette hair. A whole lock of hair. We also found a silver earring the girl's parents said the girl was wearing the day she turned up missing."

Detective Cramer sighed. "He's just a boy. I don't believe he took that girl." He bit down on his lip and thought about his own daughter, Evelyn. He swallowed hard. "But we've gotta bring him in."

"Shouldn't we wait until after the burial?" A burly red headed cop asked.

Detective Cramer nodded. "Yes. Read him his rights and cuff him when he gets home."

\*\*\*\*\*\*\*\*\*\*

The church pianist pounded the piano keys while he sang. "'I'll trust the Lord and talk with the Lord and pray until I finish my race."

One of the deacons lifted his cane then he let it fall with a loud thud to the floor again. "Praise God,

228

chil'ren!'"

Joining the choir in the last refrain, the pianist sang, "My brother and my sister, I'm sure you've had troubles and trials here too as you try to do what's right, as you walk with the Lord. But keep trusting the Lord. The Lord knows just what to do"

Outside, Ramsey's eyes swelled when he stepped on the church porch. "Rebecca."

They stood on the church porch staring at each other, not certain what to say, unaware that inside the church, Reverend Cleveland had stood. They both were aware that, as promised, Ramsey had made it to church before Reverend Cleveland had started to preach.

Inside the building that Rebecca and Ramsey stood, looking at each other in awkward silence, on the porch of, the congregation opened their morning worship service bulletins. Nestled beneath the shoulders of their parents and grandparents, toddlers cooed and chuckled. Reverend Cleveland gripped the sides of the podium. His large hands engulfing its top rim, he leaned forward.

The church grew silent, still. "Good morning." He paused, then said, "The Lord is in his holy temple; let all the earth keep silent before him." He studied the ruled sheets of notebook paper that his sermon was written on. "Now, if you will please turn in your hymnals to Number 155, we will join the choir in singing 'Remember Me Lord.'"

"Remember me, Lord, as I walk the journey laid out before me. Speak with me and guide me, Lord, all along the way. Let me know that you are with me, helping me to gain the victory. Remember me, Lord." Carolyn's voice closest to Richard's ear, was loudest and most off key. "Remember me, Lord. Remember me all along the way. Walk with me. Talk with me.

Remember me all along the way."

After singing three more stanzas, the congregation lifted their voices and sang the last chorus. "Remember me, Lord, as I follow you. Encourage me and strengthen me. Remember me, Lord, all along the way."

Outside on the church's porch, Rebecca crossed her arms. Raising her arms to her chest, she asked Ramsey, "Why was Jack following you?"

Ramsey took her by the fold of her arm. "Come on. Let's go in the church. I'm late enough as it is."

Pulling away from him, she repeated her question. "Why was Jack Robinson following you?"

Ramsey's gaze darted, searching for onlookers. Seeing none, he whispered, "Rebecca, you know I cannot talk about this now, not right now."

She took in a deep breath. "Then when?"

"When we get home."

They turned and entered the sanctuary, walking arm in arm.

Carolyn squirmed in her seat when Ramsey and Rebecca walk passed her. During Informal Moments, a time when the congregation greeted one another, Carolyn hurried to her grandfather Ramsey's side, stared him directly in the eye and said, "Awful about what happened to Keith, Melinda and their girls, isn't it?" She didn't give him time to answer. "Just awful." Then she moved away from him, leaving him filled with questions.

When Tammy turned from hugging one of the women on the motherboard, her gaze fell across Ramsey's face. She looked at him a long time before she wiped a tear from her eye and returned to her seat.

As people scurried to their seats, Richard lifted his head and, looking into the choir stand, he stared into the face of a visiting soloist. The woman, born and

230

raised in Greasy Plank, had taken two days off from touring with a musical comedy in order to pay her respects and attend the church's morning services and the burial. She sang Comfort Us Deeply.

"Comfort us deeply, Creator. We need you to do what only you can do. We need you to comfort us deeply, healing our sorrows, preparing us for a bright tomorrow. Comfort us deeply, Creator."

A tear went down Richard's face.

While the choir sang the chorus, the soloist hung her head and wept softly. "O comfort us, Creator. We are your children, and we are in need of your comfort. With your love, we will be comforted. Comfort us now."

When the soloist belted out the last refrain, her mouth opened wide. Ramsey stared at her and began to shake. She looked like she was screaming. Ramsey's shoulders tightened. While the soloist and the choir sang, he bowed his head and whispered, "I'm sorry."

\*\*\*\*\*\*\*\*\*\*

Detective Cramer sighed. "I hate to do this. That kid doesn't seem like he could hurt a fly. It's his grandfather and Jack Robinson I'd really like to bring into the station, but I can't get anything substantial on them. Their records are clean." He stared at the photos, the lock of hair, the earring and drawings on his desk.

"Go on," he said to the two cops standing in front of him. "Take a car and sit outside the Tilson residence. As soon as the boy comes home from the burial, read him his rights and bring him in. If we can get to him before his grandmother Tammy does, we stand a chance of getting the truth. Go on. I'll call the district attorney's office and have an arrest warrant issued before you all get to the Tilson residence." He shook his head and bit down on his bottom lip. "I really don't think the boy has done anything except draw some pictures. It may well be the kid's way of dealing with the entire situation." He nodded. "That's what I think it is. I think the boy's drawn these pictures to deal with the whole tragedy. Now his grandfather," he looked directly at the cops. He didn't blink once. "I think the grandfather knows something. And Jack Robinson." He lowered his voice. "Fellas, that's who I think killed this little girl and the Baxter girl from several years ago, but damn!" He pounded the desk. "I can't get anything on Jack. He's clean." He sighed. "We'll get the boy in here, question him, see what he knows, get his grandmother Tammy all worked up and see if she can put some pressure on the boy's grandfather. I think that's the only way we're gonna get a real break in this case."

One of the cops peered over the top of his glasses at Detective Cramer. "What about the photos, the hair and the earring?"

Detective Cramer chuckled while he looked at his colleague."They were planted. Shocked you didn't figure that out. The boy's grandfather planted them." He bit his lip. "I just wish I knew why he'd plant evidence on his own grandson."

\*\*\*\*\*\*\*\*\*\*

"Amens" and "Yes, Lords" sprinkled the congregation when Reverend Cleveland stood. Richard watched Reverend Cleveland's hands as he spread his fingers around the edges of the podium. "The scripture for this morning's sermon is taken from Daniel 3:28-29.

It reads as follows, 'Then Nebuchadnessar spake, and said, blessed be the God of Shadrach, Meschach and Abednego, who hath sent his angel and delivered his servants that trusted in him, and have changed the king's word, and yielded their bodies, that they might not serve nor worship any god, except their own God because there is no other God that can deliver after this sort.'"

Reverend Cleveland adjusted the microphone atop the podium and pulled it close to his mouth. "Focus on, if you will, the last part of verse twenty-nine, 'because there is no other God that can deliver after this sort.'" His chest went out as he took in a deep breath. "Church," he said, "There has been a tragedy in our midst."

\*\*\*\*\*\*\*\*\*\*

Alone in his office, Detective Cramer raised the drawings and photographs up to the light. The similarities in the photographs of the girl's body and the drawings were striking. When he sat back in his chair, he pushed the photographs and the drawings away from him. Then, he turned and looked out the window.

\*\*\*\*\*\*\*\*\*\*

The thick coating of cement that Ramsey had covered the latest hole in the cellar wall with began to dry and overcome the stench of blood, bringing the house on Nettleton Avenue back to its former circumstance. The drying, hardening cement gave Ramsey comfort. It allowed him to settle into the thought that he would never be caught, and he had lived with blank stares for so long, those he knew he could withstand.

Only one thing unnerved him. It was something that his granddaughter, Carolyn, said to him the last time that she stopped by the foundry throwing out questions, hunting for answers. Before she left the foundry that day, she looked straight up at him. She asked, "If bodies return to the earth when people make that last great change and spirits don't need bodies to exist, only to reveal themselves more clearly to us, where do spirits go when bodies return to the earth?" She moved so close to him that he felt her breath against his skin. "And if somebody takes a body from its spirit at a time that is too soon in like, for example, a murder, will that spirit come back to resolve the matter?" She stared at him until a chill raced up his spine, then she shouted, "Inyanga."

**********

The police car pulled in front of David's and Margaret's house. The driver turned off the ignition and leaned into the spine of the seat. After he glanced in the rearview mirror and watched the other squad car pull behind his, he turned and looked at his partner. "I would have never suspected that kid for anything. Gotta admit, I think that Tammy is a bit much. She thinks too highly of herself, but they're a good family. I just can't figure it."

His partner chuckled. "She ain't no different from her mother. My pop told me that ol' Tammy Tilson's mother went around talking like she had special powers." He tossed his hand into the air. "Always going around talking about root."

"Wasn't she close to that Bobbie Long, the little Negro girl that turned up murdered years back?"

234

"I don't know. My pop told me cops never did spend much time on that case. That girl was retarded from what I've heard. I guess they figured she wasn't the child of anyone important, so they did a little searching around for answers, then just let it be."

"How was she killed?"

"Don't know. Happened in the thirties. She was missing for days." He shook his head. "She was missing for the longest time. Then, one day some kids was up by old man Lenox's barn playing and they found Bobbie's clothes and shoes tore up under a tree. You know that church lapel pin that girl wore was still blowing in the wind when they found her clothes and shoes? A week later, her body was found drowned in the river, over by the railroad tracks."

"So what's Bobbie got to do with Tammy Tilson?"

The cop laughed. "Quiet as it's kept, Tammy's father never did take to staying around the house, if you know what I mean."

\*\*\*\*\*\*\*\*\*\*

Reverend Cleveland's brow tightened. "For so long God blessed our circle and made death behave. This morning we find our circle broken? And why? Because evil roams through ..."

Handkerchiefs and torn pieces of Kleenex waved through the air.

"Church, we need God to stop by just a little while."

A chorus of 'amens' and 'say that' were heard throughout the congregation.

"We need God to come by here, Lord," Reverend Cleveland said.

Richard focused on the "Hallelujah's" "Amen's"

and "Please Lord's" rising about him.

Reverend Cleveland searched faces in the congregation. "We need God to stand and be in our midst until our enemies see not only us, but the Son of God amongst us. We need God to show up in our lives until when trouble, sorrow, depression, weeping and heartache try to grip and toss us into the fiery furnace, they see God standing at our side. We need others to see God standing able, ready and willing to fight in our stead, to fight on our behalf, to fight our battles and to win us awesome and excellent victories."

He looked at Tammy and Philip, "God shows up when you dare to have the courage to apply faith to what you want. Faith is like electricity. It puts a power-energy at work on your behalf. Remember where the Bible says in Hebrews 11:6 that 'without faith it is impossible to please God'. We have got to condition ourselves and our children to believe in the very best, to know excellence is our home!"

His fist shot into the air. "Jesus, the Christ, made it clear that our thoughts are like the clay that makes us. As a person thinks, so is that person." His fist banged the podium. "Stop being a coward!"

Taking in a deep breath, Reverend Cleveland raised a fist then brought it down against the podium. "Yes! Yes! In times like these, as in all times, we need God! Aren't you glad, church! Death has no sting except the sting you allow it to have in your mind and in your heart. The grave has no power over the risen savior and those who too believe, that in Christ, they can rise above any circumstance or situation, even death. Aren't you glad about it, church! Because if you're missing Keith, Melinda, and their two precious daughters, and you have been washed in the blood. If your wrongs, though red as crimson, have been washed in Jesus' blood and made white as snow, then, in just a little while, when you hear God call your name, telling you to come on home, you can be glad to see Keith, Melinda, Janet and Lisa again."

Richard started to cry.

"Church, be glad that we, you, if you do, have a god who can deliver only like God can. I tell you, church, 'there is no other god that can deliver after this sort.'"

**********

An idea came to Detective Cramer and he rounded the corner and went into the file room. His fingers crawled through the files.

Papers pressed together then separated so fast before he finished his search that he had four new cuts on his hands. "Damn!" He bit his lip. "I knew I shouldn't have brought that file down here. I told Leonard." He shook his head. "Someone took the file." He clinched his fist. "Someone took the file on Jack Robinson."

**********

Reverend Cleveland stepped back from the podium and worked to catch his breath while he pushed a folded handkerchief down the sides of his face, wiping salty sweat from his skin. When he stepped toward the podium and the microphone again, he raised his hands and said, "The doors of the church are open. Remember what God said to us in Romans 10:8-10 where it says, "But what saith it? The word is nigh thee, even in thy mouth, and in thy heart: that is, the word of faith, which we preach; that if thou shalt confess with thy mouth the Lord Jesus, and shalt believe in thine heart that God hath raised him from the dead, thou shalt be saved. For with the heart man believeth unto righteousness; and with the mouth confession is made unto salvation.'"

Reverend Cleveland stretched forth his hand as if he was waiting for someone to approach the altar. "Won't you come back home to God? Won't you come?" he called out.

Six people joined the church. After he welcomed them to the New Mount Holly Baptist Church family, Reverend Cleveland delivered the benediction and church was dismissed.

Members of the motherboard and the deacon board surrounded Tammy and Philip. While they did, younger members of the congregation talked at the edges of the church doorway.

Richard walked beyond the chattering crowds, people he'd grown up with, adults who'd known his parents for years. He went out from beneath the church roof and into the rain. The cool water wet his skin. He tilted his head upward and stared at the gray sky. He stood behind the elm rooted in the middle of the church yard. Standing behind the tree, he was glad that no one saw him, for he knew that, if they did, they would call him in out of the storm.

He stayed out in the rain until his mother told him to get in the car so they could drive to the cemetery for the burial. Richard sat stiff beside his sister, Carolyn, while their father drove away from the church.

The procession to the cemetery was long, slow. Cars and trucks lined up and drove, one behind the other, to the place where people separated forever from the troubles of the world had their bodies laid into the

238

ground.

Richard thought about his aunt, uncle and cousins non-stop during the long, slow journey from the church to the death plots. Chills raced up his spine. Each time they did, he shook his head and told himself that he didn't believe in ghosts. And yet he knew he was haunted.

At the cemetery, there were tears and hard moans. Tammy and Philip didn't begin to wail until Reverend Cleveland spoke the words, "Ashes to ashes and dust to dust."

It hurt worse than any pain that he'd ever felt when Richard turned and looked at his grandmother Tammy. He winced while he watched her cry. It was a scene he'd never seen before — his grandmother, the proud, strong matriarch of the family, broke up ... broken like a dream that had found its way into the ether of forgetfulness. His cousins, aunt and uncle had become memories. That's what they were now.

Richard knew. He knew as he turned and followed the slow procession as it moaned and wept and moved away from the cemetery and back to the line of waiting cars and trucks.

Richard felt like clay as he climbed inside the back of his parents' car alongside his brother and sisters. He didn't feel himself breathe again until he turned and looked out the window. He watched the rain fall. Its pace had picked up since they buried Melinda, Keith, Lisa and Janet.

When David pressed the accelerator and Margaret took another roll of Kleenex out of her purse to wipe her eyes, Richard leaned forward and rubbed his hand across the foggy window until the shape of his hand created a circle. His mouth went open when he looked through the circle. He stared. He'd seen the man parked in the BMW before. He'd even heard his name spoken with reverence about town. Even Reverend Cleveland spoke highly of the man and how he mixed and mingled with Negroes, how the man was fair and forthright, how much the man could be trusted.

Richard looked at the man and thought about his grandfather, Ramsey. He'd introduced the man to their family years ago on a day not unlike today. It had been raining — hard. Thunder boomed and lightning flashed in the sky on that day.

Richard leaned closer to the window and mouthed the words, "Mr. Robinson," as David pressed the accelerator and their car sped down the road.

The sky was dark like night when David pulled the car into the driveway. Margaret had wanted to stop by her parents after the burial, but David flatly denied her. "The kids need us to be with them right now," he told her while he watched her brow tighten and furrow.

When the car stopped, he glanced in the rearview mirror. It pained him to look at his oldest son. He wondered if Richard had noticed that the drawings were missing. He'd taken them out of Richard's bottom bedroom dresser drawer two nights ago. He'd removed the drawings because of what Ramsey had told him. He'd stopped by Margaret's and his house on his way home from the foundry. "David," Ramsey had said. "You've got to protect Richard. I think he could be in trouble. When Rebecca and I visited last weekend, I went into the boys' room ... ah ... you know ... just to make sure Richard had enough drawing paper and what not."

David recalled Ramsey mostly looking at the ground while he'd talked. "I found some drawings up there." He shook his head. "Not good. It's like Richard knows something about that new girl that's missing.

They're awful pictures." He shook his head. "Just awful. You gotta hide them. Burn them or do something with them. Maybe put them somewhere nobody will ever find them. I don't know what that boy knows." He stared at David. "Or has done, but you gotta protect him. He's your son."

David's heart had raced when he saw the drawings. They were exactly where Ramsey said they'd be. He grabbed them by the armful and carried them into the closet where he stuffed them inside a box that was full with old clothes, rags and a few toys the kids had played with when they were toddlers. When he closed the closet door, he pressed his hand against his chest and squeezed until knife- like pains stopped lashing at his chest.

Not until now, sitting in the car, just come in from burying his sister and her family, did it occur to him that, "Ramsey's never been upstairs in our home since Margaret remodeled last Spring. How would he know where the drawings were?" He grimaced. "Damn. I shouldn't have told him where I hid the pictures."

"David?"

"I'm sorry," he said turning and facing Margaret. "I was thinking about something."

"I was wondering if you were going to get out of the car."

He nodded at his wife. "Yea. I am." Then he looked over his shoulder. "Come on, kids. Let's go inside."

They weren't halfway up the front walk when the four cops sitting in unmarked cars across the street from their house approached them.

"Excuse me," The first officer said, extending his hand and pushing his badge in front of David.

David turned and pulled Ruth, who walked next to

him, close to his side. "Yes?"

"If you don't mind, we'd like to speak with your son."

David looked at Margaret with intent. She turned her back to him.

"Why do you need to speak with my son, and which of my sons do you want to speak with?"

All four officers stared at David. "We'd like to speak with your oldest son," The second officer answered. He examined David's countenance. "We wanted to wait until after the funeral."

"Don't try to get me on your side. You have no reason whatsoever to speak with my son, with any of my children."

"I—"

"--What's this all about anyway?" David asked, cutting the officer off. He wanted to look at Margaret, read her eyes, watch her cringe, but he couldn't. Her back remained toward him, and she was gazing at the ground. He wanted to grab her by the shoulders and pull her around until she faced him, but he didn't. He knew, like him with his mother, she was but her father's child. He knew she wasn't her father. He knew he couldn't blame her for wrongs that her father had done.

When the third officer looked at Richard, shame knifed his conscience. "Why don't we go inside, Mr. Tilson."

David snatched his arm away from the third officer. "Don't touch me. And we can discuss whatever needs to be discussed out here. I'm not going to let you hide your nasty ways from my children. They're going to see what the law enforcement around here is all about right out in the open, right here. You have anything to say to or about me or my son, you'll have to say it out in the open." He looked over the officer's shoulder and met the gaze of the three other policemen. "Officers."

"Daddy," Carolyn suggested. "I think it's best if we all go indoors."

A bird fluttered its wings in a corner of the house roof.

Richard looked up at the bird, then he twiddled the hem of his suit coat. He hadn't peered up since the cops approached his family. He followed the sound of his sister Carolyn's voice and the up-down, up-down rhythm of her feet as his family moved closer to their home.

Carolyn turned and glanced over her shoulder. "Hold your head up, Richard. You haven't done anything. God knows it. Soon these cops and everyone is going to know it. You don't have anything to hang your head about. In fact, after all our family has been through, you should be proud that you are finding the strength to keep moving. A lot of folks would be too scared to even keep moving. I bet you," She looked hard at the cops. "These cops' sons wouldn't have the courage to face a situation like this. Being innocent and being escorted up the front walk by a band of ignorant cops when you're just coming home from your uncle's, aunt's and cousins' burials." She narrowed her brow and stared at the cops. "I bet you."

Once inside the house, the cops followed David and Richard into the dining room. Excusing herself from the cops, her husband and their children with "I don't feel good." And "This has really been a pressing day. I feel like I might faint. I want to run upstairs and splash cool water on my face," Margaret went upstairs to David's and her bedroom and got her mother on the telephone.

243

"Mama, it's all coming undone," she said into the receiver, her hands shaking. She talked fast. "The cops are here right now. They are talking to Richard. The kids are beside themselves. I couldn't even look David in the eye. I couldn't face my own children." She lowered her voice and whispered into the mouthpiece. "Mama, you have to talk to Dad. You have to get him to open up and tell what he knows. If he doesn't, my son could go to jail."

Rebecca sat in silence. Then, she took in a deep breath and said, "Everything's going to be okay, Margaret. Don't panic. You simply cannot panic."

"Mama," Margaret shouted. A second later, she glanced toward the bedroom door and wondered if the cops had heard her all the way downstairs. Leaning toward the telephone, she whispered, "This is my son we're talking about."

"I'll talk with your father."

"When?"

"Give me half an hour."

"Call me back in exactly half an hour, Mama." She swallowed hard. "I mean it."

David followed the cops and drove Richard to the police station. Two hours later, Margaret jumped when the telephone rang. She ran across the living room floor and snatched the receiver out of its cradle.

Carolyn watched her mother move with pursed lips and a furrowed brow. "If that's your father, I want to talk with him," was all that she said to her mother.

Margaret turned and looked at her daughter gape-eyed. Then, she faced the telephone again. "Hello?"

"They want to book him. Say they've got—"

"Who's this?" Margaret asked, her brow way up.

"It's me. David."

"I didn't recognize your voice."

He pointed each of his words. "Did-you-hear-me?"

"Yes," she answered, playing with her blouse collar and glancing in the living room at Carolyn. "I heard you."

David lowered his voice and leaned against the police station wall. He glanced over his shoulder to make sure that no one was within earshot. "You better do something different for the first time in a long time, Margaret. You better call your father and tell him to get his ass down here to this police station. If my son spends one second in jail for something your father knows about or was involved in, I will personally cause him more pain and grief and hurt than ten billion Jack Robinson's ever could."

He slammed the receiver into the cradle and stomped away from the telephone and back to his son's side. What he didn't tell her was how deeply he regretted not going to the police and fingering Jack Robinson all those years ago, when the Baxter girl first turned up missing.

He sat next to his son on a bench that was pushed against a wall at the police station, wondering for the first time if his wallet falling out of his pocket that night up on the railroad tracks wasn't the way things were meant to be. If the cops had only found his wallet, he'd have had no other choice but to come forward, identify himself and tell them what he saw and heard that night, but he didn't see it that way then. A few days after Evelyn returned him his wallet, he did place an anonymous call to the police telling them that he'd seen a group of men, including a man with a cane, up on the tracks the night the Baxter girl disappeared, but nothing ever came of it.

Across town from the police station, Margaret's hands shookwhile she dialed her parents' home while she sat on the edge of David's and her bed. She'd closed the door to their bedroom.

Rebecca answered on the first ring. "Margaret?"

"Mama, did you talk to Dad?"

The answer was slow in coming. "Yes."

Margaret pushed resolve into her voice. "Well, what did he say?"

"Margaret, Richard is young. Your father is getting old. He was a good provider for all of you kids. If it wasn't for him and the many sacrifices he made, who knows where our family would be. He never put a hand on any of you children. Except for that one time he was deathly sick, he never missed a day of work. Your father's a good man, Honey. Now he's getting old."

Margaret swallowed hard. "Mama."

"Richard's so young, Honey. He knows how to trust God. He'll hold up just fine through all of this. You watch and see. He'll hold up"

"Mama, this is my son we're talking about--"

"--And my husband--."

"Mama, please."

"Margaret, I talked to your father. He said he'll try to talk to Jack. See if he can get him to post bail if it comes to that."

"Mama, when is Dad going to stop being so afraid of Jack Robinson? He covered for Dad that one time Dad took that little girl for a ride in his truck all those years ago in Louisville. If you ask me, Dad should have told about giving the girl a ride. He said he never touched her. He said he just wanted to talk to her. All he did was pick her up while she was walking home from school. He just didn't want to see her walk those long miles home from school. That's all. He never was going to hurt that girl. He just tickled her and made her laugh. That's all. He said he only kept her in the truck after she asked him what his name was, then asked him to let her leave because he got scared. He said he never hurt her."

"Dad has always trusted children, opened up around kids. He's never felt comfortable with adults. Everybody knows that. But that doesn't mean he'd hurt a kid. That little girl is fine and well right to this very day. She's a happy, grown woman with a family of her own. Dad loves children. His guilty conscience cost him all this. He didn't do anything to that little girl all those years ago back in Louisville. I know he didn't do anything. He didn't hurt that girl or anything. Dad might be a little closed mouthed, but he wouldn't hurt nobody. Dad would never hurt a little girl. His conscience wouldn't let him go and now it's come to this. One little cover up and then a string of hard favors for Jack."

"It didn't start this way," Rebecca said.

"It was all a part of Jack's plan. Didn't you and Dad ever stop to wonder why Jack would appear out of the blue and come to Dad's aid just-like-that? Why would a man come out of the blue and post Dad's bail and then go so far as to demand Dad's arrest record be expunged? Didn't you and Dad ever stop to wonder about that?"

Rebecca raised her voice. "Jack Robinson is the reason you all ate food on more than a few nights. He's the reason we had a roof over our heads for more than a year. I can't count the times he stepped up and bailed your father out of a tight spot. Whatever we really needed, Jack made sure we got it. He paid for your wedding, Girl."

"Mama, that was his way of paying Dad to cover for him."

247

"Margaret, I'm not going to go over this with you. Your father did what he could."

"And now he's got to help keep my son out of this. Richard is truly innocent, Mama."

"Exactly. And that's the reason he'll be free to walk. He's done nothing. Everything will work out fine. You'll see."

Margaret sniffed hard. "I can't believe you're going along with this."

"I have no choice. Do you think I have a choice?"

"Mama?"

"Richard is young. He will get through this."

When Margaret hung the receiver in its cradle, she lowered her head into the locks of her shoulders and wept so hard that her shoulders heaved and her throat became sore until it felt like she'd been swallowing gravel.

That night, David came home late for the first time in Margaret's and his fifteen-year marriage. He was mute when he walked through the door.

Margaret stared at him while she watched him walk across the living room floor. A moment passed before she asked, "What happened? Where's Richard?"

Without so much as glancing at her, he lowered his head and walked up the stairs to their bedroom. He went directly to bed.

An hour later, Margaret climbed the stairs and followed him to bed. She wasn't laying down five minutes when David left the bedroom and went downstairs to sleep on the sofa.

Upstairs in their bedroom, Margaret knew their marriage was over. They wouldn't divorce. They would never be officially apart, but the trust, the passion, the affection, the respect was gone. David would no longer choose to love her as deeply as he had all the years before. He knew more than he let on. She wondered if her father had revealed secrets to David while they'd been out fishing, something the two men hadn't done in nearly a year. She'd tried to work it out of David ... why he and her father no longer spent quality time together, but he shut her out of that part of his life.

Today the fabric to their marriage completely tore. Their son was in jail and they both knew he was there in her father's and Jack Robinson's stead.

Margaret closed her eyes and worked at sleep. Hours later, she sat up and wondered if she had been dreaming. She heard voices downstairs. It was one o'clock in the morning.

Climbing out of bed and slipping her feet inside her house shoes, she crept to the top of the stairwell and, craning her neck, listened to the sound of David's voice.

"I demanded that Margaret talk to her dad," she heard David say. "She didn't. She said she called her mom. Her father still won't step up and tell the truth, tell what he knows."

It surprised Margaret when she heard Tammy's voice in the house. She heard her say, "I told you, I told everyone about those people. I knew something was wrong with that Ramsey. I knew it all along."

"Ramsey and Jack."

"That's exactly what I'm saying. Before Ramsey moved his people here, you never saw all these going ons. And," she paused. "I did some digging. Jack and Ramsey knew each other when the Armstrongs lived in Louisville."

"You're kidding."

"Son, I wish I was. I really do." She sighed. "Jack paid a lot of their bills. He helped the Armstrongs out when things got tight. Twice he kept them from losing their home. I think they thought they owed him something. When a little girl turned up missing in Louisville, I'm told Jack started coming around Ramsey a lot more. He mostly came to the foundry where Ramsey worked in Kentucky. Matter of fact, word has it that Rebecca didn't find out about Jack's and Ramsey's relationship until it was too late. She was so used to protecting Ramsey for being so quiet and withdrawn, it came natural to her to cover up when people started talking about why Jack was making out so friendly with Ramsey. I think she's the reason Jack's been able to get away with this for so many years."

"Whereas people might not trust Jack or Ramsey, they sure do trust Rebecca," Tammy continued. "I'm told she ain't so much as stepped on an ant a day in her life, and being around her all these years, I can say I believe it."

"I can't see Ramsey killing nobody," David said.

"I can't either. He seems too timid, too scared," Tammy agreed. "That man's scared of his own shadow. Jack knows it too." She chuckled dryly. "Heard it told that the first time that Jack had ol' Ramsey dig a grave, it shook Ramsey so badly, he found himself in need of a psychiatrist." She chuckled. "Of course, Jack picked up the fee, and Ramsey went on feeling like he owed the old man that much more."

"I wonder if Ramsey didn't marry Rebecca just so he'd have a spine to lean into from time to time, being as he doesn't have one of his own," David said.

250

Tammy winced. "I told you all, but nobody wanted to hear me. I've been saying it all along. Why do you think I didn't want you to marry that girl?"

Margaret covered her mouth with her hand. "Mama."

"Now look what a situation our family is in."

"You should have seen his face, Mama."

"Whose face?"

"Richard's."

She turned away from David.

"He looked so scared, Mama. He was shaking something awful. I kept telling him that everything was going to be all right. He was shaking so badly. I don't care if they did put him in a section for kids. He doesn't belong there, Mama. He knows it too. He kept telling me 'Dad, I didn't do nothing except draw some pictures.' He kept saying it, Mama. Over and over again. He said he didn't see nothing. He never saw that latest missing girl and he wasn't alive when the Baxter girl turned up missing. Why the pictures he drew looked so much like that last missing girl, I don't know. I just know my son is innocent. I know it, Mama. I know he is. He always comes straight home from school. He ain't had no time to hurt nobody. He doesn't have hate or meanness in his heart. He's a good kid. I've never had trouble out of Richard."

He searched his mother's face. "He was trying to be strong when I left. He hugged me and told me he was gonna be all right. He tried so hard to look like a man, but Mama, he's only thirteen years old. But he was trying so hard to be strong. It tore me up, Mama. Tore me up all on the inside. Those cops grilled him until I wondered if he'd fall apart, but he held up good. He was shaking and stuttering, but he held up. It's hurting me something awful to know he's in jail. I can't let this go on. He's my son, Mama. He's my boy. Mama." He paused. "We gotta get a lawyer. I can't let my son stay another day in jail. Mama, I just can't."

Tammy pulled her purse into her lap. "Your father and I cleaned out the tin box we keep under our bed. Cleaned it bone dry. We even took money out of our bank account at Shant's. We're gonna post bail first thing in the morning."

David sniffed hard. "Mama, I'm sorry for all those years I turned away from you and Dad. Sad thing is I think I saw something in Ramsey that I see in me. I think that's why I felt close to him. He was like a mirror."

"No."

"He was like a mirror, Mama."

Tammy raised her voice and put starch in it. "No."

Turning and walking from the top of the stairs back to her bedroom, Margaret lay down on the bed and wiped away a tear. She closed her eyes and whispered, "Who'd of thought my dad's fear would open David's eyes to fear of his own? Who'd of thought my dad's fears would drive my husband and Tammy back together? Who'd of thought?" Then, she closed her eyes and wept quietly for a long time.

Across town, her oldest son lay curled on his side on a soiled mattress in the Youth Detention Center. His lip bled where he kept biting it to lock in his tears. The following morning when the sun came up in the sky, Philip, Tammy and David hurried to the courthouse with their family attorney. In a few short words, signed courthouse papers and with fifty thousand dollars, they bought Richard's leased freedom.

He raced inside their arms. They hugged and cried on the steps of the Youth Detention Center for a long time. As they moved off the steps, Richard turned and looked over his shoulder.

Several boys had their noses pressed against the barred windows. Many had never seen their biological parents. Many had never seen adults embrace before. To them, the scene was come straight out of a science fiction story. They stared at Richard and his family gape- eyed.

Richard waved at an ebony skinned boy who had a long scar going down the center of his forehead. "He was nice to me," he said to anyone who would listen as he walked alongside his father and grandparents down the detention center's front steps.

"Where's Mom?" Richard asked when his father and he entered the house.

David was silent for an awkward moment. "She went home to talk to her father."

"Dad?" Richard's gaze darted from the ceiling to the floor to the front door. "Are you and Mom okay?"

After he cleared his throat, David said, "We have things to work through, Son." Then he smiled thinly. "Looks like we all do."

Chapter Twenty-Two

The trial lasted three months. It was a time that took more off of Richard's life than any other crisis that he or his family met.

Every river in Memphis from Monroe Avenue down to the Mississippi Delta was searched and dug through. The body of one of the city's prominent business owners was found badly decomposed at the bottom of one of the rivers, but not one child was found.

Dogs were sent into the woods that stretched along the back of Greasy Plank. Helicopters and detectives on foot combed the area around the railroad tracks. Never before had Greasy Plank seen so much passion and urgency pushed into an investigation.

Each day, while he was moved from his parents' house to the courthouse, Richard thought about his Uncle Keith, his Aunt Melinda and his cousins, Lisa and Janet. He wondered why no one searched for their killer. He wondered why police didn't knock on doors and ask residents if they saw anything out of the ordinary on the day that their house burned to the ground.

Each week that the trial extended, stress and worry caused Tammy to age another year. It pained Philip to watch his wife's light dim. He wished that he had done more to make life comfortable for her. Although they brought in enough money operating the grocery store to retire and travel, they continued to work because they wanted to provide a bright future for their children, grandchildren and great-grandchildren.

They made large donations to The University of Memphis, Knoxville College and Tennessee State. In addition to tithing and investing sixteen percent of their earnings in the stock market, they continued to put money in a special account.

They only made withdrawals from the account to help a Greasy Plank resident who had lost their home, a child who needed money to purchase books for college, or a woman recently widowed and alone with children to raise. Because of their philanthropic efforts, they figured that they wouldn't be able to retire for another one to two years.

While he sat next to his wife in the courthouse, Philip kept peering at Tammy. Advancing grays in her hair, pink tint in her eyes and the tender skin beneath her eyes worried him. He was starting to believe that the court case stress, not trouble in their relationship, was beginning to take her away from him. He knew how much Tammy wanted to take out vengeance on Ramsey, even if she had to do it through his daughter, Margaret.

At night, while they lay in bed, Tammy, her voice tight with anger, would tell Philip, "Can you believe David took that Margaret back? She didn't even love her own son enough to make her father come clean. If that coward Ramsey had told the truth, we wouldn't be sitting in a courtroom praying and doing all we can to keep our grandson out of prison." After a gasp, Tammy would continue, "I know he's our son, but David is so dumb. I warned that boy that marrying that girl would bring trouble into our family."

**********

Margaret had been living at home with David again after a three-month separation. She'd moved back into their family home the day after Richard's trial started. "We need to be a united front," she'd argued after she'd asked her father to drive her to the house that she'd

255

shared with David for more than fifteen years.

It took an entire night of debate, Margaret ensuring that she did the majority of the talking, but David eventually agreed with Margaret. "You're right," he'd told her. "It's best that Richard see us together right now."

Margaret had fallen into David's arms late that night, weeping at the fact that he'd welcomed her back inside their home, however reluctantly. What she didn't know was that whatever she told him that pointed back to the crime, he relayed to Brian Patterson, their son's attorney.

Brian knew that Ramsey had been seen by a psychiatrist while he'd lived in Louisville. He also knew that Jack Robinson was the psychiatrist's first cousin and that Jack had paid for Ramsey's weekly visitations. Brian knew that Jack had bought a ten-acre ranch in Louisville under the aliases, John Barker. He knew Jack's mother dropped him off at a boy's home in Chicago when Jack was only ten years old. The last things she gave her son on that day were words — hard words. "You're impossible to control. You're manipulative, bright, calculating and lost. You're mean. You're evil." Then, she'd turned and walked away from her ten-year-old son.

Brian knew that Jack had escaped from the boy's home when he was twelve years old and that Jack had hitchhiked from Chicago to Louisville, performing sexual favors for men who picked him up so that he'd have enough money to eat with. He knew that Jack bought his first construction firm when he was only twenty-three years old. He knew that, through hard work, charm, threats and manipulation, Jack had worked his way into multi-millionaire status.

Brian knew that Jack made sizable donations to the

mayor's and the governor's re-election campaigns. He knew that Jack attended the chief of police's summer barbecues, annual Christmas party and that Jack was invited to attend each of the chief of police's sons' and daughters' wedding ceremonies.

From his discussions with Margaret, Brian gathered that Jack had been married to a young Japanese woman for twelve years. He knew that the marriage had ended after a burglar had entered their home and took not only jewelry, savings bonds and cash that Jack had stored inside a steel safe at the back of their bedroom closet — Brian knew that the burglar had also carried away the Robinson's six-year-old daughter. The burglar had demanded one million dollars, in exchange for Jack's daughter. Despite the burglar's ongoing demands for the money, Jack didn't bite. Two months later, his daughter's body was discovered floating along a riverbank off the coast of Florida. Toll from the ordeal, created a gulf between Jack and his wife that the couple could not bridge.

Brian also had letters and a legal document that he hadn't told the Tilsons about. Most chilling among the documents was the birth certificate for a girl named Bobbie Long. Her mother's name was Jennifer Robinson. Joe Thompson, Tammy Tilson's father, was listed on the birth certificate as the girl's father.

Times when Brian sat in his plush office looking across his desk at Tammy, he couldn't bring himself to show her the birth certificate or the handwritten letters from Joe to Jennifer begging her not to abandon their retarded daughter. Then, there were the letters from Jennifer to the Home for Retarded Children in Memphis.

*Contact a Joe Thompson at 5555 Ambrose Street if you*

*need money for Bobbie. I'm sure you understand why
we had to legally give Bobbie a surname different from
either of ours. Joe has other children, but he is a
responsible man. He loves Bobbie and has advised me
to inform you that he will do whatever is necessary to
ensure she is well taken care of.*

*Jennifer Robinson, October 12, 1926*

Chapter Twenty-Three

It was September 15, 1960. The courthouse swelled with heat. Men and women waved cardboard fans back and forth in front of their faces. This was Richard's second trial in as little as eleven months. "If they say I'm guilty this time, I just want to go and do the time. I'm so tired of fighting something I didn't do."

"Richard," Tammy told her oldest grandchild, her large, warm hands pressed atop his. "It's going to work out fine, this time, Child. You watch and see. You're innocent and this is all going to be over soon. Like the Good Book says, each of us reaps what we sow. You didn't sow any hate or evil, so you can't reap any hate or evil. You're a good boy. This is all going to be over soon and our family will be back together."

Richard held onto his grandmother's words while he sat on the witness stand.

"Where were you on the morning of May 15, 1959?" the prosecutor asked while he paced the front of the witness stand.

"At the park flying kites with my friends—"

The prosecutor stared at Richard. "Early in the morning?"

"No."

"So, where were you?"

"I was at home."

The prosecutor jammed his hands to the bottoms of his suit coat pockets. "You were at home," he nodded and snickered. "First, you were flying kites at the park, now you were home. A little girl, one of your peers, was kidnapped and murdered and you don't remember—"

Brian leaped from his seat. "Objection."

Judge Harrison nodded her approval. "Sustained."

The prosecutor smiled at Richard when he approached the witness stand carrying a small envelope. "Do you recognize this lock of hair and this earring?" He held the hair and the earring up for the jury to see. "Do you recognize these, Son? Do you?" he badgered Richard.

Richard stared at the jury, his gaze darting across their faces. His bottom lip quivered.

"Do you recognize these, Son?" He peered up at Richard. "The hair from the missing girl that was found in your bedroom? An earring from the missing girl that was found in your bedroom?"

"I-I-I've ne-never se-seen the earring or the hair before. I-I-Idon't know where they came from." He shook his head. "I-I've ne- never se-seen them before."

"Never seen them before?" The prosecutor chuckled. "They were in your bedroom." He stared at Richard.

Richard shook his head again. "I-I-I don't know. I've ne-never seen them before. I don't know that girl. I-I-I don't know who she is. I've never seen her—"

"Son, just answer the question, please." The prosecutor glared at Richard.

Richard glanced at Tammy, David and finally, at Margaret. He sat up straight in the witness stand. "Ye-Yes, Sir."

After the prosecutor entered the earring and the lock of hair as evidence, he picked up the drawings. He flipped them in front of Richard and the jury. "Do you recognize any of these drawings, Son?"

"Ye-Yes," Richard stammered.

"Which drawing do you recognize?"

"All of them."

The prosecutor raised his voice, as he moved away

from the witness stand to the jury box, back to the witness stand. "All of them?"

"Ye-Yes," Richard nodded. "I recognize all of the drawings."

"Where have you seen all of these drawings before?" He turned and showed the drawings, one by one, to the jury. "Where have you seen all of these drawings of a little girl with rope tied around her neck?" He peered at Richard.

"I—"

"--Speak up."

"I—"

"--Speak up," the prosecutor snapped.

"I-I—" Richard gazed across the courtroom. He watched his sister Carolyn sit tall and straight. He watched his mother stare into her lap. He watched his grandmother Rebecca hold his grandfather Ramsey's, hand. He watched his grandmother Tammy tear a piece of tissue into tiny bits.

The prosecutor approached the witness stand. "Son?"

"I drew them."

"Son, you'll have to speak up so the jury can hear you."

"I-I-I dre—drew—I drew them."

"You drew all of these pictures of a little girl, your peer, being kidnapped and strangled? You drew all of these? Every last one of them?"

The judge leaned forward and looked intently at Richard as he answered, "Yes."

"Yes. Yes what?"

Brian leaped from his seat. "Objection. Counsel is badgering the witness."

"Overruled." The judge leaned forward on the bench. "Answer the question, Son."

"I drew them."

"He already said that," Carolyn snapped.

The judge's gavel banged the bench. "I will not have outbursts in my courtroom. Another word out of you, young lady, and you will be dismissed from this courtroom."

Carolyn sat back and pursed her lips, scowling at the judge.

The prosecutor smiled. "Thank you, Your Honor." Then, he turned and looked at Richard. "When did you start drawing pictures of a little girl being kidnapped and strangled, Son?"

Richard moved toward the microphone. "I'm not your son."

"What did you say?"

Richard cleared his throat. "I said I'm not your son."

The prosecutor shrugged. "Fair enough." After a pause, he asked, "Richard, when did you start drawing pictures—"

"--I've been drawing since I was a kid."

The prosecutor chuckled. "You're still a kid."

Richard mumbled, "People don't treat me like it."

"Well, when you do grown up things—"

"—Objection," Brian shouted.

"Sustained," the judge said, looking at the prosecutor. "I'll have to ask you to refrain from idle discussion with the witness, Counsel. And I don't want to have to remind you again."

The prosecutor nodded at the judge. Then, he returned his attention to Richard. "When did you start drawing pictures of—"

"--I've been drawing since I was four or five years old."

"Two little girls in this town are kidnapped and

murdered—"

"Objection," Brian stood and said. "Your Honor, a body has never been found."

The prosecutor faced Brian then he looked at the jury. "And very well may never be." He pointed at Richard. "This here is a calculated killer, Ladies and Gentlemen. The precious, darling, innocent little Baxter girl miss—"

"—Objection," Brian argued. "The Baxter case has nothing to do with this case. Nothing. My client wasn't even alive when that kidnapping occurred."

"Drawing disturbing pictures—"

"—Objection," Brian said, pounding the courtroom desk.

"Counsel, I'm warning you," the judge admonished the prosecutor. "If you so much as introduce another shred of unrelated evidence in this courtroom, I'm going to hold you in contempt."

The prosecutor straightened his tie. "Yes, Your Honor." Then, he neared the witness stand as he addressed Richard with, "Son, since you were four or five years old, you're telling this courtroom that you have been drawing pictures of a little girl being strangled—"

"--No."

Carolyn smiled when Richard interrupted the prosecutor.

"I haven't been drawing pictures of a little girl being hurt since I was four or five years old."

"How long have you been drawing such pictures?"

"Since I was about nine years old."

"Why nine? What happened to cause you to draw the pictures then?"

"I started having these dreams about a man who visited my grandfather a lot."

Silence entered the courtroom.

Rebecca released Ramsey's hand. She almost turned and looked to the back of the courtroom where she knew Jack Robinson was sitting.

"What's your grandfather's name?"

"Ramsey. Grandpa Ramsey."

Rebecca bit her bottom lip.

Ramsey stared at Richard with a clenched jaw.

"And what's the name of the man who visited your grandfather Ramsey a lot?"

Richard almost pointed to the silvery-gray haired man leaning over a cane at the back of the courtroom. "Jack Robinson."

The judge picked up the gavel and banged it against the bench. "That'll be enough. I want to see counsel in my chambers immediately."

Richard never did discover what the prosecutor, his attorney, Brian Patterson, and the judge discussed. The trial didn't resume that day. In fact, two days passed before the trial reconvened.

Carolyn visited the courthouse with David the morning that Richard was to resume his place on the witness stand. She cried while she talked with her brother as they stood outside the courtroom that day. "They're gonna make sure you go to prison. Grandpa Ramsey's a part of this too, you know."

Richard looked at her.

"I know you know," she told him. "We all know. I am getting so many visions and so many dreams about this trial. It's like electricity is going through me. I just feel--" She wiped her eyes, but the tears kept falling. "I always knew something like this would happen. I tried to stop it. Me and Aunt Janice and Aunt Melinda even went to the police. We tried." She began to sob. "I can't count the times I walked to the foundry on my way home from school and begged Grandpa Ramsey to tell the truth. I knew he was hiding something awful."

She wiped her eyes. "He still is." She stiffened her spine and sniffed hard. "I hate him for how afraid, how timid, he is. I hate him for believing that Jack Robinson has more power than he has. I hate him for being a puppet, not even the shell of a man. I hate him for being a coward."

She looked at Richard. "You're gonna come out of this okay. It's gonna be a long time, Richard. A lot of years are gonna pass before you're free, but I'll be here. Every single day I will."

She peered into her lap. "They already know what they are going to decide. I bet Jack has paid everyone in that courtroom. He's paid the jury. He's paid the judge. He's paid the prosecutor." She chuckled. "He probably even paid your attorney. You see how many dumb mistakes your attorney's been making." She shook her head. "I can't believe how much power and control one wealthy man can have in a town as big as this."

She buried her face in her hands and cried. "Grandma's not going to make it. Grandma Tilson's not going to come through this all right. She's been fighting for so long. She worked so hard to give us a better life. She wanted us to have it so much better than Grandpa Tilson and she did. That's what she worked for all those years. Now I know why she was always so tough. But she's falling apart. Grandma Tilson is falling apart right in front of my eyes. Everybody in our family is getting old in this courtroom. Everybody. They're trying to kill us all, one by one." She wiped her eyes and sniffed hard. "But we don't die. That's what they don't know," she sniffed. "We keep rising up and coming back again and again."

She tapped Richard's hand. "You're going to be alright. You're my brother. You have what it takes to make it through this. We've got good root, Richard." She smiled weakly. "You know that." Then, she faced the courtroom door, preparing to enter. "I love you," she said while she hugged him.

**********

Carolyn was right. A week later, when the verdict was announced, Richard was found guilty again. That night, Tammy sat in her living room gazing out the picture window. An owl was perched on a limb of the sycamore tree rooted deep and tall in the front yard. Tammy listened to it hoot when cars went by. She didn't turn away from the window until she heard Philip call her name. "What?" she answered, her voice near a whisper.

"You alright down there?"

He'd asked her that for the last sixty years whenever a crisis had entered their family.

She almost chuckled. "I love you, Philip," she called back up the stairs.

"What?" he asked, moving to the edge of the stairs. He leaned over the banister so that he could hear her better. While he did, he massaged his lower back where a bad patch of arthritis had set in. When he stood again, he pushed his glasses up on the bridge of his nose. He held the banister tightly while he made his way down the stairs.

A slither of light was coming through the living room window, resting against the side of Tammy's face.

Philip told himself to run, but his seventy-nine-year-old legs wouldn't allow. When he reached his wife's side, he felt a gust of air move over his forearm.

Day after day in the courthouse, he'd watched his wife's candle grow dimmer. The last few months, at night when she stopped snoring, he shook her until she woke. Then, he asked her if she was alright. He didn't go back to sleep until he heard her snoring again.

While he cradled her in his arms, he knew she was gone, but he wasn't ready to say good-bye. She was his sweetheart, the only woman he had ever loved, the only person he had ever let get to truly know him.

They fell in love when they were teenagers. They grew old together. He never thought he'd bury her.

The last few years when he knelt at the side of their bed and said his prayers, more than a dozen times, he'd asked God to take him before Tammy. Living without her would be too hard. He didn't want to look up and not see her sitting across from him at the kitchen table. He didn't want to work at the store without her by his side. He didn't want to sleep alone. He didn't want to have to watch his wife die.

He knew his heart would never mend. Tammy had been a most wonderful gift to him from God and now she was gone. Crouched at her side in the living room, he held her head gently inside the crease of his arm. Then he called out, "Tammy. Honey? Sweetheart? Tammy? Darling?"

When she didn't move, he told himself that she was just sleeping the same way that his mother had just been swinging from the barn loft all those years ago when he was a little boy. He tried to fool himself by rocking Tammy in his arms and whispering, "She's not dead." Not his sweetheart. Not his best friend. Not the love of his life. She was just sleeping.

He held her for a long time. "Love shined on me the day we met," he started to sing, his voice dry and rugged, as he stroked her hair. "Light from your eyes brought a joy to me that I'd never known before," he continued to sing as he rubbed her face.

Her body dangled over the side of the chair, her head leaning close to his as if she was trying hard to hear the words to the song that he sang.

"I love you, Tammy. I love you, Sweetheart," he cried out into the lonely room. Tears began to wet his face.

He didn't move until he heard a knock at the front door. "Who is it?" he called out, refusing to leave his wife's side.

"It's Carolyn, Grandpop."

"You got your key?" he asked, seconds before he kissed Tammy's face.

"No. I left it at the house."

Pressing his face against Tammy's, he closed his eyes and breathed in deeply, treasuring the remaining heat coming from Tammy's body. He hated to leave her, so instead of going to the door, he called out, "Hold your horses," while Carolyn banged on the door. He held onto Tammy for a moment before he stood.

"What's your big hurry?" he asked after he moved away from Tammy and unlocked then opened the door.

"Where's Grandma?"

He stared at Carolyn gape eyed. Then, they fell into each other's arms and wept. "She's with the angels," he said while he shuffled across the room to be at his wife's side.

"She had a heart attack."

He glanced over his shoulder at Carolyn. "What?"

"She had a heart attack," Carolyn said, her expression downcast as she entered the house. She hurried to her grandmother's side. Before she knew it, her shoulders had given way and she was sobbing as she held onto her grandmother's limp hand, the one closest to the living room window.

Across from her, Philip knelt close to the floor, massaging Tammy's other hand.

It took Carolyn an hour to get Philip to allow her to call the paramedics. While she'd tugged on his arm, pleading with him to let her call the paramedics, she kept telling him, "You gotta let her go, Grandpop. You can't sit here on the floor holding her like this forever. She's gone. You gotta turn her loose."

The instant the paramedics entered the living room, they knew that Tammy, to them merely an older woman sitting in a chair next to a picture window, was dead.

The owl outside the window hooted as the paramedics rolled Tammy's body down the front walk on a stretcher. Philip shuffled behind them with Carolyn holding his hand.

Chapter Twenty-Four

Life, at times unkind to Philip, had allowed him
to reach his eighties, this despite the fact that he no
longer had Tammy with him. Philip survived the first
ten of the twelve years that Richard spent in prison
with a single aim – "make it through another day".
Gone were Philip's dreams of launching a Tilson
Scholarship Foundation. Hopes that he'd shared with
Tammy for decades had faded, withering into mere
memories, of which an aging Philip often forgot.

He read letters that Richard sent him from prison
like they were essays he couldn't stop re-reading. He
carried the letters to Tammy's tombstone and read
them out loud while he stood above her gravesite.

*Dear Grandpop, How's it going? It rained here
yesterday, but the sun's out today. I went for a run at
the prison track. I usually run about three miles a
day, but today I ran five miles. I felt so good
running. It's a way to feel free.*

*Carolyn and Ruth told me you're still operating
the grocery store. You're some kinda man,
Grandpop. I'm glad you got help at the store and
that you are mainly just keeping the books. That's
enough for anybody to be doing. Arthur told me
Buster's grandson went home to glory, and that
you've decided not to get anymore dogs. I guess they
did enough leaving their paw marks all over the
back of the house and around the back door.*

*I heard Karl's really come along. Ruth said he's
doing good in college. Grandpop, these kids grow up
fast! Heard Karl's an outstanding basketball player
and that he's earning academic honors in college.
Arthur and Carolyn told me they think Karl's going
to make the first round in the NBA. Good for him.*

*You and Grandma sure did a good job of putting solid foundation down for each of us to build our lives upon. I can't thank you two enough for that, Grandpop.*

*Carolyn tells me Jack Robinson's health is failing fast. Like Reverend Cleveland would preach, I suppose trouble don't last. Carolyn also said Rebecca and Ramsey are trying to come around more. Said they stop by Margaret's and Dad's on their way home from church twice a month. Carolyn said Dad always finds someplace else to be when they visit. Dad always did have a habit of pulling away from folk when he didn't see eye to eye with them. As far back as I remember, he's been that way.*

*I heard Alex is using a walker a few hours a week. Some new technology Ruth was telling me about. Miracles happening every day. One thing I've learned, Grandpop, is that life goes on. Change is inevitable and life goes on. I don't feel sorry for myself anymore. I can't waste my life spending another day doing that. God's fighting my battles. Always has. I've learned to trust the way you and Grandma always did. I'm so proud to be your grandson. I don't know where I'd be without my family. Somebody's here every day to visit with me. Sometimes I get two and three visitors a day. Gotta laugh. Carolyn — she's so much like Grandma Tammy, you know — well, she probably made up a schedule and has everyone rotating when they come to visit. That's a joke.*

*In all seriousness, I get so many cards, letters, phone calls and visits, sometimes I have trouble keeping up. I started taking college courses. They've got these new computers where you can take some courses off the computer. When I get out, and I really*

271

*believe that God's going to make that be soon —*
*anyhow, when I get out, I want to take some art*
*classes at The University of Memphis. I don't know.*
*That or I might go to Knoxville and take some art*
*classes at the University of Tennessee. I do know I'm*
*going to college when I get out. I'm sure read up*
*enough to do well in school. I read-read-read while*
*I'm in here. I also started meditating, and yes, I pray*
*and read the Bible every day.*

*Well, Grandpop, I'm gonna go. Please tell*
*everyone I said 'Hi'. I love you all. Thanks for being*
*who you are and for giving me love and support*
*since the day I was born.*

*Richard*


In his letters home as well as when family visited
him at the prison, except for what he confided to
Carolyn, Richard not once mentioned the frequent
fists and pipe beatings he endured at the hands of
men whom had been at the prison years longer than
he had. Even before he was transported from the
Youth Detention Center at the age of eighteen, he
heard that "lifers" could be amongst the cruelest and
the kindest inmates at Forthright Prison.

Richard wasn't at the prison, a former slave
plantation, a year when he began to think that ghosts
roamed the grounds. After he was at the prison for
two years, he was certain that spirits walked the
cement and steel corridors. Sometimes he stayed up
late at night, his back sinking into the soiled
mattress, just so he could watch the shadows pass,
hear footsteps that came with no body.

"They'll protect you," Carolyn told him the
afternoon he leaned close to the plexiglass that

separated the prisoners from their visitors. "That's why you can sense them. That's why you can hear them. You're connected, Richard. Watch. They'll look out for you. They're from our root."

After enduring two years of beatings at the prison, Richard watched the leader of the gang that jumped him the night he first arrived at Forthright be taken to the infirmary with double pneumonia. It was then that Richard started to believe Carolyn.

He peered through the cell bars while guards pulled the stretcher that the gang leader lay on. When they passed in front of Richard's cell, the gang leader gripped his chest and started spitting up blood.

Feeling a breeze cross his face, Richard looked down at his hands. His shirt sleeves were blown up, as if he was outdoors in a storm. It was then that he knew that Carolyn was right. He was not alone.


Twelve years into his prison term, Richard came up for parole for the fourth time. He'd missed so much since he was jailed. He heard about Tammy transitioning from Ruth. She cried until her eyes were beet red the day she visited him and relayed the hard news.

He missed driving to New York to cheer for Karl when he earned a first-round draft pick into the NBA, getting picked up by the Milwaukee Bucks. He did watch the draft on TV in the prison recreation room. He smiled when he heard his cousin's name. When the television crowd cheered, Richard clenched his fist and pumped it in the air.

Richard also missed writing his grandfather, Philip, letters. He'd written him long letters for ten years. Then, his cousin, Arthur, visited and told him that Philip had transitioned.

Thatwas a couple of years ago.

Richard hated himself for three weeks for not crying once when he heard that Philip had transitioned. Then, the hate turned into fear. He feared that living at Forthright had hardened him to pain, robbed him of the ability to feel deep emotion.

That's when the running dreams started. In his dreams, when he looked over his shoulder, he was alone for miles. For the last six months, he wondered if he was running from himself and, if so, why.

While he worked in the prison laundry room, sweat dripping down his brow and the sides of his face, he wondered if he'd ever fall in love. He wondered if a woman would ever love him, allow him to hold her warm body in his arms — if she knew where he'd been.

He scrubbed his skin hard when he took showers. He tried to wash the thoughts off, but they stayed with him.They haunted him. He was changed. That he knew. He could only imagine the man he would have been had he not gone to prison.

This was his reality, bitter as it was. And although it hurt him to look in the mirror sometimes, he told himself that he was ready to be paroled. He wanted to be free. As he had the other three times that he'd gone before the parole board, he washed his hair the night before, was careful to press every wrinkle out of his prison uniform, brushed his teeth for several minutes, and manicured his fingernails.

He walked toward the parole board with his shoulders taut and his head held high. He walked the way his Grandma Tammy walked when she went to face hard criticism. His confidence, his good behavior and his faith paid off.

On August 12, 1973, a week after the parole board review, Richard walked proud as he rounded the corner from his cell, nothing more than a paper bag with cards, letters and old family pictures in it tucked inside the crease of his arm. He followed the guard down the long corridor, around another corner, down a long hallway and around yet another corner. He swallowed hard when he passed the visiting area. This was the first day that no one sat at the bench waiting for him to come toward the Plexiglas.

The guard stopped walking.

Richard's stride opened. His pace quickened. Before he knew it, he felt the wind brush his face.

Carolyn, Ruth and Arthur screamed, "Richard," as soon as he stepped outside the prison gates.


"Jack Robinson's dead," Carolyn told him that night while they sat on their parents' front porch.

"How did—"

"--Don't know," Carolyn interjected. "All I know is I was walking in front of his house on Madison one day and next thing I knew I read in the paper that he was dead."

"You didn't—"

"Richard."

"Well."

"I would never kill anyone. I just walked by his house. That's all. Whatever happened, spirits did the rest." She turned and looked hard at her brother. "Did you know Jack was Bobbie Long's brother and Grandma Tilson was Bobbie's sister?"

Richard gawked at her.

She nodded. "Sure was. Your attorney told me after

Grandma Tilson died." She nodded. "Sure did. You thought I stopped asking so many questions?"

Richard almost laughed.

"Grandpa Tilson never knew. It was best that way. But I think Grandma knew. She wrote checks in Bobbie's name to the Children's Home until the year she died. I don't know if Jack knew they were kin." She gazed into the night. "No one ever found out what happened to Bobbie."

"You think Jack killed his own sister?"

She sat silent for a long time. "I don't know." She sighed. "My heart tells me he did. But all folks know for sure is that she drowned." She shook her head. "I don't know. Heard that Bobbie was fine until Jack came to Memphis one day. He came here to buy Grandma Tilson's mother's old house. Bobbie was killed while he was here. Jack was only here one day. He stopped by to visit that old home for retarded children that day - the home Bobbie was staying at. That's all I know." She shook her head.

"Jack hated his mother. He never forgave her for leaving him. I think he would have killed anything his mother cared about to torture her." She paused. "Jack Robinson was one of those people who choose to only feel their own pain. When things go wrong for people like Jack, they convince themselves that only they are suffering and no one else in the world has hurt like them. Psychopath. They only see themselves. It's like they believe the world was created to serve them."

She shook her head. "After Jack's first daughter was kidnapped and murdered, the rest was etched in stone. He was going to make everybody he could pay for the pain he felt when his first daughter was kidnapped then killed. She was the daughter he had with a Japanese woman he'd been married to. In his

276

mind, the whole world had done him wrong and he was going to make the world pay. Jack was a cold-blooded killer. He'd been bent on death since he was a kid."

She went silent. Then, she looked at her brother. "Jack was one of those clay people, Richard. He was a coward." She smiled. "I was wrong for the times I told you that you were a coward when we were coming up." She placed her hand atop his. "I apologize. You aren't hardly a coward, Richard." She shook her head. "Not hardly."

"What happened to make the parole board let me out this time?" Richard wanted to know.

"Besides Jack dying, can you believe it, the first missing girl's father came forward. He opened up like a can of beans. He told everything he knew. His name's Leonard Baxter. He gave your attorney every shred of evidence he'd collected over the years on Jack and Ramsey. He paid for your remaining legal fees too. Paid them down to the last cent. He said he had never stopped trying to find out what happened to his daughter and wouldn't stop until you were free. Detective Cramer helped him a lot." She stared across the yard. "I never knew," she began. "Leonard Baxter's wife and Jack used to be lovers. The Baxter girl, that little girl that turned up missing before we were born, was Jack's daughter."

She nodded. "Madness. The only one not related to Jack was the last little girl who was taken and they pinned that on you. Word on the street is Grandpa Ramsey put a word out that our family knew who the killer of the Baxter girl was. I don't even know how he knew she was dead being as a body was never found. Anyhow, folks got in a fury and next thing we knew, Melinda's and Keith's house was burned down. I told Aunt Janice that Jack saw us that night we went

277

looking around at the tracks. There's even talk that Jack killed four other girls when he was in Louisville." She shook her head. "But that little Baxter girl, no one believes she was ever in the river. That river was dug and no girl's body was ever found. On account of her sweater and shoe being found down by the woods, investigators think the girl might have been down there longer than people thought. "

"Jack could have taken her back to his house. Nobody knows. They never found any bones beyond what I found below the ridge that one time Aunt Janice and Aunt Melinda and me went down there. The girl wasn't in the river. It was just a decoy. Jack was calculating. I guess he must have saw somebody up on those tracks that night Jocelyn took off running and threw something big into the river to make folk think it was a body. He was smart and calculating."

"What about—"

"--Grandpa Ramsey's still not talking. Aunt Janice and I went back to the ridge twice, but there was nothing there. I stopped having visions and so did Aunt Janice. When Jack Robinson died," she said. "It just stopped. The hauntings. The kidnappings. The murders. Everything. It just stopped." She paused. "At least I hope it's stopped. I don't think we'll ever know what happened to those missing girls. This thing will do what Bobbie, Jocelyn and that other little girl did, go to a grave without much of a trace."

"Did the cops—"

"--Ever resume the search after they put you in prison?"

He nodded. "Yea."

"What do you think?"

They sat in silence for a long time.

## Part VI

<u>Chapter Twenty-Five</u>

Gerald Ford was President.

Richard was grateful to have a college work-study job.

"Seems like I'm always late for a class," Richard complained to Arthur when they connected over the telephone. "I need to get a car. I gotta start building up my credit. It's not that I have bad credit. I don't. I don't have any credit."

"Why don't you buy a used car?"

"I want something that's going to last."

"Some used cars hold up better than you think."

Richard laughed. "I don't feel like hunting for a four-leaf clover, Bro."

"Do what you want. But you're right. You gotta start building up your credit, especially if you want to become a serious artist. You're gonna need money to buy those expensive art supplies and attend art festivals to get your name and work out." Arthur sighed. "Man, I sure am glad that you listened to Dad and started drawing again."

"Yea. Dad always looked out for me when it came to my art."

"If you decide to buy something on credit, I'll co-sign for you. We're brothers. On top of that, I believe in you."

"Thanks, Man. I'll work on getting credit, but I don't want a co-signer. I want to do it on my own, but thanks again. Plus, with the parking around here--" He released a deep breath. "Ain't no place to park around here." He shook his head. "I mean, like nowhere. You have to get to campus about six o'clock in the morning to get a decent parking space."

"Start with something small. Buy some clothes on credit, but I still say you should buy a used car. Just do it, Man. You know Mom and Dad aren't going to let you drive their cars. Leave it to them and you're just going to have to keep catching the bus." He laughed.

"They want me to move out the way Carolyn did. They want me out the way you're leaving this weekend for Atlanta. They don't want me living at home. Dad wants me to be independent, take off on my own. Mom. She just wants me out. I remind her too much of things bad. Together, they're trying to make things as tough for me as possible, so I'll just pick up and leave."

The brothers laughed.

"And?"

Richard pulled the telephone close to his mouth. "And it's working. Plus, I don't feel close to Mom anymore. It's going to take me a long time to work through that. I just feel like I'm someone who's being nice to her when I don't really feel I should be. I don't want to let that go down too far into my mind until I take it out on someone else. I could never hurt Mom, but the feelings, deep hurt and anger toward her, Rebecca and Ramsey are still there. I wonder if they'll ever go away." He sighed. "I wonder. I'm just glad Carolyn and Dad told me the truth. I had a right to know. And I kinda felt that's the way things went down anyway. It's just good to know for sure."

"Jack Robinson is dead now."

"Yea, but we both know there are more Jack Robinsons in the world. I hate that Ramsey never stood up to him. Ramsey wouldn't have survived one day in prison, not one day, maybe not even an hour."

"I think he knew that, Richard."

"I hate him, Arthur. I hate him for what he did to me, but I'll work through it. I've seen what hate does to people and I don't want that stuff to happen to me."

"Just focus on your art, Man."

"That and getting a better job so I can move out."

"Why don't you just go to school out of town?"

"I've been thinking about that. U. T. has a good art program. I've been thinking about moving to Knoxville and going to school there."

\*\*\*\*\*\*\*\*\*\*

It wasn't just Richard. Each of the children thought of ways to escape home.

Ruth, anxious to distance herself from Margaret's prudence and David's distant emotions, was engaged to be married in six months.

Arthur kept his word, packed his belongings and moved to Atlanta where he enrolled in Morehouse College.

Margaret and David beamed with pride the morning that Arthur drove to Atlanta. Margaret packed Arthur so many bologna and peanut butter and jelly sandwiches, a tinge of embarrassment pinched her conscience when she handed him the paper bag that the sandwiches were stuffed inside.

"Mama, I'm only going to Atlanta," Arthur pleaded when she shoved the bag inside his hands and kissed his forehead.

"Yes. But you never know what will happen when you're out driving," she said. "Give some of the sandwiches to your friends when you get to Atlanta if you don't eat them all on your drive to the city."

Moments later, she stood next to David waving until Arthur drove down the street and disappeared around the corner.

"I always wanted to go to college," she told David

as they walked, side by side, up their front walk.

"Why didn't you," he frowned as he strode ahead of her into the house, leaving her on the sidewalk alone.

Upon reaching the house, she stood on the front porch peering across the driveway, wondering if David would ever forgive her for helping her father escape prison. The way that she saw it, her father was innocent. He never killed anyone and the police never did find a dead body, not even one. There was only talk and speculation.

Jack Robinson, the man who had the answers, was dead. She didn't know why David couldn't just forgive her and forget what had happened. She didn't know why he wouldn't allow them to go on with their lives, putting all of that pain behind them. Richard was free. He had survived prison. His mind and his spirit were strong. She yearned to run inside the house and beg David to, "Forgive me. Forgive me so we can get our marriage back," but she just stood on the front porch staring across the driveway.

Of their children, Richard had the most promising and the most painful future. Three of his award-winning clay designs and a sculpture of elementary aged boys playing stickball earned a spot in the student center at the University of Memphis. Twelve of his water and oil paintings decorated the sides of Tennessee's state and federal buildings. He accepted the attention with a shrug. The noise of praise stirred him little.

Carolyn, the one in the family to proclaim, "the year of the Lord," was a promising high school teacher. She worked with neurologically challenged junior high school students at Memphis High. She took the students on out-of-town field trips to places like the New York Stock Exchange, the Harriett Tubman House, Bethune-

Cookman College and to science museums. She read them well researched books about places like Africa, France, Egypt, Italy, China, Alaska and Mexico. She taught them the basics of trigonometry until she molded them into star pupils. An honest woman, like Ruth, Arthur and Richard had while they were growing up, Carolyn's students trusted her.

Richard looked to Carolyn most. He knew she would never repeat intimate details of his life that he shared with her. After a couple of years of majoring in advanced art at the University of Memphis, Richard found himself looking to his sister again. He was facing a new trauma, suffering brought on from his best friend's lifestyle.

"Carolyn," Richard sobbed into the telephone, the wind howling outside the exterior phone booth that he leaned against, "Maxwell is dead."

Richard was met with silence.

"Carolyn?" he tried.

Silence.

"Carolyn?"

"I'm here."

"Did you hear—"

"--I heard you. What happened?"

"He overdosed."

"What?" Carolyn sat up on the edge of her bed.

"I was at his apartment helping him with his chemistry. He had a final coming up and he was failing the course badly. It was so cold out."

"Richard, when did this happen?"

"Tonight. Not too long ago."

"Did you call the police?"

"Yes. They've come and gone. You should have seen his eyes."

"Whose eyes?"

"Maxwell's, Carolyn."

"Okay. I know this isn't easy, but try to keep your wits. Are you somewhere that I can come pick you up?"

"I'm calling you from a phone booth." He glanced across the street. "In front of a restaurant called Mabley's."

"On the corner of Fourth and Vine?"

"Yea."

"I know where that is. Do you want to keep talking or go home and call me from there? I can drive over now or pick you up in the morning if you want."

He shook his head. "No. You stay with your family." He lowered his head. "I'll be all right."

"You sure?"

"Yea."

"Well, tell me what happened. Get it out, Richard. Don't hold it in."

"I had just hung up from talking with LaWanda," Richard began. "You know LaWanda and I used to date. Ever since I told her that I'd served time in prison, she demanded that we only be friends." He waved his hand. "She told me that she'd put a lot into her life and that she couldn't afford to mess her life up. But you already know all of that," he grimaced.

"Besides LaWanda," he continued, his voice trailing off, "Maxwell was the only person, besides family, who I was close to. As you already know, Maxwell and I both have served prison time." He chuckled. "After we got out of prison, we'd play cards and shoot pool together."

"We even took some of the same college electives. Right before I headed to Maxwell's today, I told him to make sure that he had his chemistry books out when I got there. I had on my hooded sweat jacket. Maxwell's eyes were glossy when he unlocked and opened the chain-latch on his front door to let me in." Richard sighed. "Right away, I knew Maxwell was stoned. I wasn't at Maxwell's apartment half an hour when Maxwell looked at me and mumbled, 'Hey, Man, I've got to go to the bathroom.'"

Listening absent intent, Carolyn didn't utter a word.

"Carolyn, he wasn't in the bathroom five minutes. I didn't let him stay in there long. I kept telling him — I can't count the times I've told Maxwell — stop doing drugs," Richard shouted.

When Richard covered the side of his face with his hand, the receiver almost slid to the booth floor. He had started to cry. "But he wouldn't listen."

Carolyn leaned across the edge of her bed. "Maxwell was such a beautiful person, but he didn't see himself that way," she said. "If he had, he would have left drugs alone."

"I had this eerie feeling," Richard said. "So, I went to the bathroom door. I turned the knob back and forth, knocked and called out, "Maxwell. One minute turned into two, three, four minutes. Before I knew it, I was banging on the bathroom door. Finally, I stepped back and ran with all my might into the door. The door swung open."

He stopped talking, hung his head, then raising his head, he told her, "Carolyn, you should have seen his face. His eyes were like marbles. His skin." He pulled his arms around his shoulders. "His skin was frozen. He was starting to look like clay. As soon as I looked at Maxwell, I knew he was dead." He bent over and sobbed. "I called 911. The cops came right away. They asked me questions, then theylet me go." He wiped his eyes.

"Richard?"

He stood in silence before he said, "And, Carolyn--:

"What, Richard? Tell me."

He wiped his nose with the back of his hand. "I had another dream. I can't help thinking that seeing Maxwell struggling with drugs triggered the dreams. Stress," he said, gazing upward. He sniffed hard.

"Another one? That's the second one in a week."

"It's been years since I had one of those dreams. Worrying about Maxwell triggered it, I'm sure," he said. Then, he stood firm and said, "Carolyn, I heard you say it once. Do you think it's true? Do you think one of the girls is alive?"

Carolyn was quick. Sitting erect on her bed, she told Richard to, "Meet me at the Armstrong's this Saturday. They're vacationing in Florida this weekend. We'll have the house to ourselves. Spirit will guide us when we get there. We'll know just where to go once we get in the house. All these years," she said. "Before you said what you just did, I had forgotten. I had a dream about a girl being alive. It was a dream about a cellar and a pipe. We were all still kids then. I was sweating when I woke from the dream. I woke up screaming, but no one came to help me. It's coming back, Richard."

"Yeah," Richard nodded. "Let me go back to my apartment. I'm calling you from a pay phone. I'll meet you at the Armstrong's Saturday morning."

"Okay," Carolyn agreed.

As soon as Richard entered his own apartment, he went into the den, the room that he'd turned into an arts room, and pulled a large, blank canvas onto an easel. Oil paints in hand, he spent the next hour painting a large broken winged eagle. The eagle's face looked like that of a Black man.

To Richard's unawares, that evening, Carolyn talked their father into getting the key to Ramsey's and Rebecca's house from Margaret.

That Saturday, Carolyn and Richard stood in Rebecca's and Ramsey's living room surveying the area. The furniture was new.

Carolyn and Richard looked at the knick-knacks, decor and furniture as they made their way from the living room into the dining room, into the kitchen. At the edge of the kitchen, Carolyn opened the basement door and they descended the stairs that led to the basement and the cellar. Once they reached the cellar door, Carolyn and Richard turned and stared at each other.

"I'm going to get a chisel and a shovel. There's got to be a shovel in the garage," Richard told Carolyn.

"She's in there," Carolyn said, staring at the wall. "She's in the cellar wall."

They dug for six straight hours. Despite their labor, they never did find a body. Fatigued and frustrated, they gave up and returned to the kitchen.

As he stood next to the kitchen sink, Richard shook his head. "She was in there. One of those girl's is still alive. I can feel it."

Carolyn looked at him. "So do I. I can feel her spirit." She nodded. "I bet there's a water source that kept that girl alive long enough for her to get free." She paused. "Richard?"

"Yea?"

"The creek," Carolyn shouted. "There's got to be a pipe in the cellar that leads to the creek."

They ran into the back yard. A smile tugged at their mouths the instant that they spotted the pipe that they used to play near when they were kids. Water gushed out of the pipe into the creek. "She's alive."

Richard started laughing. "She got out. That

pipe's big enough for a little girl to fit through."

Carolyn and he fell into each other's arms. That afternoon, they placed anonymous calls to the police from pay phones, relaying that, "The girl from the Tilson trial is alive. Check the pipe at the back of the Armstrong house at 542 Nettleton Avenue, the pipe that runs into the creek."

For the next three weeks, they called the police station from different pay phones. Their anonymous message never changed. The police recorded each of the calls, but they never sent an officer to the Armstrong house.

Numbness brought on from his best friend Maxwell's overdose gone, Richard painted less. For the first time in his life, he found art boring. He spent his afternoons walking through what remained of Handy Park. There, with peanuts and popcorn filling his pockets and a writing pad, pen and letters in his backpack, he watched children fly kites, young and elderly couples eat their lunches from paper bags on park benches, and runners jog the park's outer circumference along a path long since beaten into place by other athletic enthusiasts.

Besides watching people, Richard went to Handy Park to read and respond to letters from his cousin Karl. It gave him something to do, feel that he had a reason to be alive.

*"I won rookie of the year, Man,"* Karl's letter began. *"Considering that I started college late and am older than a lot of guys I play against, I'm gonna take the award as a compliment. I wish you could have been here."*

*"People were everywhere. Mom and Dad flew up to Milwaukee to watch me and my teammates play*

for the Bucks. Mom and Dad look good. I can't tell you how happy I felt looking up and seeing them in the stands. They were cheering from ear to ear, Man. Each time I scored or blocked a shot, people just went freaking nuts. I felt like I was in the twilight zone. After awhile, I almost stopped and asked the crowd who they were cheering for."

Switching gears, he wrote, "Carolyn and Ruth said you weren't feeling too good. You gotta take care of yourself, Man. A n d , t o answer the question you asked me in your last letter, no — I'm not chasing women. I almost laughed when I read that. You know I ain't never been no gigolo. I'm not changing just because I went pro. I'm not dating Monique anymore though. She was tripping. She had too hard of a time dealing with me having gone pro. She would read gossip magazines and believe what people told her on the street — all kinds of junk about me being with a ton of different women."

"She was always on the phone with this girl or that girl asking questions and listening to gossip. Every time I called her or she visited me, she'd drill me with questions. Man. I finally got enough of that. I've been talking to this lady named Tracy. She's cool, but I'm taking it slow. After Monique —you know we were together for five years and she still couldn't trust me. Well, after Monique, I'm taking it slow."

"I'm saving my money. I'm not buying a big house when I'd be the only one living in it. Nah. I'm leasing a condo. It's cool. It's enough for me. You know Grandma Tilson drilled, "Count your blessings" into our heads."

"Enough about me. How about you? I hope you're painting again. Man, you can't allow

*anything to stop you from being in the flow.*
*Remember that. Cool? And hey, yo. If you ever want*
*to come to a game, give a Brother a holler. I'll hook*
*you up."*

*Your Cuz K*

While joggers ran in front of him, Richard pulled
a pad and a pen out of his backpack and wrote:

*"Congratulations, Cuz. Yea. I heard about you*
*holding it down in the NBA. You know Ruth told me.*
*I don't care what you would have done, she'd have*
*told me. You know Ruth can't hold water. Because of*
*Ruth, I already knew about Monique and you*
*breaking up. Told you the woman can't hold water.*
*She told me that a few weeks ago. Sorry to hear it,*
*Man. I know you two had a lot of years together.*
*But trust is important, so you more than likely did*
*the right thing. Be careful out here, Man. There's a*
*lot of slick folk out here who'll come off as your*
*best friend until they get what they want from you.*
*You're young, and you're smart. Don't let nobody*
*run a game on you. Stay sharp, Man."*
*"And, nah. I wasn't feeling too good. You know*
*my friend, Maxwell? He OD'd. I was at his*
*apartment when it happened. I can't count the times*
*I tried to get him off drugs. I'm not trying to be your*
*cousin grilling you, but don't you ever do drugs or*
*start drinking. I'll come up there and beat you for*
*myself. I mean it, K."*
*"I'm going to take you up on your offer to watch*
*you play. Let me know when the Bucks play the*
*76ers. That's the game I want to see. You know*
*Arthur's a big time 76ers fan. You can't tell him Dr.*

290

*J. is not the coolest and best basketball player ever. I have to admit, Julius is good. He can find his way around or through anybody. Art wears Dr. J. jerseys and he only wears Converse sneakers. He won't hear of putting another sneaker on his feet."*

*"Dr. J. has a sweet game, but I have to cheer for Spencer Haywood, because he's from down South. You young bloods are holding it down, Man. Wilt ain't playing no more, so there's room for the rest of you young bloods to make a name for yourself on the court,"* Richard wrote.

*"Kareem's lethal with that sky hook. But you know, Man. My favorite all around baller is you. I loved it when the Bucks took it to the New Orleans Jazz last Wednesday night. I watched the game on NBC. You all shut the Jazz out, Man. Y'all steam rolled over them. I was sitting in my place eating cheese doodles and laughing until my sides hurt. But yes, me and Arthur can come check a game out together. If the 76ers lose, you might lose a cousin. Art might not speak to you again."*

*"Well, Karl, I'm going to end this. I have a class to get to. Just between you and me, I'm quitting school after this semester. As old as I am, do you know my mother would flip if she knew I wasn't going to finish college? College is a drag and I can land work without a degree."*

*"Keep holding it down both on and off the court. I'm proud of you, Cuz. You're headed in the right direction."*

*Rich*


Richard did drop out of college at the end of the

semester. He also moved from Memphis to Knoxville. He wasn't in Knoxville six months when he began to walk Knoxville's streets and, as chance would have it, he met up with his best friend — a brown and white striped mutt.

When the weather was good, Richard walked to and from McPhearsons Business Associates, an advertising firm where he worked as the firm's top artist. Neither a suit and tie or "yes, sir" man, not long after his first three months at the firm, the owners threatened to release him. Yet, the art talent that God gave him forced management into silence and to renege on their threat.

Money that Richard earned working at the firm he used to pay his tithes and his bills. Money that he earned from freelance artwork, he contributed to the community, prison reform programs and to support substance abuse prevention and intervention initiatives, Boys and Girls clubs, the Big Brother/Big Sister program and childcare centers in Knoxville, particularly East Knoxville.

Once a month, he sent money to The Home for Retarded Children in Memphis in the memory of Bobbie Long. He also sent a sizable check to the National Foundation for Missing Children.

A few weeks ago, when he telephoned home, Margaret answered the phone. "You're just like my father," she'd told Richard that late afternoon.

"I don't want to hear about your father," Richard responded flatly.

Margaret chuckled. "You're running from your past. I still remember Mama talking about how Dad used to run—"

"--Mom, I told you I don't want to hear about that man."

"You have to face facts about who you are—"

He raised his voice. "--I am nothing like your father. I do not use people. I am not a coward. I really would appreciate it if you would never speak your father's name in my presence again. Thanks."

"You are so good at being polite. You're so much like your father."

"Thanks for the compliment."

"Richard—"

"--Mom, the possibility for us to have a close mother-son relationship was lost years ago. You took that away from both of us. It was a choice you made when I was still just a kid. I can't go back and change that and neither can you. I'm sure you already know that each of us has to live with the choices we make and that our choices bear fruit. Sometimes soon, sometimes late, but our choices come back bearing fruit. Root, Mama. Root."

"I don't need you preaching to me—"

"--I know, Mom. You're a good Christian. You always have been. You and your father and your mother. Never missed a day of church. Always at Sunday school, Bible study and prayer meeting, but too scared to do the right thing. I know, Mom." He shook his head. "I know you don't need to be preached to. I just felt like talking. Thanks for listening."

She pulled in her quivering bottom lip. "Bye, Richard."

"Bye, Margaret." He returned the receiver to its cradle. Then, he turned and watched an ant inch its way toward his kitchenette.

Chapter Twenty-Six

After living in Knoxville for seven years, Richard calls upon the streets to serve as his second home. The phone in his small apartment rings off the hook. His family tells him when they see him that they telephone often, but that he's never home. He has a twenty-inch color television set that he seldom watches and attractive contemporary furniture.

Art magazines stretch the length of his livingroom floor. He is an avid book reader and has mastered the consumption of creme filled chocolates. Just last year, he allowed himself to be swept up in the jogging craze.

He hasn't touched a woman or had anyone to hold him since LaWanda made it clear that growing close to him would ruin her life. He spends his nights alone and has for years. He eats alone. He sleeps alone. He laughs alone. He works alone. He cries in the dark alone.

His only companion is the mutt, a dog he named "Friend". Thinking of age as little more than a number, he bench presses Monday, Wednesday and Friday at the YMCA downtown, the place where he lived for four years before he started renting the small storefront apartment. He quit the advertising firm years ago. Under an alias and with the assistance of his agent, he supports himself off his paintings and has enough spare money to continue contributing financially to the community.

His family remains close. They don't see one another as often as they did when Richard was younger and living at home. Tilson's Grocery Store closed its doors for the last time in 1972. A large Southern based grocery store chain bought them out, a financial transaction that left the Tilsons multi-millionaires.

294

Against Margaret's wishes, Ramsey and Rebecca moved to Fort Lauderdale, Florida. The day they moved, Ramsey went through the house like his body had no weight. He swatted at images of the girl he'd dragged in the cellar until the images left his conscience ... forever. It was the first time since he was a kid that he felt free.

He and Rebecca spent their retirement years walking the beach and spoiling their two Siamese cats. Ramsey vowed never to return to Memphis or Kentucky — ever — and he never did.

Margaret and David, people who not once crossed the stateline, packed their belongings in a U-Haul five years ago and didn't unpack until they reached their destination, a plush, high-rise apartment on Monroe Avenue.

"The house is too big," Margaret kept telling David. "The kids are all grown and moved out."

David didn't argue. It pained him too much to look inside or walk passed Richard's old bedroom. Although he didn't tell Margaret, he had to move.

Janice and Greg moved to Atlanta two years after Richard was released from prison. They adopted a little girl the year Richard went to prison. She was a cute, bright, pigtailed girl.

Carolyn and her husband moved from Memphis to Jackson, Mississippi to Baltimore, Maryland, ending up in Baltimore in the mid-1980s after Carolyn gained employment with the University of Maryland where she taught Advanced English at the graduate level.

Ruth and her husband live in Knoxville where Ruth works as a loan officer at the third largest bank in the city. Her husband owns a small cafe.

Arthur and his wife lived in Los Angeles for a few years before they hitched a moving van to the back of their RV and moved to Trotwood, a middle class suburb outside of Dayton, Ohio. It put them within an hour of their two sons and two daughters. Arthur's wife secured employment at Miami Valley Hospital as a dental assistant. Arthur works for a local television station as an electrical engineer.

Though the years have passed and middle-age has come upon Richard and his siblings, for the most part, the Tilson children remain unchanged. Carolyn, softened by her husband's gentle demeanor, is yet strong headed and wise. Her faith in God has been strengthened by the trials she has labored in prayer to get beyond, and she laughs more than she did as a child.

Ruth simply replaced her band of cackling girlfriends with her husband, from whom to receive pampering. She whines when she chips or breaks one of her polished, manicured fingernails. She and her husband have four credit cards, all maxed out and all in her husband's name. Ruth does all the family shopping.

Arthur is very much the "boss" in his house. He often demands that things be carried out in a set fashion. His wife proves herself to be his perfect mate. Satisfying Arthur is her top priority.

The ghosts of Memphis no longer haunt Richard. A year ago, a woman came forward and revealed her true identity. Although the story never made television or radio, local Memphis newspapers carried a small article on the woman. Included with the article was a letter that the woman wrote to the newspaper.

The letter read:

*"My name is Amanda Daly. I was born in Memphis in 1952. My family lived at 763 Madison Avenue. My father was a physician. My mother was a homemaker. The summer of 1959, I was playing at a park close to my home. A middle-aged Black man called to me. I went to him. I don't remember everything. I just remember I ended up in his truck. He took me to a deserted area and dropped me off with another man. The man was nice to me until it started to get dark and I started asking about my parents and when he was going to take me home.*

*I can see the man even now. He had white hair and walked with a cane. I'd seen him on television many times when I was a child. I don't know what he did to me. I don't know how much time passed before I woke up in a wall. I was covered with dirt. I stayed in that wall drinking water that dripped from a leaky pipe.*

*Then something told me to start crawling. I crawled and I crawled and I crawled. For days. I did. I just kept crawling. I crawled my way to a creek. I don't know why my parents never came forward with the story all those years ago, but if that Black boy who went to prison for me missing is still alive, I'm begging you to let him go free."*

Visit author Denise Turney online at —
https://www.chistell.com

## Read More Books by Denise Turney

Love Pour Over Me

Portia (Denise's 1st book)

Long Walk Up

Pathways To Tremendous Success

Rosetta The Talent Show Queen

Rosetta's Great Adventure

Design A Marvelous, Blessed Life

Spiral

Love Has Many Faces

Your Amazing Life

Awaken Blessings of Inner Love

Book Marketing That Drives Up Book Sales

Love As A Way Of Life

Escaping Toward Freedom

**Visit Denise Turney online** – www.chistell.com